MARY E. HART

A Graceful Christmas

For Joshykins. We all miss you forever.

For little dude. Who loves our weird conversations and my Pinky T-Rexadero antics.

Contents

One

Grace

"Watch where you're going!"

I could only look on in horror as the remnants of my half-full iced coffee dripped down the formerly pristine white shirt and houndstooth vest of the older man standing in front of me. Ugh. I shouldn't have been thinking so much about my dinner plans with Jordan and checking my texts to see if anything had changed for tonight or if he'd said "happy anniversary" yet, but nothing.

Usually, on my way to teach my community art class, I was laser-focused on what I'd be talking about. That sure wasn't the case today. My mind could only think of tonight's date and if Jordan was going to ask me to marry him. That wasn't exactly likely when I hadn't even heard from him today.

My kingdom for a time-traveling device that would bring me back to a few moments ago and I could make myself just look up as I rounded the Rec Center hallway corner. That way, I wouldn't have smacked straight into this guy.

"I'm so sorry," I said, digging into my vintage brown leather handbag from the 1920s that I'd found at a local thrift store years ago. At the bottom, underneath my class supplies, I found the three Daylight Donuts napkins I had tucked away just for klutziness like this and handed them out to him with a grimace. There was no way those napkins would be able to mop up the iced coffee, but it was a start.

Thank heavens he wasn't one of my students. If that was the case, I'd feel even worse. I did have some people in their 50s and 60s in my class, and he looked to be in that age range, but I didn't recognize him.

His salt and pepper hair was thick, and shorter on the sides than the top where it was flipped into a side part. I could see him being the CEO of some company because he had that look, but I'd never want to work for him as he had a haughty and almost arrogant expression on his face.

Okay, so that could have been due entirely to the situation. I would be feeling the same way if the situation was reversed, but I hope that I'd be nicer about it.

He grabbed the napkins out of my hand without thanks and attempted to dab his shirt, which only served to spread the coffee further. Yeah, that wasn't going to work at all.

"I'm sure there are paper towels in the janitor's closet," I said, as I took a step away from him to head that way. Anything to help out and get me away from this disaster. "Let me go get them."

"You've done more than enough," he replied with an icy tone. "I'm going to try and clean this up in the men's room and, if I can't, I'll grab my coat from my car and attend my meeting while wearing it."

C'mon floor. Can you open up and take me away? This is horrible. Why was

I always such a klutz?

"I'm sorry. Really." I turned away from him and sprinted down the hallway to class, grateful that I'd arrived so early that none of my students had yet arrived. The gratitude was twofold — I had a few minutes respite to compose myself and none of them had witnessed that horror show.

Once class started, it was like a switch activated in my head and I went straight into what I liked to think was engaging, amusing, and informative teacher mode. The students were there to learn and I was there to teach them about art and how to paint.

Today's painting was a vase of tulips, and the class was lively as always as I showed paintings of tulips from artists like Claude Monet and Paul Cézanne. The students were just getting started on their own paintings when there was a knock at the door.

Opening the door, I found the man standing there, wearing the buttoned-up coat that he'd mentioned. Ugh.

Did he want me to pay for his dry cleaning? Couldn't this have waited until after my class was over?

"Can I speak to you for a moment?" he said. His face was a blank canvas, showing nothing of his intent. Helpful.

I nodded, and turned to the class.

"I'll be right back. Paint away."

Stepping out into the hallway, I lightly closed the classroom door behind me so they wouldn't overhear.

"What can I do for you?" I asked.

"I think you've already done enough," he replied. "But I need you to be a bit more quiet when you're talking as your loud voice and laughter is flowing straight down the hallway. You're so loud that none of us can hear each other and this is a very important meeting."

I was aghast. What? I was being too loud to the point that people down the hallway could hear me through a closed door. Was he serious?

I thought back to the class before he'd interrupted. We'd been talking about how tulips were my favorite flower because roses were schmaltzy and were ruined for me due to "The Bachelor". That had prompted Ethel, who frequented the senior center, to admit that she watched the show with her friends. She'd gone off on a hilarious rant about the latest episode, which caused me to laugh. And okay, maybe my laugh was louder than it should have been. Ugh, this was embarrassing.

"I'm so sorry," I replied. "The last thing I want to do is interrupt anyone. I didn't realize that we were being so loud. I'll keep it down."

I thought about explaining further that it was a humorous conversation, but I got the sense he wasn't at all a fan of "The Bachelor" and wouldn't find it as amusing as I did.

"Please do. If at all possible, which I highly doubt."

Ouch. He was really pissed.

My face flushed and I stammered, "I'll keep my voice down. Again, I'm sorry."

I found myself saying the last sentence to his back as he had headed back down the hallway for the rest of his meeting and closed the door firmly.

That conversation had made me feel like I was two inches tall. Yes, I'd spilled coffee on him before what was an important meeting, but I had apologized. There was no need to berate me for being excited about teaching and art. Attempting to shake it off, I got back into teaching and made certain my voice wasn't loud. I'm sure my students wondered why I wasn't as jovial during the rest of the class, but I wasn't about to share.

After, when I was back in my car, the memory of the coffee spill and that chastising in the hallway returned along with a flush to my cheeks. I glanced at my phone and saw a text had come through from Jordan:

See you tonight, babe.

It wasn't the gushing text I'd hoped for, but that wasn't Jordan anyway. He was never the demonstrative type. He had confirmed that we were still on for dinner, though, so that was what was important. At least tonight, I'd be out with him, and if things went the way I'd hoped, I'd have a wonderful memory to round out today.

~~~~~~~~~~~~~~~~~~~~~~~~~~~~~

"You're breaking up with me?"

This was all wrong.

Jordan and I were out to dinner at the Rustic Steak, where we had gone on our first date a year ago today. I'd prepped for our dinner by splurging on a fresh blowout, had worn a new little black dress that showed off the curves I liked, and camouflaged the ones I wasn't as fond of. I knew I looked good, and like someone who was used to romantic dinners out.

Heck, we even had the same table we had on that first date, which was tucked away back in the corner. It was perfect for a private proposal, or at the least,
~~~~~~~~~~~~~~~~~~~~~~~~~~~~~

asking me to move in with him with plans to get engaged down the road.

Instead of that, though, our private oasis served as the perfect place for a breakup in a public location, where Jordan knew I'd never make a scene. Not that I would have done so anyway, but still.

As soon as we were seated by the hostess, Jordan reached across the table, took my hand, and looked in my eyes. I thought this was the moment I'd been waiting for—when he'd show his romantic side and declare his love for me.

My heart thumped with anticipation as he opened his mouth:

"This has been a long time coming, but it's the right time now. I know this is going to be tough to hear, but we need to take a break from being exclusive."

I sat there stunned silent.

What?

Why didn't I see this coming? Jordan had been off the last couple of weeks, but I had assumed he was nervous about taking the next step in our relationship.

I'd been dating Jordan for a year now after knowing each other for a few months before that. We'd met each other's friends at various events together and he was supposed to finally meet my parents in a month at Christmas. Heck, he had even told me three months after we started dating that I was the only woman he was seeing and he wasn't interested in anyone else.

Looking at Jordan, I stayed silent, waiting for him to laugh and say he was kidding. He had to be kidding. It would be the worst joke ever, but I'd be okay with it as long as it meant I still had him.

Instead of looking at me, he was looking behind me and shaking his head "no". Our waitress must have been on her way over to take our drink orders.

"You're great, Grace," continued Jordan, "but I'm not sure we're the right combination for a long-term merger at this juncture. Maybe we can come to a new understanding by seeing other people. We can still see each other, but not as regularly. So, how about we leave our options open and we can reassess things in a few months. Great. I knew you'd understand."

Understand? I hadn't said a word.

He was talking like the salesman that he was trying to negotiate a deal, and I was sure he fully expected me to agree. But continuing to date Jordan while he dated other people wasn't any type of a deal I'd agree to.

"I'm an all or nothing kind of woman, Jordan," I said, extricating my hand from his and rising to my feet without looking him in the eye. "I thought we were dating exclusively. In fact, I thought you were going to ask me to marry you tonight, which makes me a deluded fool. I don't want to date other people. All I want is you. But, since you don't seem interested in dating just one person… or at least you don't want to date just me anymore, that means we're done. Goodbye."

How did I manage to get that out without crying? I didn't want to draw any attention by raising my voice, so staying calm was my only option. I turned to leave.

"Grace, wait…"

Could he have changed his mind and realized that I was really the only one he wanted? I turned back towards Jordan, hoping he'd tell me he loves me and he was wrong. Instead, I saw what he was holding and my hopes were dashed.

"Don't forget your purse. You'll need your keys."

As I took my purse from him, those unwanted tears came to my eyes.

No.

Stop it.

No crying. Get out of here with your dignity intact.

Let the other restaurant patrons think I'm just going to the bathroom to powder my nose. They didn't need to know that, instead, I was walking past the bathroom and straight out the door.

I was grateful we'd taken separate cars to the restaurant from work, so I wouldn't have to call a car or, even worse, have Jordan drive me back to my apartment, knowing I'd never see him again or be persuaded to accept his offer to keep dating. Nope. That wouldn't work.

As much as I loved my apartment, the thought of going back there right now and being alone made me want to dry heave.

What I wanted was a moment of peace and I knew exactly where to find it. I drove over to my favorite mini-waterfall and sat in the lot, watched the waves as they tumbled down, and cried for what could have and should have been.

Why didn't I see this coming? Jordan was perfect for me. The first time I met him at my community art class sign-up table at the Town Recreation Fair, I felt sparks. That was unusual since I typically needed to get to know someone before I was attracted to them. But he was tall, handsome, and looked like a Ken doll with golden blonde hair, a perma-tan, strong forearms, and blue eyes.

As a salesman, he was confident, a smooth talker, and acted on what he wanted—and what he wanted when we met was to date me.

Okay, so yes, there were issues. That confidence could come across as arrogance, and while we talked all the time, it was mainly surface level or me asking him questions without any questions directed to me. When we went out, it was always to his favorite places and to do his favorite things as he assumed we felt the same way about everything, and I never corrected him.

I thought things would change as he got more comfortable around me and he'd ask me more questions about me and my likes/dislikes. But that didn't happen. Either he never hit that comfort level or he just didn't care.

Whatever the reason, I clearly wasn't enough for Jordan if he needed to date other people.

It was the continuing story of my life from my middle school days all through high school, college, and now. When would I be enough and have that moment of finding the perfect person who loved me for me, solidified with a picture-perfect first kiss as snow or rain (depending on the season) lightly fell?

Okay, enough wallowing, self. It was time to reach out to my friends and my growling stomach also reminded me that I hadn't eaten dinner.

I dug into a protein bar I found in my purse as I scrolled through my phone to glance at photos and videos on QuickPic to see if friends had posted recently. Jordan and I were friends on that site, even though he had set his settings so he couldn't be tagged in any pictures or posts, and any posts to his page were only viewable by him. I figured he wasn't big on social media so I understood, but now I realized that was probably so no one would know he was dating someone.

Unfriending him would look petty or like I was devastated (okay, so I was) but it was easy enough to unfollow him so I wouldn't see his posts if he suddenly started posting pics with another woman. Now I'd just have to not go to his profile. That would be more difficult.

As I scrolled down, I saw a sponsored post by a fashion influencer for the dating app, Connect. Hmm, that's the one my friend, Abigail, was using when she met her boyfriend, Ethan.

Before I could double-think, I clicked on the "Swipe up to sign up" arrow and downloaded the app.

Once the app finished downloading, I opened it, started a new profile, and uploaded a few pics from my phone where I looked cute.

Next up was the dreaded opening sentence. I needed something eye-catching that would possibly draw the man of my dreams to me, or at least someone who'd be fun to date for a while for holiday festivities.

Would I even have time to date with Christmas so close, along with teaching at the high school? After next weekend's class, my community art classes were done til next year, so that freed up some time and also would hopefully keep me from bumping into Mr. Drenched by Coffee at the Rec Center again.

Plus, I'd found time to date Jordan, and that was no more, so yes, I'd have time to go on some dates here and there if I found anyone interesting. Okay, I needed to do this and put myself out there again.

Otherwise, I'd spend my nights at home watching my not-so-guilty pleasure Hallmark Christmas movies and crying over Jordan.

As I thought of those movies and why I adored them, inspiration struck for my opening sentence. I typed…

"Be like a Hallmark Christmas movie: Sweet, corny, and predictable."

Was that too much? Would men know what I meant by "predictable"? I didn't mean "boring".

I don't want someone who does the same thing every single day down to having the same cereal for breakfast every morning.

By "predictable", I meant that I want someone I can count on. Someone I can turn to and he'll always be there for me. Someone who wouldn't let a day go by without being in contact with me. THAT kind of predictability.

I had to find out if that guy was out there, especially after that awful dinner with Jordan. Clearly he had moved on or was about to. It was time for me to do so, too, especially since we lived in the same town and could possibly bump into each other somewhere—probably when I looked like crap and he had a stunning woman on his arm.

With that thought, the tears that had stopped started welling up again. I took a deep breath and looked out at the waterfall and let that relaxation wash over me.

Breathing slightly easier, I texted my best bud, Josh (who I had started calling "Joshykins" years back when we met and it had stuck), asking him if he had any funny videos to send along.

My next text was an SOS to my best girlfriends, Abigail and Dani, asking to meet up for dinner this week. Hopefully they'd be okay with that since it was late notice, but I needed my girls since I no longer had Jordan.

Ugh. Why did this have to happen to me?

Two

Chloe

"No! Why did this have to happen to Grace?!"

I snarled, watching the scene play out below on Earth through one of our heavenly display monitors. Even my short angelic wings and long blonde curls shook with anger.

Grace Webster, my first charge, and Jordan were fated to be together.

I knew it from the first moment they met at the Silverton Recreation Department's community fair.

Jordan had stopped by Grace's table to sign up for her Learn How to Paint class. The sparks lit up the room that day from their chemistry when he introduced himself and they shook hands.

When I saw—and heck, felt—their electricity, I knew they were meant to be and needed to spend more time together. The class had just filled up and there wasn't space for Jordan, but Grace had said that she'd put him on the waiting list if he was interested and anyone canceled.

So I gave a teeny little thought nudge to Grace's friend, Josh, who had also enrolled for the class, that he instead wanted to take a cooking class.

And look what happened. Josh dropped out of Grace's class and took the cooking class. During that class, he found he had such a knack for cooking that he quit his job as a project manager in advertising to pursue his dream. He was now a full-time assistant chef at the local bistro working under the executive chef, who had taught the class and saw his talent.

That left the space open for Grace to reach out to Jordan through the waiting list and spend more time around him during the class, which led to drinks after the last class and then dating for the past year.

They're perfect for each other. I need to fix this.

I ran out of the monitoring room and went to find Emerson, my guide and mentor, who was meeting with the newest angels.

"Emmy! Help me! I need to go to Earth!"

Emerson turned calmly towards me, assessing me with a glance of her pale gray eyes that stood out against her long white dress, pale skin, bald head, and full majestic wings. The look on my face alerted her to an issue, so she turned to her mentees, told them she'd be back in a moment, and came over to me.

She was always so peaceful—probably because she was used to outbursts from fledgling angels like me who were still learning the ropes.

"Chloe, my darling girl, what's wrong?" said Emerson.

"It's going all wonky. I need to intervene so Grace and Jordan wind up together as they should be. They don't belong with anyone else."

"What exactly happened?"

As she spoke, Emerson put her arm around my shoulder, steering me to a white plush couch in the corner so we could speak semi-privately.

"Jordan's dating other people," I replied. "That's not how it's supposed to be. He's meant to be with Grace. I know it, Grace knows it, and he must know it deep inside. I just need to get to Earth to be around both of them to give them a nudge that's strong enough to get them back together."

"How do you know they're truly meant to be together?"

I knew that she was concerned about how involved I was with my charge, and okay, probably about my interference like prodding Josh to take the cooking class—and getting Jordan to make plans for Grace when it didn't look like he was going to, like last night's dinner.

His saying he wanted to date other people wasn't my doing at all, though.

"Their chemistry lights up a room. It's evident just by looking at them, and people with that kind of chemistry are fated to be together."

"I know that's how you feel, Chloe, because you've been telling me that since your first day when you saw them meet. But it's not that simple, and going down to Earth is a big ask…"

Tears were threatening to fall, so I squeezed my eyes shut for a moment to squash that.

"Please, please, please. I just need to see if I can help Grace and I can do that better from down there than up here. She needs help and guidance to have the life she deserves. You don't want her to be forever alone, do you?"

Emerson looked up in thought for a moment before speaking again.

"I'll let you go down there on two conditions…" she started.

This was going to be easy. I was certain the conditions would be doable. Well, hopefully.

"Anything!"

"First, you have to bring Mitchell with you."

"Perfect! He's my best bud! I love that. And he can befriend Jordan and they'll become best friends and he'll talk Jordan into not dating anyone else but Grace and maybe he'll meet some cute guy down there…"

Emerson placed her hand lightly on my arm. Oops. I'd been rambling and bouncing up and down from excitement. Time to rein myself in a bit.

"Chloe, I know you're excited, but you cannot interfere. You can go to Earth and you can even be around and talk to Grace, but you can't make any big changes to her life nor impact anything big in her life. Do you promise me?"

"Of course. I won't interfere. Well, no more than my usual little nudge of a suggestion. You can count on me. Or you can count on Mitch…"

"What about me?" said Mitchell, as he walked into the room.

I broke into a grin. Seeing my bestie always made me smile. No matter where we were or how crowded a room was, Mitchell was the first person I would see—his jolt of blonde, almost icy white, hair always caught my eye.

It probably also helped that we were the same height at close to 6 feet tall, which made us stand out in the angelic realm.

We'd been inseparable since we were toddler cherubs frolicking around in the clouds and were so close through the years that the other angels always thought we were dating. But that had never happened. Angels could date, sure, and I'd had some boyfriends over the years, but nothing serious.

When those breakups inevitably happened, there was never any bad blood because that just wasn't the way. I always remained friends with the guys because we were just better friends than partners. Mitchell, though, never expressed any interest in any of the girls around us, despite sometimes blatant interest from some of them, and never dated.

I assumed that due to his lack of interest in the girls around us, he was interested in guys and was too shy to pursue anything, but I never asked. Mitch would tell me if he wanted to. He was my stalwart pal, so I was thrilled he'd be coming to Earth with me.

"Mitch" I yelled, and then lowered my voice, remembering Emerson's wish to have her rooms known as quiet places. "We get to go down to Earth! Isn't that exciting?"

"What?" Mitchell replied. "Wow! You've wanted to go there forever. But why do we get to go?"

I started to talk but Emerson got there first.

"As part of working towards your full angel wings, you and Chloe will be going to Earth to be around your charges and ensure they're making the right decisions in their lives… without interfering."

Emerson looked firmly at me with that last statement, and I vigorously nodded my head.

Continuing, Emerson said, "Luckily, they live in the same town, so you won't have to travel and can help each other out as well."

"I'm honored," said Mitchell. "Thank you for giving me this opportunity to prove myself. I won't let you down, Emerson."

"I know you won't. You'll also help Chloe with her charge to make sure that goes well. The two of you will go down to Earth in three days. By then, I'll have the nudges in place to set up a two-bedroom apartment and positions at the Silverton Recreation Center for you. Plus, you'll both have full wardrobes in the closets, since you can't really be wearing your all-white tops and pants down there."

Something had flickered in my brain while we were talking, and it finally hit.

"Emmy, thank you for agreeing to let me go down to Earth and for Mitch to come with me. I appreciate it more than you ever know. But you mentioned a second condition…"

"It's really a second and third condition. On Christmas day, you have to be back up here. And if you do anything that goes beyond a little nudge of your angelic influence, you will BOTH be stripped of your wings and remain down on Earth."

I gasped as the price for interfering hit me, and the little amount of time that I had to get Jordan and Grace back together. "Oh my goodness! That gives us just one month! How can we possibly….?"

My words trickled off as I saw the stern look on Emerson's face. Mitch put his arm around me, drawing me to him, and to get me to shush before I got us in trouble.

"That is the perfect amount of time," said Mitchell. "We won't let you down. And, just think, Chloe, we'll be down on Earth for all of the pre-Christmas festivities."

Mitch knew just how to distract me from being troubled about the timeline and condition. My mind swirled with the possibilities of all the romantic ways I could get Grace and Jordan back together: ice skating; caroling; a holiday stroll.

"You're right, Mitch. It will be simply perfect. Thank you, Emerson! Come on, Mitch, we have so much to plan!"

Three

Grace

My plan for a night out with my girlfriends was just what I needed to forget that news from Jordan. Well, first, I'd vent about Jordan, of course, but then we'd talk about other things.

I pulled into the parking lot for Subtle Savors, the hottest bistro in Silverton, and was happy to find a spot far away from the entrance, so I could get some steps in both before and after dinner. As a teacher, I wore flats almost exclusively, so walking wouldn't be an issue. And my sleeveless mustard yellow 60s-inspired ModCloth dress, black tights, and black cardigan worked well for both teaching and dinner.

Normally, I wouldn't have been able to get reservations for Subtle Savors, but it helped that Joshykins was their sous chef, so he pulled some strings.

As I walked through the front doors, the aroma of tomatoes and garlic filled the air. My mouth watered thinking about their bruschetta. Some restaurants added balsamic to the bruschetta, which turned me off, but Subtle Savors used olive oil and garlic for the seasoning instead.

Looks like I've decided on an appetizer already. Now, where are my girls? They're always early, so I knew they'd already be seated. I glanced around the bustling bistro to find them.

"Gracey! We're over here!"

Just one person gets away with calling me Gracey…

I turned in the direction of the voice to see Abigail and Dani waving at me from a table.

Abigail Godwin and I had wound up in the same intro to psychology class our Freshman year at Littlewood College, and had become close friends after we realized we were in the same dorm, but on separate floors. She asked me to join her for lunch one day after class and that became our daily routine, chatting about psych and how different college was from high school. Over time, we opened up about our lives. We were there for each other in both little and big ways, like when I had my heart broken sophomore year by someone whose name I couldn't even remember now, and when her grandma had a heart attack our junior year and Abigail needed a ride back home.

As for Dani Wilson, we'd met during my senior year at college when I was assigned to an internship at her then just-started art gallery in Boston. The internship was the usual busy work of making copies, but Dani learned that I was a dabbling artist and included one of my pieces in her first student art exhibit. That was a thrill, and we'd become friends during the internship—a friendship that continued to this day.

Dani had loved Boston and would have stayed there, but five years ago, she was in a car accident that left her in a wheelchair. Due to that, she needed a more accessible gallery location than she could find in Boston for a reasonable rate, so she moved the gallery up north to the next town over from Silverton in Willowdale.

Arriving at the table, I hugged both of my friends. Abigail, as usual, seemed to be caught in a sunbeam with her yellow silk top (accompanied with a navy skirt), golden highlights in her light brown hair, and constant light tan thanks to frequent trips to the beach that left her gilded year-round.

Dani always wore black or gray to serve as a complementary backdrop for any art that surrounded her in her gallery, and today's outfit was a satin black spaghetti strap tank top and black belted pants. Due to her long sleek black hair, light gray eyes, and dark skin, she was often compared to Rihanna in looks. Can't say I'd complain if I got that comparison, but with my reddish-brown wavy locks, I was more often compared to Anne of Green Gables if anyone.

"Sit down and order a drink and then tell us what happened," said Dani.

"Aye aye, cap'n," I joked as I slid into the booth next to Abigail, noting the margarita in front of her and the bottle of Sam Adams by Dani.

I started to open my mouth and spill about Jordan, but caught a waiter heading towards our table.

"Hi!" said the waiter, who was tall and stocky with curly black hair and horn-rimmed glasses. "Looks like your whole table is here now, and I'm guessing you're Grace as Josh described you as the one who looks like a darker red haired Amy Adams, and told me I better be on my best behavior."

I laughed and replied, "Well, that's a new one. Why has Joshykins never told me that? I've always heard Anne of Green Gables, but I'll take Amy Adams any day!"

Dani and Abigail both glanced at me as if to assess the resemblance, and Abigail spoke up.

"You know what? I see it. Your long reddish brown hair and pale-ish skin. Yeah, that description works. Good job, Joshykins. I've never heard that I have a celebrity resemblance, so I probably don't."

The waiter looked thoughtfully at Abigail.

"Ever watch 'Night Court'? Remember Markie Post—the blonde from that show? You look like a younger version of her."

"Wow. I used to love that show, and thank you, I'll take it—especially that younger part considering we turn 30 next year," said Abigail.

"Speak for yourself, missy," said Dani. "I turned 32 this past year and I still consider myself young. Plus, my 30s so far have been fabulous."

"I've got you all beat," said the waiter. "I'm in my late 30s, and I'll agree that 30s are the best decade by far."

"You're the best, mister waiter dude," I said.

"Thank you, miss, and I'm sorry, I just realized I never introduced myself," said the waiter. "Because of Josh, I feel like I already know you. I'm Jeremy and I'll be taking your orders tonight. Can I get you something to drink, Grace?"

"Thanks, Jeremy. You've made my night—or Joshykins did with his description of me that you shared. I'll have a glass of Malbec. Can we also get some water for the table?"

"You've got it. I'll go get that for you and then be back to take your orders and I'll start calling Josh 'Joshykins'. Don't miss me too much!"

"That dude is hilarious," said Dani. "Before you got here, he was regaling us with his stories of his other gigs. In one of them, he restores antiques with his partner and they even won some contest on TV."

"Shut up!" I said. "That's awesome. Go, Jeremy."

"Yes," said Abigail. "And Grace, he's also starting up a historic tavern bus tour in Boston in the fall. We are so going."

"Amazing. Yes, we'll have to find out more when he comes back."

Oh, no need," said Dani. "I gave him my card and told me he has to send me his website when he gets started up. We'll be one of the first to book a tour. He's already promised me he'll make sure all the taverns are accessible for our tour. Plus, I may do a show at the gallery of his restored antiques."

"Just how late was I? Kidding. That's awesome. You are always networking, Dani. That's why you're so good at your gallery."

"Thanks, babe. And that reminds me…"

"Eep. Hold that thought," I replied as Jeremy came back with my Malbec and set it down on the table.

"I'll give you girls some time to talk more and look at the menu, but I'll be back in a few minutes with some bruschetta for the table, compliments of the chef."

"Oh, that rocks," I said. "I've been thinking of that bruschetta since I walked in. Joshykins knows me too well. Thank you!"

Jeremy walked away and I turned back to Dani and Abigail.

"Okay, yes, we'll discuss the gallery. I know what you're going to say, but first, let's look at the menu. Also, I'm proposing a toast. Cheers to my awesome girlfriends for coming out with me tonight. I can't thank you enough."

We raised our glasses and clinked them together and then scoured the menus for a few moments of silence. When we all had closed the menus and set them at the side of the table, I spoke up.

"First, the reason for tonight and why I needed my girls. It's Jordan, to no surprise… Long story short is that he suddenly went from being exclusive to wanting to go out with other people, and he informed me of that the other night during that dinner when I thought he was going to propose. I'm such an idiot."

"That jerk," said Abigail. "You know I've always had my concerns about him because, and I'm just being honest, but I don't think he really ever 'got' you and was just seeing what he wanted to see, or what you wanted him to see instead of the awesome you that you really are."

"I agree with Abigail," said Dani. "You, my dear, are unique and creative and funny—and you look like Amy freaking Adams—and any time I've been around you and Jordan, he comes off as not all that interesting. He's all about appearances and talks at people instead of talking to them. You deserve way better than that, and I know that in a year from now you will be trying to remember what you ever saw in Jordan."

Ouch, but they're not wrong. I have thought at times that Jordan chose me just because I was single, happened to be there, and he just needed someone to check off the boxes of what he was looking for on a superficial level rather than choosing me for me.

When we were together, I acted like I thought he wanted me to, listened attentively, and put the focus on what he wanted to do instead of anything I wanted to do. When I thought about it, I really stifled myself to be the "perfect" girlfriend that he'd of course want to be around long term and propose to because I was just what he wanted.

But that wasn't really me, was it? It was a facade.

On the rare occasions when I let my sense of humor and personality come out, he seemed irritated or like he was only half paying attention. I wonder if that was the beginning of Jordan realizing I didn't fit in with his world.

"This is why you guys are my besties," I replied. "You don't spoon-feed me what I want to hear and instead tell me what I need to hear. Thank you, and I know you're right. It's just tough to hear, but that doesn't make it untrue. Also when I think about it, Jordan constantly commented on my klutziness and would say I wasn't living up to my name. I always thought he was just joking, but maybe there was a vein of truth in that humor and he wanted a dignified Grace Kelly rather than a goofy Amy Adams."

"I hate hearing that," said Abigail. "We can get away with joking about you being a klutz because we've known you for close to a decade now; we love you; and it's what makes you the loveable you that you are. Jordan doesn't get to judge you for that."

"Thank you. Doesn't much matter now because I told Jordan that I wouldn't be seeing him anymore and that I was done. And I mean that. Or at least I hope I do. I don't want him to suck me back in and I feel like he could by paying me the slightest bit of attention or showing even a possibility of wanting to be exclusive again. But to that end, I signed up for that dating app, Connect, right after that dinner that wasn't, to maybe at least find someone to have a fun night out with."

"Yes!," said Abigail. "That's what you need. Attention and interest from someone who isn't Jordan. And you will have chemistry with guys besides Jordan. I'm sure of it. Plus, you never know. I met Ethan through Connect."

Abigail had been dating Ethan Morse for the past two months. He was an English professor and dressed the part with button-down shirts and herringbone tweed vests as a constant staple in his wardrobe.

"Ethan is handsome and he clearly worships you, as he should. If all the guys are as quality as Ethan, I'll be a happy girl, but I'm guessing that won't be the case. Oh, that reminds me…"

I reached into my purse and pulled out my phone, placing it on the table.

"Abigail, I know you have a rule against us having our phones out and normally I'd agree with that, but don't you want to see if anyone has shown interest in my profile? I haven't looked at it since I set it up the other night because I've been too nervous to do so. You can help me vet the guys. Just don't reject all of them…"

"Shoot," said Dani. "If Jessie was here, she'd be all over this idea. She's going to be so mad that she's not feeling well."

"How is Jessie?" I asked. Dani's girlfriend usually came along to our get-togethers, which I loved. "Sorry she couldn't make it tonight."

"Thanks. Just allergies. She's probably napping right now, but she's going to be annoyed when I get home and tell her she missed out on grading your potential guys. Neither of us have ever used an app, but we're not about to leave each other to see what the online dating world is like."

"Wait. A subscription to a dating app isn't the proper get well soon gift? Dammit. Be right back, girls. I have to go make a call to cancel that order before she signs up…"

I feigned rising up out of the booth, causing both Dani and Abigail to laugh.

"Shut it, you," said Dani. "She sent her love, but just didn't want to fall asleep or sneeze all over you guys."

"And thank her for that," said Abigail. "I get enough germs from the kids and parents at Silverton U when I meet them in Admissions."

"Please tell me you slather on hand sanitizer after those handshakes," I said. "I'm getting all itchy crawly thinking about it."

"Of course! And I wash my hands all the time, but still…"

Jeremy came back with our bruschetta.

"Okay, girls. I see those menus closed and moved, so does that mean you're ready to order?"

"Yes, definitely," I replied.

Perfect! But before you order, I'm supposed to tell you, Grace, that your buddy created the chef's meal of the day just for you."

"Oooh, I'm intrigued. Tell me."

"Our chef's special is the lemon parmesan risotto with peas…"

"You can stop right there. Nicely done, Joshykins! Yes. I'm in. That sounds perfect, and now I'm starving even more. So glad the bruschetta is here."

I reached over and took a piece of the delectable grilled bread, tomatoes, and garlic and devoured it. It was as delicious as I knew it would be.

Jeremy turned to Abigail, who ordered the chicken piccata, followed by Dani, who ordered the Bistecca alla Fiorentina, which was a steak grilled with rosemary and sage.

"Thanks, girls. I'll let you get back to chatting away, and I'll get those orders in for you."

After Jeremy left, Dani looked at my phone and then looked at me.

"You know I'm itching to get my hands on that app and see what horrors await us, but first, Grace, let's talk about the gallery and how perfect your work would look on those walls…"

I held my hand up, knowing what was coming. Dani had been trying to get me to have an art gallery at her show for years now and I kept putting her off.

"Don't say it. I know exactly what you're going to say, and I don't know if I'm ready."

"You are! I know you've got a bunch of paintings stored at your parents' house, your apartment, and probably at the school."

"I do," I admitted. "Teaching art at the high school and the rec center is giving me a lot more time and reason to paint than I had right after college when I was working for that ad agency, so there's a lot there. But I don't know if it's the same quality as when I was interning for you."

"Stop it," said Dani. "You're too hard on yourself. Your work is amazing."

"Dani's right," said Abigail. "I've seen the ones you have hanging up at your apartment and they've only improved over time. In fact, they're even better than your work in college. You've got this. Have a show. You deserve it!"

"Aww, you're sweet," I said. "And Dani, I really do appreciate that you want to feature my work. I just don't know. Maybe it is time…"

Dani cheered.

"Yes! You heard that. Right, Abigail? I've got a witness now, girl. From you, that's basically a go ahead to start planning for your show, so this is happening."

Oh, what have I agreed to? Imposter syndrome was starting to kick in. Am I ready for my own gallery show? The school board and the rec center would probably love the publicity unless it was a complete bomb.

"Okay, yes," I said. "Oh, get that mock shocked look off your face. You must have known I'd say yes eventually, especially now that I have even more paintings from my rec center classes."

"Whoop! I was hoping, but didn't want to book it," said Dani. "Okay, so I totally did block off a date already for next Friday night, and may have put together flyers already and hung them up in and around the gallery…"

"You are so sneaky! It's a good thing I love you and know your gallery always gets a good turnout no matter how inexperienced the artist is. But what if I'd said no or the night didn't work?"

"Stop it! It's going to be a success. I knew that if anything, you'd try to find a way out of it, so making it a week from now gives you much less time to do that, or to get nervous and change your mind. So it's happening. YAY! And now we are going to swipe through these dudes, right, Abigail?"

"Yes, I'm okay with it, since I deleted the app with Ethan a month after we started dating, so I'm curious to see if it's changed at all. Plus, it's fun selecting guys for other people."

I picked up my phone and unlocked it, going to the app. Taking a big breath, I clicked on it, and turned the screen towards Abigail and Dani, so I didn't have to be the one to look. Yes, I'm a wimp.

"You have 15 winks already, missy!" said Abigail.

"What the heck is a wink?"

"That's how you express extra interest on this site. If you like someone, you swipe right on them, but they won't know if you did or not unless you also hit that 'wink' button there. That helps you to stand out—well, kind of, because now almost everyone sends a wink when they also swipe right. If neither of you send a wink, you won't know if they swiped right or not until you swipe right on them and it tells you that you're a match. Then you can message each other. And it will also show you a bunch of people besides the ones who winked at you, so you can wink at or swipe right on other people, too."

"Okay, so a wink is good," said Dani. "I'm just gonna sign up, start winking at people, and then when they write to say 'hi', I'll tell them to visit my gallery and buy some paintings. New advertising method unlocked. I'm kidding. I'm kidding. Don't either of you tell Jessie I was joking about that."

"We won't," I said. "Okay, so how do I look at the guys who winked?"

"Here," said Abigail, turning the screen so I could see it as well. "I'm going to click on the first guy on the list that winked. If you like the look of his pic, and think you'd be interested in dating him, or at least in messaging him, swipe his pic to the right. If you swipe it to the left, that means you're not interested."

I looked at the first guy. His grin seemed a bit too sure of himself, and like there was no way I would ever measure up to his lofty standards. Okay, so I was reading a bit too much into one picture, but still.

"He reminds me of Jordan. That's not ideal. Swiping left on him."

"Umm, Grace," said Dani. "I know I'm sitting across the table, but I'm pretty sure you just swiped right on him instead."

"That ya did, babe," said Abigail. She made a left swipe and right swipe gesture with her fingers. "This way is left and this one is right."

"Oh, no. Well, hopefully he'll never message me, because no."

I moved on to the next guy. He was holding up a fish in his pic. Hard pass. He probably also camped. Nope. My idea of camping was a Motel 6, and that was pushing it.

"Nope, nope, nope," I said. "Even I know that's a sign of a guy without a personality who just does what he thinks will impress the ladies, but is instead a dud."

"You're right," said Abigail. "Bummer because he's cute."

I held up my fingers to form L and swiped towards that way, making sure not to make the same mistake again.

Swiping continued and it seemed like it was the same guy over and over again, or at least the same look. Someone who was just like everyone else and didn't have a strong personality of their own. I'd already dated that. I wanted someone different. I moved on from the guys who had winked to just random guys.

The next face came up and I stopped swiping. A handsome guy with glasses, dark brown hair, a slight beard, and a warm smile was looking up from my phone.

"Oh, wow, I like him," I said. "Wyatt..." I let his name roll around my tongue, saying his name again and again to see how it sounded.

"You can click on his other pics," said Abigail. "That won't leave his profile, I promise."

Clicking on his picture, I took a look at the other pics he'd put up. In one, he was wearing a clown nose while standing in front of a large whiteboard.

I looked closer at the pic. "I can't tell if that's a meeting room or a classroom. It doesn't look like the high school ones."

"I'm pretty sure you'd have noticed that guy walking in the hallway of your school, even though you were dating Jordan," said Abigail.

"You're right. There's no way. I may be oblivious at times, but he would have caught my eye."

Swiping to see his other pics, I saw another that was from a Halloween party where he had dressed in a beret, a red and white striped tee with suspenders, dark pants, and was holding a baguette but had on face paint.

"Holy cow," said Dani. "That makeup is like Gene Simmons. I'm thinking he was 'French Kiss'. That's clever and he's not afraid to look goofy. I like that for you."

I grinned because I was thinking the same. Could this be the corny guy I was looking for? I clicked the wink button and swiped right before I could accidentally cause him to go off into the ether or, worse, swipe left.

We continued swiping through, but none of the next ten guys gave me the same feeling I had when I saw Wyatt's pictures.

As I swiped left for the tenth time, Abigail took the phone out of my hand and looked at me.

"I know you got warm fuzzy feelings about Wyatt, but dating apps aren't a love at first sight kinda thing," she said. "You can't just swipe right on one guy because he probably swiped right on twenty women to play the odds. And yes, you aren't finding the other guys attractive right off the bat. That's normal. Just don't brush them off just because they're not the ideal. You might not think they're hot right away but then you meet them and suddenly they're the most handsome guy in the world. I almost swiped left on Ethan because I thought he looked like a snob, but he's not at all. If I'd swiped left, he and I would never have met."

She handed my phone back to me, and I glanced at the guy I'd been about to swipe right on. I tried to picture myself dating him and the interest just wasn't there.

"Solid point," added Dani. "Plus, the idea is to go on a date with a few guys and see who you like. I am aware that's a do as I say, not as a I do thing since I dated Phoebe for five years and then met Jessie like a month later after Phoebe and I broke up, so I've never been one for dating multiple people at once. But I hear that's what people should do."

Dani's ex, Phoebe, was my old shopping and gossiping buddy. I always knew I'd have a good time while she was around and was bummed to lose that friendship when they broke up, but Dani came first.

"Aww, Phoebe," I said. "I wonder what she's up to. I always liked her."

Seeing Dani's face, I felt a pang of remorse and quickly added, "But of course I love Jessie more."

"Jessie's not going to up and decide to take a job offer in Arizona without consulting me like Phoebe did. At least I hope she's not."

"She wouldn't do that," I assured Dani. "You and Phoebe were good together, but you and Jessie are even better."

"We are. With Phoebe, I felt like I always had to fight with her job or anything else for her attention. With Jessie, we understand each other and there's that comfort level and love there that I didn't have when I was with Phoebe."

"That's what I want—what you and Jessie have; and what you and Ethan have, Abigail. Hopefully I'll find that for myself with Connect, since I don't think I'll be able to find it with Jordan."

"You will," said Abigail. "But first, I'm going to fix something on your phone to help. Hand it back over."

Without a word, and because I trusted Abigail, I gave her my unlocked phone.

"I'm changing Jordan's nickname here so you'll be less inclined to answer his texts," she said as she pecked away.

"Oh, no. I'm scared to ask."

Abigail gave me back my phone with a saucy grin. "Go pull up your text exchange with him. I promise I didn't read it. I just made an adjustment to his name there and in your contacts."

I grimaced, wondering what might await me, and opened my texts. The text convo with Jordan was still there, underneath the group text with Abigail and Dani, and my last text with Joshykins.

When I saw Jordan's new name, I couldn't help but let out a snort laugh.

"'Just say no' sums it up well, my friend. Nicely done and thank you for the reminder because I'm sure I will probably need it."

"Abigail was nicer than I would have been," said Dani. "His thread would be deleted entirely and that number would be blocked, or there would have been a few swears or very unflattering words used for his new name if I had done so."

"I almost did just that," said Abigail, "but then I remembered Grace works at a school, so I didn't want anything rude coming up on her notifications in case she left her phone out somewhere."

"Very smart. Thank you. Okay, I will not answer if he texts because he's not worth it. Although I think we all know that, even though I'm strongly saying this tonight, I might not be feeling the same in a few days if he texts. Okay, or even a few hours. That's where that reminder of his new name will come in handy."

We all saw Jeremy come back towards the table with our food.

"Ooh, here comes our food!," Dani said." I'll get him and his guy to attend your show and also have them spread the word."

All of the meals looked scrumptious. I couldn't wait to dig in, so I took a bite of the delicious lemon parmesan risotto as soon as it was in front of me. Heavenly!

"Have you ladies been gabbing about how great I am this whole time?" said Jeremy.

"We sure did talk about you," said Dani. "I was telling Grace all about your work and your tavern tours and how you're going to have a show at my gallery. It's going to rock. Grace knows that for a fact. Her first one was back in college at my Boston gallery years back. Now she's painting again and she's going to have her second ever show at my gallery as well next Friday night. I hope we'll see you there."

"Well now," said Jeremy. "That's definitely worth celebrating. Cheers, ladies!"

"Thank you, Jeremy," I said. "Your show will be in really good hands with Dani. She puts on one hell of a show and knows tons of PR and news people to get it noticed."

"So, you're my new best friend," said Jeremy, turning to Dani. "I've got your card and will be in touch about booking a time to come see your gallery and set up a show. And I want the info about Grace's show because that'll be a must attend. Now you ladies enjoy your meal and holler if you need anything."

"Thank you, and let Joshykins know this risotto is delish, by the way, since he can't come out to say hi" I said. Turning to Dani, I added with a grin, "And you should probably send me the info about my show, too."

"Yeah, yeah. I will. I'm so glad you're doing so! The show is going to be epic! Now let's eat!"

Four

Grace

After dinner, I went home to swipe through Connect and look through my paintings before bed. As I walked down the hall, I noticed the door to the apartment across the hall from me was open with sealed boxes being stacked up inside by moving guys. What the heck?

"Grace!" Kelly, my apparently soon to be former neighbor, came out of her apartment. "I was hoping I'd see you before we left tonight."

"Tonight?! I had no idea! Where are you going? I'm so bummed you're moving out!"

"Remember that cute little house we had an offer on, but they didn't accept it because they got a higher offer? Well, they called us today saying that the other buyers decided to stay in their current house after all at the very last minute, and it was ours if we wanted it! Since the inspection and everything was already set, and the former owners of that house had already moved out, we can close on it and move in first thing tomorrow after the closing."

"Oh, my gosh. That's wonderful for you, and what kismet for it to work out that way, since I know how much you loved that house. Plus, it's perfect for you since it's closer to your jobs and the mountains for all of your hiking."

"Yes, I'm sorry we won't be neighbors anymore, but any time you want to go for a hike, you're welcome to come visit. I do mean that, Grace. John and I will miss living across the hall from you. Now we're going to have to get to know people in the new neighborhood."

They'd been such great neighbors. When I'd moved in, Kelly had arrived at my door with two rolls of paper towels and disinfectant wipes, since she remembered that's what she had run out of first when she moved in. Our apartments had been cleaned before we'd each arrived, but wipes were the one thing I'd forgotten to pack so she was a godsend.

"You'll be missed here, and I can only hope the person or people that move into your apartment are as nice as you guys were."

"Thank you! You'll find that out soon enough, actually. When we gave our notice to the apartment manager, she said our timing was perfect as she had two people looking to move into a two-bedroom, but didn't have any available until we moved out. So, they'll be moving in on Sunday."

"Hmm, two people? So that rules out a single guy. Well, maybe it'll be two single guys… and with my luck they'll be gay, or way too young or old, or commitment-phobes. Okay, so I hope an elderly cute couple moves in instead. Either way, I'll miss you guys!"

"We'll miss you, too! Stay in touch, please! You have my number."

Kelly and I hugged our farewells and she went back inside her apartment to make sure everything was under control with their move.

I unlocked my door and stepped inside my cozy two-bedroom apartment, tossing my purse and keys up on the wall hook. The door I used most opened straight into my kitchen with the other door that opened into my living room a few steps down the hall. I liked the open floor concept of the kitchen and living room only because it didn't feel as cramped that way.

As a renter, I couldn't change the ivory paint on the walls, the tan vinyl flooring in the kitchen and bathroom, nor the oatmeal polyester carpet in the living room and bedrooms. My friends wondered if I would get bored with the neutral colors surrounding me, but I made my own splashes of color with orange, blue, and other hues throughout the apartment.

In the kitchen, I placed bright blue canisters and a tea kettle on the shelves and stove and a navy blue rug in front of the sink. My fridge featured a number of artistic magnets, including a few Van Gogh pieces. For extra oomph, I always had a fresh bouquet of bright flowers in the middle of the kitchen table. The living room featured two burnt orange couches with ivory and dark gray patterned throw pillows and an ivory throw blanket on each. Those came in handy when I wanted to snuggle up and watch TV at night.

During Halloween, I had added pumpkin pillows for the season, but I replaced them earlier this month with light orange square pillows with a white outline of a reindeer on each along with a red Santa pillow for a kitschy feel.

Seeing Santa made me remember that I had to get my fake tree out of mom and dad's basement soon enough.

I had the ornaments and skirt for my tree in boxes in my spare bedroom closet, but there wasn't much space for the large tree box with my paintings strewn around that room. My folks were glad to let me store whatever I needed in their basement because it meant I had to stop by when I needed something from there. Of course, I loved visiting my parents anyway because my family home was always filled with light and love and music.

It suddenly felt a bit too quiet in my apartment, so I turned on the radio and Tom Jones' "It's Not Unusual" filled the air. That was better.

Because I can't hear that song and not dance, I did the Carlton on my way into my bathroom to take out my contacts and then headed to my room to change, since I was in for the night.

My bedroom featured a plush icy blue microfiber coverlet that felt like I was stepping into a comfortable long velvet gown each time I got into bed. As an accent, an ivory comforter draped across the bottom of the bed to pull up if there was a chill in the air, which there usually was as I liked the room to be in the upper 60s when I was sleeping. And I always kept the ceiling fan on for some white noise and breeze.

On the wall above my bed, a silver spiral sunburst mirror captured the eye. When I had my apartment-warming party after moving in, Dani said that my mirror looked like a portal to another realm. I always liked that idea because my dreams were always so vivid that it felt like they were real. At the time, I joked that I probably did take a spin somewhere else while I was sleeping and Dani had replied that would explain my creative side.

Typically, a TV would be across from my bed, but since I lived on my own, I preferred just watching TV in the living room and having my bedroom as my oasis for sleeping. Behind the dresser along that entire wall, I hung up sky blue long drapes for an ethereal feel and to make the room more mine and less like a generic apartment.

Making my way through my apartment on my way into the living room to watch some TV, I stepped into the spare bedroom first to look at my paintings there. Yes, I could have saved money towards a down payment on a house by going with a one-bedroom apartment over my two-bedroom, but this room served as my art studio oasis where I eased stress and frustrations by painting.

I didn't have a guest bed in there, nor any furniture, but that room didn't need any extra color. It was colorful enough since that's where I hung and stored my paintings. I turned on the light to look around at the paintings on and propped up against the walls, and the one currently on the easel—which was a scene of a cottage on a beach. It was my most recent painting, and the one I was most proud of to the point that I was okay with having a show of my own at Dani's gallery.

That painting was inspired by a girls' weekend trip to the Cape with Abigail, Dani, and Jessie. We tried to get away every year, and this last year was no exception. Early fall was my favorite time to be near the beach so we could walk it any time of day without dealing with crowds. Instead, we basically had the beach to ourselves. As I walked one evening before dinner with Abigail, I caught this cottage in the distance. Something about it drew my attention and I wanted to check it out further. Thankfully, Abigail was okay with walking down to the cottage and back with the promise of having dessert along with dinner, since we'd walked so much.

The walk had been so worth it. The sun was setting at that moment, so the sky was a haze of blue, purple, pink, and dark gray. Just that alone would pique my interest and make me want to paint it, but the rustic weathered light gray cottage looked so peaceful and like a stalwart against the battling colors of the sky. I was instantly drawn to it and stood there for a moment taking it all in, while Abigail checked out QuickPic on her phone.

When we got back to the house we'd rented, I excused myself for a moment and grabbed my sketchpad from my bag. I hadn't been sure if I'd need it when I was packing, but at that moment, I was glad I had it with me. I quickly drew up a rough sketch of the cottage and sky with my colored pencils so I'd have it to work from upon my return from our little vacation.

That painting was one of the quickest ones I have ever created. It just seemed to flow out of my paintbrush. I hadn't shown it to Dani yet, but I hoped she'd love it when I brought it to the gallery for the show.

Thinking about the art show, I shook my head to clear my reverie about creating my painting. I couldn't believe that Dani wanted me to have my own show at her gallery. Looking around the room, I tried to imagine my paintings on the walls with people standing in front of them. Would they like my artwork? Or would they judge it as the work of an amateur?

Putting my palms over my face, I sighed. There was no way for me to know the answer to that until I actually had a gallery show, so I guess I'd know in a week. Which reminded me that I would get to see my folks sometime over the weekend as I'd need to get my old paintings that I had stored at their house to bring to the show.

I walked over to my purse to dig out my phone and call my parents. Unlocking my phone, I found a few notifications awaiting me. One was a text from Dani that she got home safe. The other notifications were all from Connect, including a message there from Wyatt. Oooh.

I couldn't believe I'd heard from him so soon.

Five

Chloe

"Can you believe we're going down to Earth?!" I said to Mitch while we walked past a sparkling blue river with the sun shimmering on the water. It was a gorgeous day, but all days were like that up here. What else would the weather be like? The lush green grass on the riverbank had a permanent sheen of dew, and the water always flowed smoothly. Today, there was a tree stump and branch resting on top of the water. I wondered for a moment if that was a tree that had been chopped down on earth, so it had made its way up here as its landing spot. I'd have to ask Emerson later.

"I actually can," said Mitch, "but only because you wanted it so much and I know you well enough to know you get anything you want."

"Oh, that's not at all true. I'm just persistent. You should try it more. Think about something you really want and then just tell yourself that it's going to happen. Sooner or later it will. What do you want more than anything in the universe, Mitch?"

"There is something…"

I only partially heard Mitch as I saw a large black puppy appear on the banks of the river ahead of us. Squealing, I walked quickly over to it and held my hand out. The puppy tentatively sniffed my fingers, licked my hand, and laid down, putting its head against my leg.

"It's okay, pupster. You're safe now. Aww, Mitch, this ball of floof is shivering. He must have just crossed the rainbow bridge and has no idea what's going on."

"Let's get him to Braddox, since he registers all the new pets that wind up here. Want me to take him?"

I couldn't take my eyes off the dog, who looked a bit like a Newfoundland from what I'd seen of other dogs up here. Its fur was so soft and ruffling my fingers through it made me happy.

"He looks pretty big, so there's no way I can carry him, as tall as I am. But I think you can. Maybe? Come over here slowly and let him sniff your fingers. That way he'll hopefully trust you and let you pick him up."

Mitch slowly bent down to a crouch next to me as the puppy eyed him warily, with an arched back.

"Hey there, big fella," Mitch said to the dog. His voice was so soothing and I was glad the dog recognized that. Mitch held out his hand to the dog, who instead of sniffing his fingers, rubbed the top of its head against his hand.

"Aww, that's adorable." I couldn't stop smiling. "Nicely done. You're really good with animals, Mitch. How have I never noticed that? You're like the dog whisperer."

Mitch easily picked up the large dog in his arms without any strain, and he glanced over at me.

"There's probably a lot you haven't noticed about me," he said.

"No way," I replied. "You're my best friend. I know everything about you. I might even know things about you that you don't even know yet."

"Umm, I don't think that's possible, but I'll let you think that."

"You're such a stinker. But I'm glad I have you, Mitch. That cute ball of fluff is like puddy in your hands right now, and it makes sense because you have this soothing, peaceful presence about you. At least I always feel safe and happy when I'm around you."

"Wow, thanks, Chloe, as long as that safe part is actually a compliment. You've never told me that before."

"I haven't? Huh. Well, I do, and you should know that because it's true. Heck, I wouldn't spend as much time with you as I do if I didn't feel happy around you. But yes, being around you makes me feel safe and soothed. Not that we ever have anything to worry about up here, but I just feel more like I can be fully me when I'm around you, so that makes me feel safe."

"I'm glad. I'm happy around you, too."

Hearing that made me smile. It wasn't news to me because I'd known Mitch for years, but still it was great to hear.

"Well, duh, I'm awesome. I kid. I kid. Kinda. Seriously, thank you, Mitch."

We walked silently for a few moments, until a thought poked its way into my head.

"Wait. I just remembered. You were saying something about what you wanted before I saw this floof. It seemed important. What was that?"

"It can wait. Maybe I'll tell you when we're down on Earth. Right now, let's get this pup to Braddox before you think of keeping him for yourself."

"You know me too well. I did indeed think that. It's not like it has a home up here yet, and it's so cute…"

"This is one time when you might not get what you want, at least right away. Remember that we're heading down to Earth in a few days. If you took the dog, you'd have to find someone to watch it when we're there anyway. Be patient."

"Easy for you to say. You're so calm and patient, and I'm just not."

"That's correct. You're basically the opposite of calm, but that's a good thing. You're full of spirit and people always know how you're feeling and what you're interested in. I sometimes wonder if I should be more that way."

"Nah. You're perfect the way you are, Mitch. And that's why our friendship works, because we balance each other out. We just work."

"You're right, Chloe. We do work."

"I'm glad you're coming to Earth with me. It's going to be so much fun."

As we walked towards Braddox's center, I wondered if the days on Earth would be as serene as my days up here were. At least I'd have Mitch with me, and that was a good thing. Being around him made me feel calm.

Six

Grace

I felt a sense of serenity knowing that I'd heard from Wyatt pretty close to right after I had winked at him. But before I read it, I needed to make a phone call. I phoned my folks and left a voicemail about the art show and seeing if they were around this weekend to grab my paintings.

Ahhhh, my art show. Ack. What had I done by agreeing to this?

Once that was done, I went back to Connect. Butterflies started swirling around in my stomach as I clicked on his message. It read:

Thanks for the like, Grace. It's nice to meet you. Your profile was refreshing and interesting. By the way, if you sneeze, I'll always say 'bless you'. I hope you know what movie that's from and I look forward to chatting further.

Biting my lower lip, I grinned. How could I not know "Singles"? It was a classic and the basis for some of my life choices, wise or unwise.

What could I write back that was short but also playful and intriguing, all in one message? That suddenly sounded like a tough call, so I went with my heart and sent:

Hi there, Wyatt. One of my favorite movies. Janet was way too good for Cliff, though. Now Linda and Steve with 'What took you so long?' That's a romance and one heck of a great line. How about you? Are you a Cliff or Steve guy? Look forward to talking more.

Okay, so that was longer than I planned, but that's how I write and talk and it was time for me to stop reining myself in for anyone.

That cleared out one Connect notification, but there were many more to check, including one more message. How was that possible? I'd only swiped right on Wyatt.

Oh, no.

No, no, no.

The guy with the smile that reminded me of Jordan. Ugh.

I opened his message with dread and found an unsolicited pic awaiting me of a part of his anatomy that I had no need to see. Well, I was sure right with my initial reaction of not being interested in him.

Okay, time to learn how to delete a message and block the sender. Ugh.

I figured that out, and then went to see the new potential matches to swipe through.

Swipe left; swipe left; okay, he's cute and is holding a book in his pic. Fine, I'd listen to Abigail and not just be interested in Wyatt—swipe right; swipe left; swipe left.

I'm pretty sure that guy is the dad of one of my students. Immediate swipe left.

Hmm, that guy has great arms. Swipe right.

A notification showed up at the top of the screen that I had another message from Wyatt. I liked that he wrote back right away instead of waiting hours.

'I was stuck in traffic.' Great choice. Those two did seem like they had a better chance than the other couples. As for me, I'm more of a mix of Steve and Doctor Jamison. By the way, I should add that I've never seen a Hallmark movie, Christmas or otherwise, but please don't hold that against me. I'm corny to a fault, sweet to my family and friends (with a touch of sarcasm thrown in), and am perpetually 15 minutes or more early to everything, which I guess means I'm predictable.

Oh, I like him already. Dammit.

I admire your honesty and not trying to make me think you're a Hallmark movie watcher, because I'd probably be able to tell that right away with just a few questions. Are you a fan of Christmas or more of Halloween? I have to admit that I don't remember what your profile line was—your face and smile is what drew me in, and then I saw that Halloween pic of you as a mime, which is what caused me to swipe right, because I like guys that can be goofy without worrying what people think.

As I hit send, my phone rang with caller ID saying it was my folks, Sarah and Jonathan Webster.

"Hey there," I said.

"Grace, we're so thrilled for you," said Mom. "Congratulations! This is huge."

"Thank you. I'm still processing it, kind of, but I'm thrilled. So are you guys around this weekend?"

"Yes, definitely. We're going out to a movie tomorrow night, but we're around during the day if you want to come by, or Sunday if that's easier?"

"Let's do Sunday. That way, you can tell me all about the movie in person."

"Sounds good. We'll look forward to seeing you then, honey. How are you doing?"

Telling my folks about Jordan wasn't interesting at all, so I brushed that topic aside.

"All good. Nervous about the art show Friday night, but wrapping up school for the Christmas vacation in a couple of weeks so that's keeping me busy."

"Understandable. I hope that goes okay, and Dad and I know you're going to do great at the art show. Unfortunately we can't make it because that's the night of our company holiday party, but we would be there otherwise."

Mom and Dad launched their own real estate business, Webster Realtors, 20 years ago, taking it from just them to now having 12 agents working for them and two admin assistants. Their Christmas party was always a huge event that I'd never miss, but I'd have to this year.

"Shoot, Mom. I'm so sorry. I must have spaced when Dani told me the date of the show. Do you want me to try to move it?"

"No, honey, of course not. We'll miss you, but we wouldn't be able to spend much time with you at our party anyway as we'll be talking with everyone. I'm just sorry we won't be able to be at your show."

"It's okay. You guys were there at my show in college, and if Dani has anything to do with it, this will apparently be the first of many shows. I know you guys support me and love me and you'll be there in spirit."

"We sure will, and I'm glad you know that. Plus, we'll see you Sunday anyway, so we'll get to catch up more there than we would at the party."

"Totally. Okay, so I'll see you guys Sunday. Does 11 work?"

"Absolutely. We'll be back from grocery shopping then. Want to stay for lunch?"

"Of course! Wouldn't pass up a meal with my folks, even if Dad will say he cooked it all himself with his toe."

"You know your dad. He has to get that joke in whenever and wherever he can. We love you, and we'll see you Sunday."

"Love you, too. Oh, and remind me to get my tree out of the basement while I'm there. Thanks! See you then."

After hanging up, I noticed I'd missed a few more notifications from Connect, including another message from Wyatt.

This is Halloween. This is Halloween. Does that answer that question? I do enjoy Christmas—a little less than I used to—but Halloween is my favorite time of year, as evident by that pic. Glad you enjoyed it. When's the last time you dressed up for Halloween?

Hmm, I wonder why he doesn't enjoy Christmas as much. Guess I'll find out if we keep talking down the road.

Haven't been to a Halloween party in a while, but every year at Halloween, the other teachers and I dress up. I haven't been too out there with my outfits, typically going with an eye patch, bandana, and vest over my regular outfit to be a pirate like this year or throwing on a black cape and hat to be a witch. Was the mime your most recent costume?

I found myself enjoying the back and forth. It was nice texting with a guy who was responsive, unlike say, Jordan. My phone dinged with a notification and I glanced at it, eager to see another message from Wyatt.

Aargh. Jordan. It was like I summoned him by thinking about him. I opened up the two texts with dread along with a spark of hope that he was going to confess that he missed me.

The first text was a gif of a penguin walking along the ice and tripping.

The second was a pic of a stuffed penguin hanging behind a bar. That text said:

Saw this and thought of you.

My eyes rolled skyward. Seriously? Not exactly news that he thought I was a klutz. He'd sure let me know I wasn't exactly living up to my name more times than I could count.

But I had to wonder about the timing. Was he out on a date at a bar, saw that penguin, and was now thinking of me and regretting that he was out with someone else? Or did she go off to the bathroom and he got bored for a moment, saw the penguin and needed attention, so he sent that my way along with the penguin tripping gif? Or was he by himself and missing me?

Okay, that last one wasn't likely.

The date being in the bathroom was far more likely but I did have to admit to getting a bit of a thrill that he saw the penguin and took the time to take a pic and find the gif and send both to me because I was clearly on his mind even just for a moment.

Should I reply? Should I not?

My heart and head always conflicted when it came to him, especially after how much he had hurt me. I decided to do so, knowing I'd regret it even as I hit send.

I can walk/trip like a penguin. Yeah, I'm singing that now. Very cute.

Another text came up and this time it was from Wyatt.

I was a bit more laid back this Halloween. Went out to a friend's party and dressed up as a 70s detective, complete with brown leather blazer, turtleneck, big mustache, and a long gold chain. So, what do you teach?

That's laid back? I had a feeling we had different definitions of that term, although I liked that he was out there or self confident enough or both to think that was low key.

That sounds like an amazing outfit. I'm an art teacher at a high school. Have been so for the past five years and I love helping students bring out their talents. How about you?

I hit "refresh" on my texts to see if a text had come in from Jordan and I'd missed it. Nope. Instead, I saw the evil "read" indicator after the message but no … to indicate he was replying. Really hate that feature. I was usually a fan of ellipsis except for when I saw those dreaded ones. I should have just deleted the text thread after I sent it, so I didn't have that message read sitting there taunting me.

Two new messages came in. One from Abigail and one from Wyatt. I clicked on Wyatt's first.

I'm a corporate property lawyer. Been at the same firm since I graduated from law school and passed the bar. The hours have been long, but they're getting more stable now so I can actually think of dating. That's how I wound up on Connect and now interacting with you. Timing's everything, right?

Oh, it sure is. He had no idea. Before I replied, I went to read Abigail's message.

Hey, hon. Great seeing you tonight. Was going to call, but wasn't sure if you were home yet.

That I was. I quickly clicked on Abigail's name in my contacts to call her and she answered after just one ring.

"Hey, Grace. You must be home since I don't hear the sound of a car."

"Sure am. Was just going through my paintings and mucking around on Connect. Great seeing you tonight. You okay?"

She was silent for a moment, which gave me pause.

"What's going on, Abigail? You sound off…"

"Yeah, I just needed to talk something out. Ethan called on my way home from dinner. We were planning on celebrating our first Christmas and New Year's together, but his parents want him and his brother to spend the holidays with them and his extended family down in North Carolina where he's from."

"Oh, shoot. I'm sorry. I'm guessing that's going to muck up your plans just a bit."

"We've only been dating a few months, so I can't exactly ask him to choose me over his parents."

"Is there any way he'd ask you to come to North Carolina with him?"

"No. That came up, but I'd rather be here for Christmas with my family, so I can't fault him for wanting to be with his family. But at the same time I just wish he'd want to be with me."

"You guys are so good together, and I have no doubt you're going to have many holidays together down the road. But I get it. It stings to not have that first Christmas and New Year's and all those fun things with him. When is he heading down?"

"His parents have this big Christmas Eve thing, so he's leaving the day before that and then would be coming back up here January 2nd."

"Oof. Okay. I'm voting now then that we ring in New Year's Eve together and spend New Year's Day sleeping in, eating all the brunch foods, and watching cheesy movies."

"You're the best, but what if you meet someone between now and then? I don't want you to give up the possibility of a romantic New Year's Eve?"

"Well, I am texting with that guy, Wyatt, from Connect, and it's going well. But no, my besties come first and I'm not choosing a guy over you. It's you and me for New Year's Eve, babe. No matter what."

"Thanks. That does sound fun and takes a bit of the sting out from knowing Ethan won't be here. I'm going to start looking up brunch food ideas and ways to celebrate New Year's Eve now."

"Awesome! I can't wait to see what you come up with, and I'll do the same. We'll talk soon, okay?"

"Absolutely. Have fun with your texting, and stay away from Jordan. Love you."

I decided to keep mum and not mention that I had in fact just replied to Jordan because Abigail would have smacked me through the phone. Or she would have driven to my apartment to do so.

"Love you, too."

I put the phone down for a moment and thoughts of a girls' New Year's Eve spun through my head. We'd have to get blingy party hats and champagne. And all the food. Pizza? Shrimp? Go big? Go low key? I should make a list. But first, I should text Wyatt back….

Wait. Another message from Connect? Who else had I matched with?

I clicked on the message. Ohh, it was that guy with the hot arms, whose name was Noah.

Well, hey there. You're hot. Let's meet up. Whatcha doin' tonight?

Slow down, dude.

Hey. Just got home from a night out with friends, so can't tonight. Maybe coffee some night next week?

My phone dinged again. Wow, I was popular tonight.

Awaiting me was a text from Dani with an attachment.

Now that you've said yes, here's the flyer. Go promote it, girl! I'm so excited.

Opening the attachment, I was surprised by the butterflies I got seeing my name listed there as the featured artist for the gallery exhibit. Aww. Yay! I quickly saved the image of the flyer and posted it on my social media accounts, making sure to change each post to "public" so it would be shareable, instead of my usual "friends" or "friends except for..." a few people that didn't need to see everything I posted.

Then, I wrote back to Dani:

Thanks, babe! You're the best. It's been promoted everywhere, as I'm sure you've now seen since we're friends on all my accounts. Love you!

Now to re-read and reply to Wyatt's message.

Corporate law? I'm impressed. Do you have to wear three-piece suits to work? Even if you don't, lie and tell me you do, since they're my weakness. Well, mainly the vests. Sounds like you've been busy. Sure you have time to meet someone, let alone date?

As I hit "send", a message from Noah came in, so I opened it.

This is Noah's wife. Yes, wife. He's married. Never text him again.

Oh, good heavens. He's married, on a dating app, and leaves his cell phone open. The first one alone would be a no go for me, but I'm considering that a massive bullet dodged that I never spoke to him more than that one sentence. Yikes.

Another notification came in and I closed one eye to look at it, fearing that it would be Noah's wife again telling me off.

Nope, Wyatt. Much better.

I do wear suits to work every day, actually. Not always three-piece suits, but there are some in my wardrobe and I'll have to remember that you like the vests. As for being busy, right now we're dealing with end of the year filings, so this week is actually kind of nuts. But then it clears up a bit. I'm free starting after work next

Friday if you'd like to grab coffee or dinner?

Shoot. That's the night of my gallery show. Of course it is. Do I invite him? He could be a horror in real life, but it would be a safe place for a first meeting.

Actually, Friday night, I'm booked. I'm having an art show of my paintings at my friend's gallery in Willowdale. You're welcome to come to that if you'd like? I know we won't get a lot of time to talk, but it would get that pesky first meeting and making sure we look like our pictures out of the way...

Was that too much? Am I putting all my eggs in one basket here by not swiping through and talking to other guys? Back to Connect I go.

I opened up the app, ignored any recent winks, and went to look at the general realm of men based on my specifics of their early to mid 30s, within a 30-mile radius of me. For height, I had kept that pretty open on purpose because I didn't want to be seen as a heightist and rule anyone out.

Okay, what do we have here?

Swipe left.

Swipe left.

Hmm, he's kind of adorable in that tux. Hope it's not a pic from his wedding. Even if he's divorced, that's pretty tacky. Cautiously swipe right.

Swipe left.

What?

I put the phone down and then picked it up again to see if I was seeing things correctly or hallucinating.

Oh, no.

Jordan?

Really?

Thanks, universe, for putting him on that list, considering he's the reason I'm on here. If he hadn't changed his mind about being exclusive, I would have happily still been dating him and we would have been talking about Christmas plans. Guess I'm glad I hadn't bought him a present yet. Okay, no swiping right on him. Just no, self. That would be ridiculous.

Swipe left.

Ack. What is this? That's Ethan, Abigail's boyfriend.

I thought they both left the site, but that's his picture. Although now that I thought about it, she'd said that she left the site. She didn't say that he did. However, his name was listed as Nick here instead of Ethan. Ugh. I took a screenshot of the profile, and swiped left.

Should I tell Abigail? She's one of my best friends and I would want to know if someone I was dating was on the site. As I thought that, I wondered if she had seen Jordan on Connect when she was swiping and hadn't mentioned it to me. No, she would have told me. Right?

It was entirely possible that the "Nick" guy was a scammer using Ethan's pic, since I've heard of that happening quite a bit with dating profiles and social media alike. But what if it wasn't?

I pondered what to do, and a banner showed up at the top of the app with a new message from Wyatt.

That sounds like fun. What time is it? I'll just need to see if I get caught in the office, but how about I'm a solid maybe? And if I don't, hopefully we'll be able to get coffee over the weekend.

Oh, hey, and here I have the flyer from Dani that I can send him. Or can I? I looked around the message window and didn't see a place to attach a picture. I could send a gif, but that wouldn't do it. Shoot. I wasn't quite ready to ask him for his number to send a text, so this would have to do.

It starts at 6 and goes til 8. I was going to send along a flyer I have, but looks like that's not doable on the app. However, you can find the info on the location on the Center Space Gallery website. And yes, coffee sounds good if the gallery show time doesn't work.

As I waited to see if he'd reply, I took the flyer about my gallery show and posted it on the high school's intranet under Events, and also sent it off to my friend Town Recreation Manager, Amber Agarwal, to see if she could post it on their sites and also print out a few copies and hang them up at the Rec Center. She and I had always worked well together for my introduction to painting classes, so hopefully she'd be interested in promoting me further.

Another message popped up from Wyatt.

Sounds good. Just found the website and made a note of it in my calendar. Hope I'm able to make it. I should probably get to sleep soon as I have an early morning pickup basketball game with some friends, but I enjoyed chatting with you tonight. We'll talk again soon. Good night.

Oh, gosh. He's sweet. I like that. Of course, Jordan was also sweet in the beginning with constant good night and good morning texts, and look what happened there.

I've enjoyed talking with you, too. Sleep well and enjoy the game tomorrow. I have some paintings to go through tomorrow and shopping to do if nothing in my closet appeals to me for the show. Good night.

With that being said, I yawned and realized I should get some sleep as it was going to be a busy couple of days prepping for this show. I was glad that the night turned out busier than I thought it would with dinner with my girls earlier, talking to my folks and Abigail by phone, and chatting with Wyatt for quite a bit. There was that text from Jordan, who I just realized still hadn't replied. That stung, but it was lessened a bit by talking with everyone else, and I had a flicker of hope about Wyatt, as weird as that was since we'd only just started talking that evening. I really didn't want to get my hopes up, but clearly they were getting up there.

Before I went to bed, I did some self-Reiki to try and counteract the stress of the day and promote good energy. And in case that didn't work, I also meditated for 10 minutes, hoping for a good night's sleep.

I wasn't sure how sleep would go, considering that my mind was running a million miles a minute. Surprisingly, I was feeling good overall, though— probably thanks in part to my dinner with Abigail and Dani, and the conversation with Wyatt, which had sparked my interest. But I still felt a bit antsy. Would I sleep at all?

Seven

Chloe

"I didn't sleep at all last night," I said to Mitch as we waited in the pristine white and silver hallway outside of Emerson's office on Sunday morning. "Way too excited to get down to Earth and it's happening today!!"

As I grinned, my shoulders bounced up and down and I shimmied to celebratory music that wasn't there, but it sure felt like it was to me. Waves of happiness surrounded me and I wondered if Mitch was feeling even an inkling of it. He was tough to figure out sometimes, despite being my bestie.

"I get it," he replied. "I'm looking forward to it, too."

"Are you really? Because you're like the epitome of calm. Why aren't you bouncing around with me? Are you regretting going down to Earth with me? Would you rather stay up here?"

"Gosh, no. I really am happy, Chloe. You know me better than that. When have you ever seen me bounce around? I just have a slightly more sedate—understatement of the year, my friend—way of responding to things than you do. Doesn't make either way wrong. Both are completely normal. But I

62

promise you that I am looking forward to our travels. And I'm also a little nervous."

"Why are you nervous? Sure, we're going somewhere new, but that's exciting and it will be so different. Not that up here is bad, because it's not at all, but down there is just something I've never experienced and I can't wait to soak it all in and just be there."

"That's the part that makes me nervous. I like things the way I know them, I guess, and this is certainly going to be different. And I see that worry in your eyes. I'm not backing out. I'm not. I'm just being honest telling you that I'm wondering how things are going to go."

"Phew! You did have me worried for a minute there that you were going to bail on me at the last minute. I would have been so sad because as much as I am thrilled that I'm going down to Earth, I'm happier that you are the one coming with me. It's going to be awesome. You'll see. Take a look at it through my eyes even for just a moment."

"I'll try. Once we're down there, I'm sure I'll be okay. I just want to know where we're going to be and what we're going to be doing and that not knowing worries me."

"I think I can help with that," Emerson said as she appeared in her now open doorway. Neither of us had noticed the door open. "Come on in, you two, and I'll tell you where you're going to be staying and what you'll be doing."

I saw Mitch's shoulders drop a bit. Wow, he really was tense over this. I needed to remember that he and I were totally different people and just because I was gung ho about something didn't mean he was, too, automatically. I promised myself that when we were down on Earth, I'd do a better job of paying attention to just how he was doing.

We all walked into Emerson's office and sat down. Mitch and I plopped down on the cloud-like white sofa, while Emerson pulled over a rolling light gray tufted desk chair to sit across from us.

"So, how are you two doing?"

"Well, you heard me out there, I'm sure," said Mitch. "I really am happy to be going but I'm nervous because I don't know the details yet."

"I'm super duper happy," I said. "And I can't wait to hear all about it!"

"Mitch, you have every right to be nervous, but I'm glad you're pushing through that and still happy to go. Chloe, I knew you'd be thrilled from the start so I wasn't worried about that in the slightest."

Emerson swiveled around in her chair to grab a manilla folder off her desk.

"This has all of the information you're going to need to know. I'm just going to go through it with you quickly, and then it will also be waiting for you in your apartment. Ready to hear the details?"

"Yes, yes, yes!" I said without any hesitation.

Mitch grinned and said, "Definitely!"

"Okay, so first, you'll both be staying in the same apartment. There's two bedrooms so you'll have your space. And that apartment is right across the hall from Grace's apartment. We made some nudges so the previous tenants were able to get a house they wanted quickly, which left that apartment open for you to move into."

"Oh my gosh! We'll be right by Grace! Yay! And I totally thought we'd have two apartments, but this is so much better! Mitch, we're going to be roomies!"

"Okay, I didn't expect that, because I think I also figured we'd be in two apartments," said Mitch, running his hand through his hair, causing it to go in all different directions. "But that's good because otherwise we could have wound up with some truly strange people as our roommates, and explaining our backstories would be, well, difficult."

"There is definitely that," said Emerson. "I know how close you two have always been, so it just made more sense to keep you together when this opportunity came up. The apartment is fully stocked with clothes for each of you and all the furnishings you need, as well as food to start you off. You'll have a car ready for you as well. Mitch, I seem to remember you have learned how to drive up here, yes?"

"That I sure have. There's not much need for driving up here, as we all know, but some of us wind up learning anyway just in case we ever wind up going down to Earth to see our charges so we can fit in better."

"Wait. Why didn't I learn how to drive?" I asked.

"If you want to learn when we're down there, I'm sure there'll be some big empty parking lot we can use and I'll try to teach you."

"Aww, thank you, Mitch. Maybe I'll take you up on that. But, really, Emmy, how come only Mitch learned how to drive?"

"You never seemed all that interested in it," said Emerson. "Mitch came to me and asked to learn a few years ago. We typically only teach those who ask and we know that they'll put in the work. Your focus has been on other things, like learning how to work with having a charge and what's involved with that, and for the past year, you've been heavily involved with Grace, which hasn't left much room for anything else. If you'd shown interest, we would have taught you as well."

Ouch. But she wasn't wrong. Still stung a bit, though.

Was I a bit obsessive? Yes, but only because I wanted things to work for Grace as much as they could. What was wrong with that?

"I understand that. Thanks for the honesty. I appreciate it."

"I can sense you're hurt despite what you've just said," said Emerson. "And I don't want you to feel that way, although you both know your feelings are always valid. That's why I said only some of the angels have learned how to drive. It's probably about half and half. Maybe in a year or so, you would have been interested and would have come to me then. But if Mitch is willing to teach you while you're on Earth, that works just as well because I know you trust him."

"Of course I do. I trust Mitch completely. He's my person."

"Thanks, Chloe," said Mitch, who was blushing a little bit. "I appreciate that. You're my person, too."

He turned to Emerson. "So, what else do we need to know?"

"You've both been set up for jobs at the same location so you can commute over and back together."

"A job! Yay! Are we going to be working with Grace, too?"

"Not quite," said Emerson. "But you'll be working somewhere that she works at every so often. I got you both jobs at the Silverton Recreation Department. They need extra help during the holidays for their special activities, so you'll both be working there handling their programs and coordinating events, etc. You'll find out more when you're there, but what you'll be doing will work to your individual personalities and skill sets, so I think you'll enjoy the work."

"You had me at special activities," I said, envisioning all the traditional Christmas things I'd heard about, like ice skating and holiday crafts and cookie baking. "I'm so excited and all in!"

"Thanks for setting this up for us," Mitch said. "We'll make you proud."

Shoot. Yes, I should have thanked her as well when I was gushing about activities.

"Yes, Emerson, thank you. I'm so excited and I know Mitch is excited, too, and we're just so happy that you made this happen for us."

"Now, remember. You're going down to Earth to watch over your charges, but let me reiterate again that you're not to interfere in any major way. Chloe, if you wonder at all if what you're going to do is major or not, ask Mitchell first, please, before you do so. I know you only want the best for Grace, but what you want and what's best for her may not be the same thing. That's another reason you're getting to go to Earth… to see that for yourself in person and to learn more about her and what she actually needs instead of just what you think she needs."

"Of course," I replied. "Yes, I do think I know what's best for Grace because it's just so crystal clear that she belongs with Jordan. Their chemistry is just off the charts and she's what he wants, so they just need to find their way back to each other, and maybe that means they need a little nudge…"

"Chloe, this is what I'm talking about," said Emerson. Her face was set sternly, which was something I thankfully had only seen before a few times. "Be careful of those little nudges because you might be interfering with something else that would be better for her and could cause her life to go in a direction that it shouldn't. I'm not saying she doesn't belong with Jordan because she's not my charge, so I'm not as involved, but from what I've seen of him, I want you to listen to your mind and your heart and try not to get as involved as I know you'll want to."

Oof. It's like she doesn't want Jordan and Grace together. They belong together. I just know it. They have that spark that I've been looking for with every guy I've dated and just haven't found it. That's what matters. But fine, I'll learn that in person and be able to tell Emerson for sure that Jordan is who Grace really needs and that they're meant to be.

"Sure thing! So, when do we get to go?"

"That's also why you're here." Emerson turned and pointed to a door that had appeared in the wall behind her desk. "All you have to do is step through that door and you'll find yourself in the living room of your apartment. We decided that was easier than having you appear out of nowhere anywhere else as we don't know who would be around and happen to see that, which would be tough to explain."

"It sure would," said Mitch, who had paled quite a bit. It looked like his nerves had taken hold of him again. I reached over and took his hand and squeezed it, prompting him to look at me, and I offered a soft smile.

"This is going to be good, Mitch," I said. "You being there with me is perfect because you're my best friend and we even each other out. You'll keep me from going off the rails and I'll bring out your fun side a little bit more. Let's go get our Earthly Christmas on!"

Keeping Mitch's hand firmly in mine, I stood up and he followed suit after a brief moment of hesitation.

"That's the spirit," said Emerson. "Go spread the faith and bring cheer to those you encounter. And most of all, help people believe and have hope. That's what is desperately needed on Earth year-round, but especially at Christmas."

We walked over to the door, which opened as we drew near. Beyond the door, I could see couches and a TV… our living room. Amazing. I glanced over at Mitch and saw that his jaw had dropped, but he looked pleased. Phew. This was going to be easier than I thought.

I stepped up to the door, bringing Mitch with me to walk through the door together.

"Okay, Mitch, let's do this."

Eight

Grace

❦

"Okay, let's do this."

With my dad's help, we lifted the last of my paintings into the mini U-Haul I'd rented, which was currently sitting in my parents' driveway by the cul-de-sac at the end of their street. That circular path was one I knew well from the many times my Dad had cracked us up, and made us slightly nauseated, by driving around and around it when we were kids instead of pulling straight into the driveway.

It was also the path I took the first time I learned how to drive, sitting in my dad's old boat-like car, the Monte Carlo, to learn how to turn around corners smoothly and slowly. The main practice happened in empty school parking lots after the school day was over, but it was around that cul-de-sac that I started to learn how to drive and how delicate the handling was to make a turn without overdoing it.

Pulling back from my reverie of times gone by, I reached up and pulled down the U-Haul door.

"Thanks for the help, Dad! I really appreciate it."

"Of course, kiddo. Your dad isn't that old that he can't help his daughter lift canvases into a van."

"I know, but I still appreciate it anyway. It was a lot easier than if I had done so myself."

"It's too bad Jordan couldn't make it. I'm sure he would have been helpful."

Ooof. Well, guess there was no time like the present to rip off the old bandaid.

"Yeah, about Jordan… There's something I haven't mentioned yet. He's not here because we broke up a few days ago. Turns out he was more interested in the thought of dating other people than he was in just dating me."

"Well, he's an idiot then and a jerk for hurting my little girl."

"Thanks, dad. He's not a bad guy. He's just not the guy for me. It happens. I'm kinda glad I hadn't yet introduced him to you guys because the break-up would have been even tougher if that had happened."

"We'll meet the right guy when he's right for you, Grace. I have no doubt in that and that you'll find the guy who deserves you instead of someone who didn't."

"Don't make me cry, dad. Thank you, though. I'll be lucky if I meet someone who's even just half as great as you are to mom. You two are my role models for what a relationship should be."

"Now you're going to make us cry," said my mom as she walked up to us from the side of the U-Haul. She must have come out from the front porch without me even noticing.

"I'm sorry about Jordan, honey," she continued, "but your dad's right. If things didn't work out there, he wasn't the one for you. And that just means the one for you is out there and you'll find him. I have no doubt. Heck, I met your dad when I wasn't expecting to, and I know that's such a cliche but it's true. I'm going to add another one, too. When you meet him, you'll just know."

I put my arms around both of my parents for a hug.

"Thanks, guys. I love you both. I should probably hit the road."

"Before you go, you almost forgot something, which is why I came out," said Mom.

"What's that? I know I got all of the paintings."

Mom pointed to the porch. As I turned the corner of the U-Haul and looked at the porch, I smacked my head with frustration at what I'd come close to forgetting.

"Oh, my Christmas tree! You dragged it up from the basement by yourself? I'm impressed, Mom! Thank you!"

"You're welcome, sweetheart. I wouldn't want you to not have that in your apartment. Now you'll be all set to decorate for the holidays."

That thought tugged at my heart, because my hope had been to decorate the Christmas tree with Jordan. That sure wouldn't be happening this year or any year. I'd get through it, but the thought was a bit depressing.

"My sweet girl," said my mom. "I see that look in your eyes. Don't think about how you'll be decorating yourself. Think instead that you're going to be able to decorate the tree and your apartment exactly as you want. You know that your father and I love each other, but oh, my, the little tiffs we used to get into about what would go where since we were each pretty stubborn about how we wanted the tree to look every year. Thankfully, we got over ourselves and realized it's just a tree and what was more important was that it looked like 'us' instead of looking like the perfect vision we each had in our head. That's pretty helpful advice in any situation, actually. Don't look for what just looks perfect. Look for what is perfect."

"The problem is that I thought Jordan was perfect, but how could he be if he gave up on us, or really gave up on me? He sure didn't think I was perfect."

"And that's his loss," added my dad. "He'll regret that someday and it'll be too late. I almost lost your mother, and I'm glad I didn't. But that's a story for another time."

"Wait, what? What do you mean? And how have I never heard this before?

Mom and Dad looked at each other as if they were wondering if they should tell me or let this be. Once their nonverbal communication was complete, my dad continued.

"I'll sum up the long story, which we'll save for another time, to say that I didn't realize what I had in your mother when I first met her and we became friends. She was wonderful, but my head was turned by someone else at the time—not someone I was dating. It was just a crush—and it didn't even occur to me to think of your mom romantically at that time because my attention was elsewhere. Only when your mom started dating someone else did I look at her differently, and I take the blame for that, because she should have been the only one shining in my eyes from the beginning. But I did figure things out eventually and that I was interested in her as more than a friend, especially as our friendship grew and I got to know her more. I wasn't sure if it was too late, but I had to tell her how I felt and risk the chance of losing her friendship if she rejected me. So I took a risk. Luckily for all of us, she'd felt the same way but she didn't think I did, so she was happy that I spoke up. Once we'd finally talked, she broke things off with the other fella for me. And I'm so grateful she did."

Dad looked at Mom with such love and caring in his eyes that I almost burst into tears on the spot. Yeah, they were goals. No question about it. Would I one day be telling a story like this to my own child or children? If only I had a time machine to find out.

"Your dad summed it up pretty well," added my mom. "One part that's missing is that I had no idea he felt the same way because I thought his type was something else entirely from me based on something he'd said, which it turns out I'd misunderstood. But I didn't know that at the time, so there was no way I was going to try and compete when I thought I didn't stand a chance. I didn't want to tell him how I felt and hear from him that he wanted someone who looked nothing like me. How embarrassing would that have been? So, I had told myself that we'd just be friends and I'd be okay with that, and that whole 'fake it til you make it' cliche is true. After a while, I was okay to the point that I started dating someone. The other guy was perfectly nice, but when I ran into your dad at the county fair and he finally told me how I felt, I knew who I had to choose. There was really no contest. Your dad's always been the one for me. And perhaps Jordan will come to the same realization over time… or maybe he's just the guy you had to date on the way to perfect."

That feeling was what I wanted. When you just knew and it was clear and there was no pretense, although I guess my parents had indeed both been pretending for some time until they took that chance with each other.

I thought of Jordan and I didn't see ever having that moment with him. How could I? Maybe I was the one instead who'd been pretending. I'd acted like I was fine and happy, but deep down, was I really, or did I just love the idea of being in love?

"Thanks, mom. That's sweet of you to say but I don't really believe it's going to be Jordan because I think he's already made up his mind and that isn't likely to change. It's a nice thought, though. But he just doesn't want me."

"You're special, and I'm not just saying that because I'm your mother. I'm saying it because it's true. If he doesn't see that and regret what he lost, he's an idiot."

"That I will certainly agree with you on. He's an idiot for sure. Okay, I'm going to get out of here before I give you his number so you can call him and tell him that whole story, because that wouldn't help anyone. I love you both so much."

"We love you, too, sweetheart. Make sure you send us a pic or video of your tree when it's up, and we want a bunch of pics from your art show."

"Of course! You know Dani's going to have a bunch of pictures. And I want all the pics and the gossip from your annual holiday party that night."

I hugged Mom and Dad goodbye and got in the U-Haul to head over to Dani's gallery to drop off the paintings so she'd have them there and be able to make various-sized prints of them for sale before my show.

On the way there, I might as well have been on autopilot, as I was lost in a reverie of being at a county fair at night, with the fairway lights blazing and the sounds of the rides whirling through the air. I was eating a fried chocolate chip cookie dough ball fresh out of the oven, and bumped into Jordan. He'd been searching the fair for me and was so happy to see me.

He grabbed me lightly by the arms and said he had to tell me that he'd made a terrible mistake wanting to date anyone else. I was the only one he wanted and he hoped that I hadn't moved on and would take him back, because he wanted me forever. Speechless, I nodded my head yes, and he dropped to one knee, pulling out a ring and asked me to marry him right then and there, which I happily accepted.

The ringing of my cell phone pulled me out of my fugue state. Dani. I hit "accept" on my steering wheel to take the call over Bluetooth.

"Hey, you. What's up? I'm on the road right now heading your way."

"Fabulous!" replied Dani. "Was calling to see what time you thought you might get here and if you wanted to come up to the apartment after for dinner with me and Jessie."

"Oh, heck, yes. I will be there in probably an hour and a half or so, as long as traffic stays as fine as it is, so yes, absolutely! Can't wait."

"Excellent! See you then! Love you."

"Love you, too, my friend. See you soon."

Boy, I was glad Dani had called when she did before I started conjuring up images of my dream wedding to Jordan in my head, right down to a sleeveless wedding dress and our wedding in an old barn, surrounded by just close friends and family, wildflowers and twinkling lights as decorations, and down home charm.

As I thought about that wedding, I wondered where the thought came from. Jordan would never want to be married in a barn. That wouldn't have the look that he'd want, which would instead be a sleek country club or fancy hotel ballroom, surrounded by business acquaintances as well as a vast array of friends and family. Down home charm would be frowned upon quite a bit.

I couldn't stop picturing that wedding in my head, though. It felt right.

Okay, self. Stop. Jordan isn't going to choose you and you're certainly not going to marry him.

Time to bring myself back to reality. First, I hadn't been to a county fair in about a decade. Second, if I did bump into Jordan at a fair, there's no doubt that it would be right as I had taken a big bite of food so I had a mouthful and he'd have his arm draped around some gorgeous model who'd look at me aghast. There would be no declaration of love and instead would just be me fleeing in horror. Ugh.

I was glad that had worked out well for my parents, but I didn't really think that was going to be my future.

Instead of thinking more about that, I told my phone to call Joshykins, hoping he'd be free for a moment or not yet at work.

"Hey! What's up?" His voice came through along with the sound of wind through his car windows. Okay, he was driving to work and not there yet. Good.

"Hey! I was just driving from my folks over to Dani's gallery to drop off the paintings and thought I'd call and say hi. How are you?"

"Good. Good! I have a funny story for you, actually."

"Oh, no. Joshykins, did you sleep order songs or sleep pay bills again?"

"No! Who do you take me for? Okay, so I've done both of those. But no, that's not what this is about. I have a new favorite snack I have to tell you about."

"Why do I think I'm going to hate this?"

"Probably, but you're still going to try it the next time you're over at our house, just like the dill pickle candy."

"Yeah, that was all sorts of weird, but it worked. And I hate pickles. I don't get that. Okay, so spill. What's this new favorite snack."

"Green boiled peanuts."

I took my eyes off the road for one second to give the dashboard phone screen the hairy eyeball at that statement. There's no way he just said that.

"I'm sorry. What? How do you boil peanuts in green? This better not be a Soylent Green kind of thing, because those are people, Joshykins. Put Zack on the phone right now."

"No, no, no. You have to google it when you're not driving. Green peanuts are ones that are freshly pulled and haven't been dehydrated. And I boil them in brine."

"Per usual, I'm so confused. Had no idea there were peanuts that weren't the usual crackly kind. I kind of feel like you've made this up."

"You know me well enough to know I don't make up random food things. I just try random food things."

"Okay, solid point. I'm still concerned at the thought of moist peanuts boiled in salty water or whatever brine is. Are these going to wind up on the menu at Subtle Savors?"

"Noo. I don't think it quite fits in with our fare. Zack loves them, though. He didn't think he would at all, but he does. And you're going to try them when you're over? You promise."

"Like I have any other choice in that matter. You know I will anyway. No questions asked."

"Perfect! Okay, I just pulled into the restaurant now. We'll have to set a date for green boiled peanut fun. And I'm totally naming my next band Moist Peanuts. Love you!"

"Love you, too, Joshykins. Talk to you later. Have a great night at the restaurant."

I hung up the phone, shaking my head. Our conversations always baffled me but amused me at the same time. Joshykins had definitely expanded my palate in the foods that I'd try.

Stopping at a light, I leaned my head back against the headrest and rested my palms on the top of my head for a brief moment of Reiki to get a bit of serenity. Talking to Joshykins was good for my soul, as would seeing Dani and Jessie, but Jordan was still top of mind.

"Bring the good. Release the bad." I recited that to myself a few times. It wasn't at all a typical Reiki statement, but it worked for me at this moment.

As the light changed, I took my focus back and concentrated on driving, telling myself to stop thinking of Jordan. There were other guys to think of.

There was Abigail's boyfriend, Ethan, who was going by Nick on Connect, who I sure didn't want to think of. I really needed to tell her about that. It wasn't fair to keep that from her, especially if it was him and not someone using his picture as their own.

But if it wasn't a catfish? No, the thought was too dreadful to consider. They were so cute together, and I couldn't just assume because of what happened with Jordan that all guys were jerks.

There were also a few guys I had swiped right on in recent nights, and had received the "You're a match" message. But nothing happened with any of those after the match or the introductory volley of "hey".

No further message. Nothing.

Which okay, was probably good since it avoided the whole getting a message from a dude's wife thing. Ghosting seemed to be so typical on these sites from what I had heard, and I guess it was true. Typical.

I'd heard of and knew too many guys, and girls for that matter, who were all about the chase. Once they got the previously unattainable person, they were no longer interested and moved on to their next conquest. That sure didn't help with making dating work, because you didn't know who was really interested in a relationship and who just wanted to play around.

So many games… It just wasn't fun.

Nine

Chloe

"This is going to be so much fun!" I said while looking around our new apartment to check everything out. We'd walked through the closet door into the kitchen with a view of the living room. It was just as cute as it looked from the doorway in Emerson's office.

In front of me were two couches and the TV was set against the wall next to big windows.

"Ooh, windows!" I ran over and raised the blinds to reveal one heck of a view.

"Mitch! Come look! Trees! And grass! And tennis courts. We can play tennis!"

Mitch came over and stood next to me looking out at the view.

"The trees and grass do look very pretty, and I love how excited you are about all of this. But, umm, Chloe, you realize it's almost winter, right? I don't think people play tennis in the fall nor in the snow."

Shoot. He did have a point there. But...

"We're here to spread joy and help people believe, right? Let's cause them to believe that tennis is for all four seasons, and not just for the spring and summer months! Wouldn't it be fun to figure out how to play?"

Mitch placed his hands on my shoulders to lead me gently away from the windows.

"How about first we explore the rest of the apartment?"

"Oh, yes! I forgot we had more than just this room and that gorgeous view! Eep. Okay, kitchen first?"

Without waiting for Mitch to reply, because I knew he'd follow me, I walked back into the kitchen. There was so much to explore, and I decided to start with the fridge.

"Mitch! You're going to love this. There's two big jugs of chocolate milk—your favorite! And a bunch of flavored water for me, but of course you can have some, too. Ooh, look at all of these fruits and veggies here. And cheese! This looks so good!"

I reached up and opened the freezer, revealing a bunch of frozen meat, meals, veggies, fruits, and pizzas along with pre-made cookie and pizza dough.

"Emerson did say she'd made sure we'd have plenty of food on hand and she was right," said Mitch, who had come up to stand next to me. "I'm glad to see chocolate milk there as well as all the rest. The cupboards are probably fully stocked as well."

He opened one of the cupboards to find pasta sauces, boxes of pasta, rice, and cereal along with a lot of cans of veggies. Yup, we were fully stocked!

"Well, I guess we won't have to go shopping for food anytime soon," I said.

I was a bit bummed because I was dying to check out stores, but there'd be time for that.

Turning from the kitchen, I walked over to see three closed doors along the hallway. One had a post-it on it with Mitch's name on it and another had my name. Leaving those two rooms for a moment, I opened the third door revealing the bathroom.

"This is so pretty!", I exclaimed.

It was colorful, which would help with waking up in the morning. The black shower curtain was covered with tree leaves, flowers, and berries in hues of deep purple, navy blue, dark orange, turquoise, mustard yellow, and burgundy red among others.

That turquoise tone carried over into the bathmat, towels, soap dish, and toothbrush holder, which held two toothbrushes—one that was pink and one that was navy blue.

Mitch chuckled as he walked into the bathroom and saw the toothbrushes.

"Let me guess. You're going to want the navy blue one just to be different."

"No way!" I grabbed the bright pink toothbrush and held it up. "It's so pretty and girly and mine! You can have the boring blue one."

"As you wish," Mitch said. He turned and walked towards the bedroom door with his name on it. "Do you want to check my room out with me or check yours out yourself first?"

"I'm going to come see yours to further the anticipation of seeing my own room. Eep!"

Mitch opened the door and walked into his room with me right on his heels. The room was pretty much what I would have picked out for Mitch and it made me wonder if the toothbrush colors were chosen to go along with the room decorations.

Mitch's bed was covered with a navy blue comforter with a navy, green, and white plaid blanket folded at the end of the bed. Two pillows—one navy and one a deep green to match the blanket—were on his bed against a dark gray upholstered headboard. The windows in his room were covered by emerald green curtains, and there were two prints of gray fern leaves on a white background above his bed. The gray tone continued in the dresser.

It was simple, classic, and comforting, so it was the perfect match for my bestie.

He walked over to his closet and opened the door to find a bunch of khakis, sweaters, jeans, and other items of clothes. All looked like they were well suited for him.

Closing the closet door, he turned to me. "I'm not opening the dresser drawers in front of you, so don't even ask."

"Aww, c'mon, Mitch. Don't want me to see that they gave you days of the week underwear, so you'll remember what day it is?"

Mitch flushed. Okay, I might have pushed things too far with that. Hopefully I didn't.

"Of the two of us, who's more likely to forget what day it is?"

"Okay, valid point. That would indeed be me. You know I was just teasing you, right?"

"Yes, obviously. I've known you long enough to know that. Speaking of forgetting something… aren't you itching to go see your room now?"

"Yes! Yes! But I want to see it with you, so can we go? Please? Please?" I tugged on Mitch's arm to drag him out the door of his room with me. It didn't take much cajoling, though.

"Of course, silly. Let's go!"

I sprinted next door and gently opened my bedroom door, expecting to find bright pink all over the place that would be a bit jarring.

Instead, I was blown away.

It was pink, yes, but tones of rose gold and blush rather than the bright pink I thought I'd find. I was relieved.

My bed was covered in a blush tufted comforter with a cream fluffy blanket folded at the end of it, and a light gray throw rug on the floor next to my bed across from the cream-colored dresser. My bedside table was a rose gold and glass table in between my bed and the windows that were covered by the most gorgeous panels. The top of each was light gray silk with beaded sequins in between the light gray and the blush part of the panels at the bottom.

"I'm in love! Everything is perfect, but those curtains? Beyond romantic. When I see them, all I can think of is a dress I saw once on someone when Grace was at an event. The dress was just like that with a light gray bodice; the sequins beneath the bodice, and then it flows into the blush silk skirt. Wow. I can't believe this room."

I could tell Mitch was happy with the whole apartment because he was smiling.

"I can picture you in a dress like that, Chloe, just from your description, and fashion isn't typically my thing. This room suits you perfectly and I'm glad you're happy with all of it. We're not looking in your dresser either with both of us in the room. But you haven't looked at your closet yet. I'm surprised. Figured that would be the first thing you'd look at."

"How did I forget that part?"

I opened the closet door to find jeans, dresses, khakis, sweaters, leggings, tunics, and..

What?

What on earth was that shiny bright pink thing hanging at the back?

I pushed clothes aside until I could get a closer look and pull it out of the closet into the light. Holding it up out of the closet, Mitch and I looked at it in shock. What the heck?

Ten

Grace

What the heck have I done? I'm going to actually have a gallery show?

After dropping off my paintings with Dani and then enjoying dinner with her and Jessie, I drove back to my apartment with the U-Haul since it was too late to return it tonight. Sitting in the parking lot before heading inside, I thought about the next day. The plan was that Abigail would meet me at the rental place after work, so I could drop off the truck and then she'd drive me back home and we'd go through my closet to figure out what I wanted to wear to the show, if anything of what I had.

I had picked up a bit of a sense of style over the years, but she always knocked it out of the park. So I trusted Abigail more than I did myself sometimes for deciding on outfits.

To get the paintings back from the gallery—unless by some chance they all sold, but I knew there was at least one I didn't want to part with—I'd already rented a truck for the day after the show.

As I got out of the truck, I stretched. I loved seeing my parents, but the round-trip was a bit of a hike for one day and my legs always felt a bit dead after I got home. Would make sure to do some Reiki to soothe my muscles tonight before bed.

My phone vibrated as I walked through the parking lot. Pulling it out of the front pocket of my purse, I saw it was my folks. Of course I'd accept that call, but I had a moment of being bummed that it wasn't a text from Jordan or Wyatt.

"Hey there! Just got home and was going to let you know as soon as I got in the apartment. I'm in the parking lot now."

"Perfect," said my mom. "That's what I was calling to check. We're going out to the grocery store to get some prep done for the party, so I wanted to make sure you got home safe before we left."

"I appreciate it, Mom. Sure did. I'm here safe and sound now and about to walk in the building, so all good. I'm glad you called, and it was great seeing you and Dad today."

"You, too, honey. You know we're always happy to see you. Okay, we're heading out now. Have a good night and know we love you."

"I love you guys too, Mom. Talk soon."

Ending the call, I walked up the stairs to my apartment. I briefly thought to check my mailbox, but then light dawned that it was Sunday. Not a mail day, Grace.

Unlocking and opening the door from the apartment foyer, I walked up the stairs to the hallway of my apartment. As I got to the top of the stairs, I stopped in my tracks.

I have to be seeing things.

Was that actually a pink dinosaur standing in the hall outside my apartment?

No. There's no way. I didn't think the one drink I'd had at Jessie and Dani's was all that strong. But maybe I was just that tired from the long day.

I rubbed my hands over my eyes to see if the apparition would go away.

Nope. Still there. Okay, so that's a person in an inflatable pink dinosaur costume waddling up and down the hallway. This is bizarre. Were dinosaur telegrams now a thing? I wonder where they're going if it is.

Wait. They're stopped in the hall outside of my apartment. This is totally something Joshykins would do. But how did they get into the hallway? Everyone in the apartment building was pretty good about not buzzing just anyone in, so that wouldn't make sense. And it's not quite like a big ol' pink dinosaur could follow someone inside without being noticed.

I pulled my phone out of my purse again in case I needed it, and if it was a telegram, I wanted to get that on film for posterity. My keys were already clutched in my left hand. I didn't really think I'd need them as a weapon, but you never knew, unfortunately.

Okay, here we go. Let's go see what this is about. I walked down the hallway slowly until I got closer to my door. The pink dinosaur had lumbered off towards the other end of the hallway but was coming back towards me. I should say something.

"Umm, hi there. Hello?"

Good one, Grace. Way to show strength and courage. That'll scare off the potential big bad. I tried again, hoping for a less squeaky voice.

"Can I help you with something? Are you looking for someone's apartment?"

The dinosaur drew closer to me and then stopped short. I glanced at its hands—well, paws. Is that what they called dinosaur hands? I didn't even know. Was there a knife hidden there?

"Hi there!"

Okay, it was a female. That was less scary than finding out it was a guy in the suit. But still bizarre.

"Hi. Are you looking for someone?"

"Oh, no! I live here." The pink dinosaur pointed to the apartment across from mine where Kelly and John used to live.

Okay, so I'm meeting my new neighbor and they're dressed as a dinosaur? For fun? Did they wear the costume all the time? That had to get hot, right?

"Ohhh, I thought you were a singing telegram someone hired or something. Hi. I'm sorry. I'm Grace. I live here." I pointed to my apartment. "We're neighbors. I didn't realize the new tenants were moving in so quickly as Kelly and John just moved out."

"Grace!" The pink dinosaur jumped up and down with excitement. "Hi! It's so great to meet you! I'm Chloe! And yes, Mitch and I just moved in."

"Is Mitch your husband? Boyfriend? Umm, life partner? Does he dress up like a dinosaur too?"

Chloe burst out laughing.

"No, no! Mitch is my roommate and best bud. You'll be able to recognize him if you see him in the hallway from his bright almost white blonde hair. He's gay, so no, not my husband nor boyfriend or anything. And nooo, he's definitely not the type to dress up like a dinosaur. That's more something I'd do, or I guess do do, since I'm currently standing here doing so. Duh, Chloe."

I was more than a little bit bewildered, but hoped it wasn't showing in my eyes.

"So, this is the first time you've ever dressed up like a dinosaur? I guess that's one way to make an impression when you go around to meet neighbors."

"Oh, wow. Yeah, one heck of a first impression I'm giving. Sorry. Let's try this again. Kelly had left a note in the apartment saying that if we needed anything, Grace was right across the hall and that she's great and the one reason why Kelly and John were sad to be leaving, so I already have a great first impression of you… and this is your impression of me."

The inflatable pink dinosaur head fell forward a bit, like it was sad. Awww. That was so sweet of Kelly to say that in the note to Chloe and Mitch, but yeah, this was definitely an odd first impression. I didn't want her to be sad, though. Heck, I knew how important first impressions were and I had my own anxiety and self-consciousness about those. I had to help Chloe feel better.

"Gosh, don't feel bad. Seeing a pink dinosaur in my hallway isn't exactly a usual occurrence, but it's memorable in a great way. I'll never forget the way I met my new neighbor the first time."

The dinosaur's head perked back up and I could see a glimpse of a face behind the clear plastic window in the dinosaur's neck. Okay, there was a smile there. Phew.

"That is true," said Chloe, and I could hear the smile in her voice. "I wasn't planning on wearing this pink T-Rex costume at all, but I'm going to be wearing it somehow as part of my new job at the Silverton Rec Department, which I start tomorrow. So I figured I'd get used to it now by walking down the hallway since there's more room out here. I was going to do so in the parking lot, but I rethought that since people might think that was a bit peculiar seeing a T-Rex roaming around. Not that walking up and down the hallway isn't odd. Yeah, I should have rethought that rethought…"

"I know the Silverton Rec! I've taught a few art classes through them. I'm an art teacher at the high school, by the way. So, you must be one of the two new hires Amber has coming on. She's so excited. You'll love working with her. She's so detail-oriented. Wait until you see her binders upon binders. But her energy level and her love of putting on events for the rec department is the highest of anyone I've ever seen. And a side note: Bring her a hazelnut coffee with extra cream, no sugar tomorrow and she'll be thrilled."

"Ooh, I'll make a note of that right now. Or actually I'll tell Mitch, who's the other new hire at the center. Hold on…"

Chloe opened the door of her apartment and called out, "Mitch! Can you make a note for us to bring a hazelnut coffee with extra cream, no sugar tomorrow?"

She looked back at me. "Did I get that right?"

"Absolutely perfect! You'll start off on her great side. Oh, actually get two because her assistant manager, Laurel, will also love that."

"Yay!" Chloe poked her head back inside the apartment, which looked a bit tough considering it was a huge inflatable T-Rex head trying to fit under the doorway. "Mitch, make that two coffees! Thanks! You're the best!"

She closed the door and came back into the hallway.

"Thanks so much for that information. That's going to be huge! I'm so glad we met! And I just realized I'm keeping you from going into your apartment. I'm sure you want to see your boyfriend or husband or roommate?"

"Nah, none of the above. I live alone. I was dating someone for a little while there, but that didn't work out. It happens." I shrugged my shoulders, feeling unsure how much I should say and wondering why I was actually saying anything about Jordan.

My phone vibrated in my hand and I instinctively glanced down.

"Speak of the devil…"

"Do you need to get that? From the look on your face, I'm guessing it's the guy you were dating. Maybe he wants to get back together…"

My heart shouldn't have skipped a beat with that thought, but it did. Darn it.

"Excuse me for one second. I just want to glance at it, because you're right on who the text is from."

"No need to apologize! I'm excited and have my fingers crossed for you."

I unlocked my phone and opened his text to read:

Was just thinking of you… Watching the game and an ad came on with "Amazing Grace" as the background song. Hope you're well.

Well, he was thinking of me. I had to admit I liked that.

"I take it the text was good based on your smile…" Chloe said.

I'd forgotten she was standing there. I'm sure my grin was a mile wide. Jordan was thinking of me and I couldn't believe it. That's what I wanted, right? Unless he was just bored and texting me was easy.

"Yeah, it was unexpected and really good. Do you mind excusing me? I should reply to this and get some stuff done before going to sleep."

"Of course, Grace. I'm glad that happened and that it made you smile. It was a real pleasure meeting you. I'm sure we'll talk again, but thanks also for the tip on the coffee for Amber."

"You're welcome. Glad to. I know her pretty well. Great meeting you, too, Chloe."

I unlocked my door, went inside, and hung up my keys on the key rack. Pulling out one of the kitchen table chairs, I slumped into it and placed my purse on the chair next to it.

Jordan texted me.

He was thinking about me, and this wasn't just him sending a klutz gif like before. Did it mean something? I didn't know, but I should reply.

Great song! Hope the game's going well. Just got home from my folks with my paintings for a show I'm doing at Dani's so I haven't watched any of it. Will probably check it out in a few to catch up. Having a good weekend?

That wasn't exactly breezy, nor short, but it would do.

My phone buzzed in my hand, causing me to almost jump out of the chair. Had Jordan replied back already? I looked and saw it was from Wyatt.

Shoot.

Seeing the text from him made me smile, but it wasn't the same rush I got when I got a text from Jordan. That wasn't fair to Wyatt, though, because there was history with Jordan. I read:

Sorry I haven't been in touch. Busy, busy week and into the weekend with a lot of work meetings and deadlines. I think I'll be able to come by your show Friday. Hopefully. Fingers crossed.

That was sweet, and a nice apology. He didn't have to do that.

And really, there was nothing wrong with me talking to him. I shouldn't feel guilty. Well, Jordan was dating other people the last I knew, so it was fine for me to meet other people. Plus, I'd really enjoyed that first conversation with Wyatt.

Awesome! I hear ya about the busy'ness. Hope to see you Friday. I'll cross my fingers.

Okay, no new notifications, which means nothing from Jordan. I got up from the kitchen chair. Leaving my phone on the table, I went to my bedroom and changed into my comfy college t-shirt and joggers for sleeping, and then hit the bathroom to wash my face and brush my teeth, which would stop me from having a snack before bed. I was full from dinner anyway.

When I came back, my phone screen had gone dark, and flared back to life as I picked it up, showing me just my home screen without any banners.

Any chance my phone was just hiding notifications? I swiped down from the top to see if anything came up. Nope. Just a blank screen showing me how much Jordan hadn't replied. Excellent. And because I was a masochist when it came to Jordan, I even opened texts to see if he had replied and notifications just weren't showing up. I saved myself slightly by covering up the right hand side of the screen so I couldn't see if he'd read my message or not.

As I hid part of the screen, I realized that he still had more of a hold on me than I thought he did, because I didn't want to know if he'd read my message and not replied. I glanced down at the bottom of the text chain quickly and only saw my message there.

Okay, no reply at all. I quickly closed out of texts before I could make myself feel worse by seeing that dreaded icon there showing he'd read it and didn't care enough to reply.

It was probably for the best right now that he hadn't replied though and that I hadn't said anything too big.

As much as he liked to tell me whatever was going on with him or any feeling he had, listening to me or replying to me wasn't top of his priority chain at all.

And what does that say, self? It says you should not be in contact with him because you want someone who listens to you and talks to you. Not someone who just talks at you and doesn't even know the real you.

I blamed that crazy chemistry I had with Jordan for ignoring that part and just assuming that over time, he'd listen more. But that wasn't the case. It was time to admit it.

I knew it was also my fault because I didn't tell him it was bothering me. When I tried once and he just kept talking like I hadn't spoken, I stopped trying.

It wasn't supposed to be that way. At least it wasn't when I saw my parents talk. They were all about talking to each other and I knew they listened to each other and cared about what the other was saying.

That's what I wanted. It was what I deserved.

Why didn't I have that with Jordan?

Without my usual overthinking, I flipped back into texts. I I needed to know if Jordan had read and not replied or not.

Read.

There was my answer. The delivered icon might as well have been beaming a spotlight at me. He'd read my text. He didn't care to reply, so he hadn't. I could provide excuses for him like that he got a call or something happened so he couldn't reply, but that's all they were. Excuses.

Enough.

This had to end. I went back to the main text page and swiped left on his name. "Delete" came up.

Did I want to delete the text thread? Maybe not, but I had to. Keeping his texts around was wreaking havoc on my self confidence, and probably also stopping me from pursuing anyone else because my mind was still stuck on him.

Like Wyatt.

Okay, decision made. I continued swiping left so the text thread would disappear and stop sitting there to mock me.

When I'd first texted with Wyatt, that conversation was a true conversation and what I thought conversations should be. By the way he responded, he seemed to be listening and replying to what I was saying instead of bulldozing ahead with what he wanted to say. It was a nice change from Jordan-centric conversations.

I really enjoyed that witty repartee with him. But I had no way of knowing if that's how he was all the time because we hadn't talked since then except for that brief text tonight.

Hopefully he'd show up Friday and we'd get a chance to talk, so I could see how he was talking in person. Although that was going to be at my gallery show. Did I really think we'd get much of a chance to talk then?

Well, we would if my show was a bomb and no one else showed up. Ugh. Let's hope that wasn't the case because even though that would give us more time to talk, it sure wouldn't be an awesome first impression.

I could just imagine it now. I'd be standing there with maybe one other person besides Dani and he'd walk in. He'd look around, wondering if he should quickly turn around but then he'd see me and feel stuck so he'd walk over with a look of pity on his face.

Oh, hi, Wyatt. So great to meet you. Look at what an awful artist I must be considering only two people showed up for my show. Yeah, totally someone you'd want to date and be around. Yup, you can just leave now. No, of course you suddenly don't have time to date. Understandable. I'd do the same thing if this was reversed. Nope, no worries. No need to ever text me again.

Yeah, hopefully that wouldn't happen. I was blushing as red as my hair from embarrassment at just the thought.

Of course, even that would only happen if he did get a chance to show up that night. Guess I'd find out Friday.

Was it too late to cancel the show? Now I was panicking that no one was going to show up.

I looked down at my phone.

No, no texting Dani and telling her the show's canceled. She did so much work putting this together for you and you're not backing out due to nerves. And especially not from nerves based on your imagination running rampant at what could be.

I quickly said a prayer:

Dear Lord, I know we haven't talked in a while. But could you help me find the strength to get through my show on Friday and if you could put even a tiny word out into the world that people should come to my show, that would be great? Thank you!

I promised myself that I'd say an Our Father before going to sleep tonight, and maybe start looking into local churches to get back into going. I'd always loved the pageantry of it all and the singing.

Getting up, I stretched. Okay, it was time to relax.

Suddenly, I heard a knock at the door. Who was it at this hour? I hadn't heard a buzzer.

Peeking out the peephole, I saw a tall young woman with springy blond curls standing there.

"Hello?" I called out tentatively.

"Grace. It's me, Chloe. Your new neighbor. Just not in dinosaur form right now. This is me."

Oh my gosh. Well, now I know what she looks like. She had a kind, pretty face. I unlatched and opened the door.

"Hi, Chloe. I'm sorry. I definitely didn't recognize you outside of your pink dino outfit. What's up?"

"So sorry to bother you, but I realized that you'd only seen me in that outfit so I wanted to introduce myself to you without it on, so if I said hi in the parking lot or hallway, you'd know who I was."

That makes sense, and good to know she wouldn't always be walking around in the dinosaur outfit. Not that I thought she would, I guess, since Amber and Laurel probably wouldn't be big on having dinosaurs roam around their office. They were both fun, but professional.

"I appreciate that you did, because yes, it was tough to see what you looked like."

"That's all I wanted. Also, are you okay? I'm sorry. I probably shouldn't have asked, but you look troubled."

"You're sweet. Thanks for asking. I'm fine. No, actually, you know what, I'm not that fine. I'm nervous because I have my first real art show Friday night and I'm scared no one's going to show and I'm going to look like an idiot. Wow, that just all came tumbling out, didn't it? I'm so sorry."

"Don't ever apologize. I'm a good listener. I can promise you that Mitch and I will be there Friday night for your show, and I can guarantee you will have a great turnout. Just trust me on this, and people are going to love your art because you're so talented. I just know it. You wouldn't be having an art show if you weren't.. Before Friday, you can just slip a note under my door with the info or something, and we'll be there."

"Aww, Chloe, you're an angel. Thank you for being so sweet. That's just what I needed to hear."

"You're welcome. That's what I'm here for. Okay, I'm going to head back to get ready for bed. Have a great night, Grace. Sleep well."

"I appreciate it, Chloe. You sleep well, too. Thank you. Really."

Chloe went back across the hall, and I closed the door with my shoulders slumped. I felt more relaxed than I was before Chloe had come over. It was like she knew, but that was silly. However she happened to knock on my door, I was grateful.

I decided that along with Reiki tonight, I was going to indulge in a bubble bath to soothe my muscles a bit more and maybe watch a bit of "Coyote Ugly", which was my favorite guilty pleasure movie. Hopefully that would help me sleep before a day of school and then return the truck tomorrow night.

As I walked over to the bathroom to get that set up, I thought of my new neighbor, the Pink T-Rex with a kind smile. I grinned. I had been worried about whether I'd like the neighbors as much as I'd liked Kelly and John. Seems I had nothing to worry about.

Eleven

Chloe

"I'm so worried…"

Mitch and I were on our way to the Silverton Recreation Department for our first day and my nerves were shot. I was glad Mitch was driving the zippy little Ford Focus because, besides having no idea how to drive, there's no way I would have been able to concentrate.

We had stopped by a local coffee shop, Daylight Donuts. on the way for two hazelnut coffees for Amber and Laurel, a large hot with extra cream and no sugar for me, and a medium regular for Mitch. According to Grace, Amber and Laurel would be thrilled. So at least we had that going for us.

Typically, I always knew what to expect and what I'd be doing every day because we had set rules for everything up there.

But now I was on Earth and starting a job there and I had no idea what I was walking into, besides that at some point I'd be wearing that pink T-Rex outfit again. They didn't expect me to wear that every day, did they? Should I have brought it? I tried to sit down in it and that just wasn't happening, so that would make anything in the office unmanageable.

"What are you worried about?" asked Mitch, not taking his eyes off the road. "You're going to be great. I know it."

"Thank you. But that's what I'm worried about. I don't know what we'll be doing. Should I have brought the T-Rex outfit with me? Am I wearing the right thing? Will Amber like me? I know she'll love you because you're awesome, but I'm not for everyone and I know that I can be too much for people. Maybe I'll be too much for her and she'll fire me. Mitch, I'm going to be fired from my first ever Earth job. Emerson's going to be so disappointed."

Mitch reached over and took my hand in his, rubbing his thumb across my palm to try and soothe me.

"Okay. Take a deep breath. First, you look great. You always do. The T-Rex costume is in its bag in the trunk. I put it there in case you need it, so it's there. Amber will love you because you're amazing. Your energy is perfect for the recreation department. And you won't get fired and Emerson won't be disappointed."

He always knew the right thing to say to make me feel better. I took a deep breath, counting to four as I inhaled, again as I held my breath, and then once again as I exhaled. That was a trick Emerson had taught me for relaxation and anxiety a couple years back and it was one that had stuck with me.

Between that and what Mitch said, I felt less anxious, which was a relief. I took a big sip of my coffee that I still held in my right hand, figuring the caffeine would help. Mitch's thumb was still rubbing my left palm gently to calm my nerves.

"I don't feel like I'm going to bolt from the car and head back from the apartment now, so thanks."

"If you ever do that, please at least wait until we're at a light and don't do so while the car's in motion, okay?"

"Yes, sir." I grinned at the thought of just hurtling myself out of the car.

Looking ahead, I saw a bunch of traffic on the busy street.

"With all of those cars, you should probably have both hands on the wheel there."

That prompted Mitch to glance down for a second and realize that he was still holding my hand. He hastily lifted his hand away and put it back on the wheel along with the other one, leaving my hand feeling a bit bare. Weirdly, the feeling of his thumb rubbing my palm stayed with me like a ghostly sensation. I knew his hand was firmly on the wheel, but the feeling on my palm said otherwise.

We sat in silence for a few moments as Mitch made his way through the traffic. Amber had told us to be at the Recreation Department building at 10 a.m. for our first day, and it was currently 9:45 with probably about five minutes to go. I was notoriously late, but Mitch was an early bird and early to everything. I was quite grateful for that especially now as I didn't want to be late on our first day.

"That must be it over on the right," Mitch suddenly said, pointing to a red brick building featuring a sign that said Silverton Town Hall. I don't know why I had pictured a bright school building when I heard the words recreation department. This certainly wasn't that.

The Town Hall was majestic and a bit imposing. And with that my nerves were flaring up again.

"I suddenly feel way underdressed," I said, looking down at my bright blue sweater and khakis. With my height, I was pleasantly surprised to find that the sweater didn't wind up looking like a crop top, which was typically the case. This was just the right length and hit at mid-hip. Mitch had decided on a dark green long sleeved polo shirt with mustard yellow chinos.

"Stop it. You look great. That sweater makes your blonde hair even brighter and your blue eyes sparkle even more than usual."

Mitch pulled into the Town Hall parking lot and stopped the car. He made driving look easy and I hoped I'd pick it up quickly so he wouldn't have to drive back and forth all the time. Instead we could take turns. But we only had a few weeks here, and I had to think about that. I wasn't actually sure how long it would take me to learn how to drive. Maybe I wouldn't learn before we left.

"Chloe? Are you coming?" Mitch poked his head into the car from the passenger door that he'd opened for me with one hand while he held the tray of three coffees in the other. He'd gotten out of the car and opened the door for me all without my noticing any of it. My head must have been in the clouds.

"Yes, of course. No idea where I just went. Thanks for opening the door."

I got out of the car, grabbing my navy cross-body purse that had been waiting at the apartment with my identifying documents. Mitch had a new wallet that contained the same for him, since we'd been told we'd need those on our first day.

Carrying a purse was new to me since we didn't need identification up there. We all just knew who everyone was. I had a feeling I was going to wind up leaving it somewhere, which wouldn't be ideal, considering that purse also had a checkbook and debit card in it.

"I know we still have a few minutes before we're supposed to be there," said Mitch. "But we don't know what floor the Recreation Department is on and that's an awfully tall building, so let's get going."

It was really cute how Mitch was reliable about being everywhere on time. He kept me in line. At the same time, I could tell he was getting antsy and seemed a bit nervous, which was weird to see, since I was usually the one on edge.

I put my hand on his shoulder to turn him around.

"I know this is reversing our roles for a moment, but now I'm going to tell you to take a deep breath, Mitch. I'm sure when we get inside there'll be a sign on the wall indicating where we're supposed to go, or a security guard or front desk person or something. You know I have no idea how Town Halls work, but that's what I'm picturing. So, let's not lollygag here and get going."

"Lollygag?" He chuckled, which made me smile, as there was no way he'd do that if he was still nervous. "We didn't come down to Earth in the 40s, Chloe. It's a good word, though."

"Wait? We didn't? Shoot. I was going to join up with the war factory and draw fake pantyhose lines up the back of my leg. I'm so glad I didn't do that."

"You'd fit in really well in the 1940s, actually. Saying goodbye to your soldier boy as he ships out to war, and writing him love letters scented with your perfume."

We were chatting while we walked over to the building, and I was glad for it as my own nerves had resurfaced.

"Oh, stop it. No way. I'd want to be out there fighting and making things happen instead of sitting at home. That sounds so boring."

"The thought of you with a gun! You'd probably shoot your foot off because you saw an animal and got distracted by its cuteness."

I smacked him gently on the arm for that one.

"Hey, while you were learning how to drive, I was taking archery lessons up there and I aced the class according to the teacher, Tony. He said I had natural skills and pinpoint accuracy."

Mitch stopped in front of the building and turned to look at me, shocked.

"Wait. What? How have you never told me that? That's pretty impressive."

"Thank you. It just never came up, I guess. But it kinda makes sense considering I'm an Amazon. Just call me the warrior princess. And you never told me about your driving classes, so guess we're keeping things from each other."

"It just never occurred to me to tell you about driving, I guess… But archery? Huh. Who knew? It's like I'm seeing you differently."

He opened the door and gallantly held it for me as I walked into the building, feeling a bit taller than I already was thanks to my memory of my archery classes.

Right in front of us, there was indeed a sign on the wall listing the various departments and what floors they were on.

"Okay, Recreation is on the second floor, so we can just take the stairs over there instead of taking the elevator, right?"

"Yup," replied Mitch. "That sounds good. Lead the way."

"Thank you, kind sir…"

We quickly made it up the sweeping Alaska gray marble staircase to the second floor.

At the top of the staircase, there was another sign on the wall to show us that Recreation was #217 off to the right, so we headed that way marveling at the marble floors, which seemed incongruent with the wood paneled walls and doors.

Before we knew it, we were standing in front of Recreation. Mitch reached ahead of me to open the door for me again, and I tentatively walked inside.

"You must be Chloe and Mitchell," said a young woman of average height at about 5'5" or so who was walking over to us. Wearing a light gray blazer with a matching skirt and a mustard-colored button-down shirt, Amber (if it was Amber) had dark brown hair that hit just below shoulder length. A skirt and a blazer? My khakis suddenly seemed like a bad choice.

"Yes, hi," I said, reaching out my hand to shake hers. "Are you Amber?"

"No, no. Sorry, I should have introduced myself. I'm the Assistant Manager here, Laurel Chen. I report to Amber just like you two will. There was a call just now that she had to take, but she'll be out in just a minute. She's over in her office."

Laurel pointed over to the back right, where I could partially see a figure through the frosted glass office window.

"Great to meet you, Laurel," said Mitch as he walked up to her and also shook her hand. He set the coffee tray down on the counter, presumably to present it to Amber and Laurel when Amber was ready.

"You, too, Mitchell. Hey, we're mustard twins with your pants and my shirt. I don't think I've seen anyone else wear that color but it looks good on you."

Was she hitting on him? Okay, her gaydar clearly wasn't working, or it was and she was looking for a new friend. Even with that, a frisson of jealousy shot through me. Clearly, I was being territorial about my bestie and didn't want to lose that close friendship we have.

"Hopefully neither of us are planning on having anything with mustard for lunch because it would wind up on our clothes," Mitch replied. "Kind of seems like we're a beacon for mustard now."

Laurel chuckled. "Nah, unless you put mustard on pizza for some reason. Amber had suggested ordering pizza for your first day. We can eat it out in the courtyard on the first floor, since it's not too cold out. Otherwise, we would have eaten it in the conference room here."

"Yummy!" I declared. "Pizza sounds great. I love pizza."

What was I saying? I'd never had Earth pizza. Hopefully it would be at least somewhat like the pizza I was used to.

"Awesome! Pizza is typically an easy choice for everyone. We're ordering two cheeses, a veggie, and a pepperoni, so that should work. Any dietary restrictions we should know about?"

"Nope," Mitch said. "We're both good with pretty much anything."

"That makes my life easy," Laurel replied.

"Making Laurel's life easy already? Well, that's a good start to your first day right there!" said a woman with a lilting voice who was coming out of the side right office. Hopefully she was indeed Amber.

She was a tall, thin, gorgeous woman with a mane of lush black hair and olive skin. She was wearing a burnt orange cardigan over a floral silk tank and short black skirt.

"Hi, Mitchell and Chloe," she said, shaking Mitch's hand first and then mine. "I'm Amber Agarwal, the Manager here of the Silverton Recreation Department. So glad to have you here, and I should tell you that Grace called me to let me know you guys were neighbors and she knew you'd be great here. I was happy to hear that, since Grace is wonderful."

"Yes, I met her, hilariously enough, when I was trying on the pink T-Rex outfit. What a first impression that must have been!"

"She definitely did mention that as well. And I should give you some information about that, shouldn't I? You're a good sport for wearing it, by the way. Some people would be too embarrassed to do so."

"Oh, gosh, no. I thought it was great and so much fun!"

"Excellent! That's the mentality we love around here. So, let's all sit down over here and we'll chat a bit."

Amber pointed at a large circular table over to the left, which looked like a typical meeting spot for the office.

Before heading over to the table, Mitch picked up the tray of coffees and brought it over. I retrieved mine that I had placed back in the tray to shake hands. It was easy to see which one was mine, as it had my lipstick print on it. I was suddenly glad that I hadn't accidentally taken a sip of one of the hazelnut ones by mistake.

"Speaking of Grace, she made sure that we arrived here today bearing the proper gifts," said Mitch. He took both hazelnut coffees out of the tray and set them in front of Laurel and Amber. "We have it on good authority that you're both a fan of hazelnut coffee with extra cream and no sugar."

"Oh, you rock," said Laurel, giving him a big smile, which set my nerves on edge a bit. Plus, hey, that coffee was also from me. "I didn't have any coffee this morning and the machine here is broken. It's getting worked on today, but I was going stir-crazy from no caffeine. Thanks so much." She put her hand on Mitch's arm as she said the last sentence. Down, girl.

"You're welcome," said Mitch. "But you should also be thanking Chloe since Grace told her and then Chloe told me. It's from both of us."

"Thank you, Chloe," said Laurel. She took her hand off Mitch's arm to pick up the coffee and take a sip.

"Yes, thank you, both," said Amber. "Grace is so sweet and it was thoughtful of you to bring us coffee on your first day. I hope Laurel has told you that we have plans for pizza lunch to welcome you."

"She sure did and it sounds delicious," I replied. "Can't wait!"

"Wonderful! Well, let's chat and go through some information here."

Amber took some folders from the large pile in front of her and passed them around. I was surprised there weren't binders based on what Grace had told me. Maybe she'd been exaggerating? I guess I'd find out as I worked with her.

"Okay, so Mitchell, you're going to be the Coordinator here, handling the clerical and admin duties for us. We'd heard that you have a sense for numbers, so you'll be doing a lot of running reports and accounting. Think you're up for that?"

"Absolutely. I love numbers and keeping things organized, so you've chosen the right person."

"Perfect! That's the impression I got, so I'm glad I was right. Laurel used to be the Coordinator before she was promoted, so you'll probably be working with her closely during your training."

Laurel looked over at Mitch and gave him a big smile. "I'm looking forward to it. Great to have a fellow numbers person around here."

Of course they were going to be working together closely. That seemed right.

"As for you, Chloe. You're going to be the Event Assistant here, which means that you're going to be working on organizing and overseeing special activities, including the annual Silverton Christmas stroll. Part of our annual stroll always includes inflatable T-Rexes walking alongside Santa's sleigh. We're known for having T-Rexes instead of reindeer, and we have a team of volunteer T-Rexes led by a dance teacher, Nadia, that you'll be part of. The volunteers also get together to dance around outside of our local senior centers and schools on a few days in December to spread some silly Christmas cheer. There'll be more than that, but that's to start."

"That sounds like so much fun! I can't wait to meet the volunteers and get started. And yes, I'm totally in for being a T-Rex. I felt so at home in that costume. I can't explain it."

"Too funny," Amber said. "That's what the volunteers say about the costumes. I don't understand it, but I have a bit of claustrophobia, so being inside a costume doesn't exactly work well for me. You'll fit right in with the whole group. In fact, there's a volunteer meeting later today after lunch, so you'll get to meet them."

"I can't wait," I said. Part of me wondered if the volunteers were going to show up in their inflatable T-Rex costumes, but it seemed silly to ask, so I didn't.

"Now, Christmastime has always been special in Silverton," said Amber. "But before Laurel and I joined, the Recreation Department wasn't all that involved. We were typically reserved for summer activities, but I just love Christmas, so I wanted to get involved, and well, I sure did."

"You could even say it's in your blood," Laurel added.

"How's that?" Mitch asked.

"What Laurel means is that my family has always been big into Christmas," Amber said. "My grandfather worked part-time as a Santa at the Silverton Mall and then when he got older and couldn't do so anymore, my dad took over for him. It worked out well because Grampy and Dad both worked overnight at the post office. They could have easily just slept during the day but they loved putting on that Santa suit and getting into the whole act and interacting with the kids. Plus, as they got older they both grew long white beards and always had rosy cheeks, so my running joke with my siblings as we were growing up was that we were actually related to the real Santa."

Visions of letters to Santa at the North Pole swirled in my head, and peppermint candy canes, and hot chocolate with sprinkles. Hmm, maybe I should have had breakfast before we left the apartment instead of just having that coffee on the way over? Lunchtime pizza couldn't come quickly enough. But thinking of the letters gave me an idea.

"I have an idea that might be weird. What do you think about setting up a special Letters to Santa box outside Town Hall or at the post office, if of course you don't have one already? I know it's soon, but we could have a table where kids could write their letters and then drop them in the box. It would have to be a red box of course and maybe we could get someone to affix or paint candy canes on it, and include some other festive things like hot cocoa with sprinkles and bells or a sleigh."

"That's a great idea, Chloe! Letters that are sent to Santa usually wind up at the post office where people go through them in case there's anything in the letters that need to be addressed, but I love the thought of that, and it would be so festive and pretty straightforward. And I know there are some old mailboxes that are no longer used in storage at the post office. One of them might be perfect! Plus, we're having the annual kids' party a week before Christmas at the rec center, along with pictures with Santa. So if kids don't want to hand Santa their letter, they can put it in the box, which we will also have there."

"Isn't Grace an art teacher? I could ask her about painting the box if you want?"

"Sure. Sounds great! She's actually who I was talking to when you came in. I wanted to make sure she was still set to teach two painting classes at our rec center the week before Christmas. The kids are going to paint a fingerprint Christmas tree in one class and a snowman in the other. Those paintings wind up being perfect handmade presents for their parents or siblings, and the class sells out every year the day it's announced. I know she'll be up for painting the mailbox. She's such a sweetheart and the art classes she does for our department are always a hit. The students just rave about her because she has a heart of gold and is just a sweet person that everyone wants to be around."

"Yeah," said Laurel. "Everyone sure does want to be around her. I learned that the hard way."

Laurel..." Amber seemed to scold her a bit with that one word.

I sensed there was more here, but I wasn't sure if I should push or not. Mitch, however, decided to ask.

"Did something happen, Laurel? Something we need to know about Grace?"

"No, it's not Grace. She can't help being perfect and how she radiates this energy that people just want to be around. There was just someone I went to high school with that I always thought was hot, and I saw him at the rec fair. He had just said that we should go out for a drink sometime and was about to ask for my number when Grace laughed at something someone was saying. He looked over and saw her and was so swept away that he totally forgot about me and walked over to her table and signed up for her class… and then they started dating after he took the class."

Well, that was just one more sign that Jordan and Grace were meant to be. And he knew it the moment he saw her—that same time I got the jolt of electricity. I did feel sympathy for Laurel though. It would have been tough to compete with that and feel like she wasn't chosen.

"Oh, I'm so sorry, Laurel," I said, shifting my chair a bit closer to her. "Do you mean Jordan?"

"That's the one. How do you know his name? Did Grace talk about him when you met? I thought they recently broke up?"

"His name came up. Not to speak out of turn, but they did break up recently. However, I am pretty sure that he is rethinking that idea since he just texted her last night while we were talking."

"Ugh. He texted me last night, too, claiming they weren't together anymore and he wanted to grab a drink. I wanted to believe him, but I knew that was too good to be true. I'm glad I decided to wait to reply, after I replied the first time saying I wasn't sure. He replied right away saying he swore up and down they were done and he wanted to catch up with me. But that kind of sounded like maybe he needed a friend or someone to vent to instead of someone he was romantically interested in. So I wanted to make him suffer a little bit."

Jordan texted Laurel last night? I had given him a little nudge to text Grace and he had, so I assumed he was still interested in her as our nudges were always well-intentioned. Did it change things that he'd also texted Laurel, and had he done so before or after he texted Grace?

"Okay, guys, let's get back to only talking about work," interrupted Amber. "Laurel already knows that I try to keep personal drama out of the office, and I'm not big on gossiping, and this seems to be quite a bit of both."

"I'm sorry, Amber. I didn't mean to even mention that, but I guess it still hurts."

"I get it. Everyone winds up with heartache and getting involved with people they shouldn't, like that guy, at one point or another. I was already annoyed with him for breaking up with Grace and now he's also hurt you, so he's fully on my list. But the thing is to not let it interfere with your work, and keep us from doing work stuff. You know I adore you and we've worked together forever, so this isn't going to change anything. And Chloe, it's your first day, so now you know that while we can chat about stuff that's outside work, I don't want to be known as a gossip factory, okay? Just like you wouldn't want someone talking about you, we're not going to be talking about other people like Grace or Jordan or anyone else's actions, either. Is that clear?"

I felt fully abashed by the little smackdown. Was I gossiping? That's the last thing I wanted to do. I just wanted people to be happy and especially my charge so I needed to know what else might be going on with Jordan's interest in other people. I'm sure that was a blip on his part and he just texted Laurel because he thought things were over with Grace, but then my little nudge made him realize he didn't want to be done with Grace. Hopefully?

"I'm sorry, too," I said. "I really am. This isn't the first impression I wanted to give. I'm such a helper that sometimes I wind up getting involved and providing advice or information that I think the other person should know.

But I know I have to rein that in and I'll be better about it, I promise."

As I said that, I looked straight at Amber. I certainly didn't want to look at Mitch at all as I knew he'd be disappointed that I got involved. There was probably an earful awaiting me tonight about this. Hopefully, Emerson wasn't looking down right now and had missed it, although it wasn't like this was me doing anything bad. I was just getting information.

"Thank you, Chloe. The recommendations I received about you and Mitchell were glowing, so I have no doubt this isn't usually the case. Let's move forward from it. How about I show you both to your desks so you can start reading up on your projects and tasks and come up with some more great ideas like the red letter box?"

"Sounds great. Thank you."

My face was probably still red, but I knew that I did need to be professional here and this was a good lesson for that.

We all stood up from the table and Laura walked us over to two small desks off to the side. Both were piled high with binders. Aha. Here were the binders that we were warned about. I couldn't wait to dive in to focus on something else.

Sitting down, I looked at the binders and saw one labeled "T-Rex Volunteers". Perfect! That's the one I wanted to read since I'd be meeting with them after lunch today.

Opening the binder, I found photos on top of past events they'd done. Oh my goodness! The inflatable dinosaurs surrounding Santa's sleigh in the parade was a sight to behold. I loved how different it was.

Flipping to more pictures, I saw the dinos dancing around inside a packed senior center with the elderly in chairs and wheelchairs around them. Every single person in the audience had the biggest grin on their face. What joyful energy! Oh, this was perfect.

I read through the details about each volunteer. Many of them had been involved with this for over a decade in various inflatable costumes, but the inflatable T-Rexes started coming into vogue just a few years back. The history of the T-Rex costumes was fascinating. They came into being when Rubie's Costume Co teamed up with the creators of "Jurassic World" in 2016 but really took off when all the T-Rex antic videos started hitting the internet in 2017.

T-Rex videos? I knew what I'd be watching after work tonight! I glanced at the computer sitting on my desk and wondered if Amber would be okay with me watching one or two now before the meeting.

Nah. I already felt like I'd pushed my luck with her earlier in the day. Didn't need to do so again or make things worse.

Moving on from the T-Rex binder, I read the one about the current Letters to Santa program where volunteers at the post office read through letters that arrived in the mail and also about the annual Christmas party. That inspired me to grab one of the yellow legal pads that were sitting on my desk and sketch out my thoughts on what the mailbox should look like.

My first iteration wasn't matching what I had in my head, so I crumbled that one up and tossed it into the trash basket under my desk. It was soon joined by four more.

As I started the sixth one, however, I took a minute to close my eyes and bring what I'd envisioned to the front of my mind again.

Stick with me this time, I pleaded to myself. All I needed was the roughest of rough sketches that showed the ideas for the Letters to Santa mailbox.

I felt a spark of electricity in my fingers, picked up the pencil again, and started sketching away. This time, the images seemed to just flow out of my brain through my fingers. Having the thought set there and wiping out everything else around me helped bring it clearly into focus.

"Oh, wow, Grace, I didn't realize you were artistic," Amber said from behind me. I didn't know how long she'd been standing there, but I was suddenly glad I hadn't pulled up a T-Rex video online and had instead been creating.

I glanced up and handed her the legal pad so she could take a closer look.

"I'm not an artist at all, actually. At least I don't think I am. But I thought I'd jot down my ideas for the mailbox. I'm sure Grace will have her own since she is the artist, but I figured some suggestions would help."

"Whoever told you you're not an artist was wrong, plain and simple. You have a good eye and a way with a sketch. Nicely done. This will definitely help Grace when she's painting and I know she'll be inspired by it."

I blushed. "Thank you, Amber. I appreciate that."

"If you're ready for something to eat, the pizza has just arrived. Mitchell and Laurel already went downstairs to our courtyard and I told them we'd be right down."

My stomach growled loudly and we both chuckled.

"I guess that answers that question. Yes, bring on the pizza!"

The courtyard was adorable. It was festooned with circular red tables with built-in surrounding benches and an orange umbrella sticking out of the center for shade. Today was somewhat sunny with a bit of clouds, but the heat wasn't bearing down at all this time of year. So the umbrellas were folded down.

Mitch and Laurel were sitting, chatting away over pizza. Telling myself to not be, or appear, clingy towards Mitch, I strategically sat down next to Laurel, while Amber sat next to Mitch.

"Glad you guys were able to join us," said Laurel. "We tried getting your attention before we left, but it was like you were lost in another world."

"It feels a bit like I was," I replied. "I was sketching my idea for the Letters to Santa mailbox, and was so focused on making that right for Grace to paint that I wasn't aware of anything else until Amber spoke up from right behind me."

"Wait until you see that mailbox sketch," said Amber. "Chloe rocked it. It looks amazing. She has art skills that it sounds like she didn't even know about until today."

I blushed, dipping my head a bit to try and hide that. "Thank you, Amber. I appreciate that. The vision was so strong in my head that I'm glad it translated onto paper. I didn't think at first that it would, which was frustrating."

"Seriously, you did great. Grace will be able to see exactly what you want from your sketch because it's so detailed. She might even ask you to help her with painting it."

More time with Grace? Well, I was all for that because of course I wanted to spend more time around my charge. But, painting? I wasn't sure if I'd be able to make that imagery spring forth again, but I was certainly willing to try.

"Thank you. Of course. I'd love to give that a try if Grace is interested, but if she's not, I fully understand because she's the one who's the artist."

"Excellent. We'll see what she says when she sees it. I'll scan the sketch and email it over to her today."

That was a nerve-wracking thought. Hopefully she would like it.

"You guys should eat," said Laurel, pushing the pizza boxes towards us. "Otherwise, Mitchell and I are going to eat all of it."

"Yes," said Mitch. "I know I was hungry because I forgot to eat breakfast, but this pizza is delicious. Chloe, try some."

I grabbed a slice of cheese and put it on a paper plate. After dabbing off some grease with a few napkins, which was something I'd seen people do through the cameras we had, I tentatively took a bite.

What we called pizza up above was very deep and doughy. This was a thin crust that was almost crisp. As much as I loved our pizza, I couldn't fault this for being delicious in its own right.

"Wow, this is so good. I've never had thin crust pizza before. All I've ever had is a deep crust."

I stopped myself suddenly because I didn't know if they had deep crust pizza down here. Mitch shot me a look, which showed he was thinking the same thing I was.

"Oh, you must be from Chicago," Amber said. "They're known for preferring deep-dish pizza. I didn't realize they didn't have thin crust pizza as well, though."

I sent a silent prayer upwards in thanks for Chicago's pizza style.

"Chicago, huh?" asked Laurel. "So what brought you here to Massachusetts?" She shot a quick look at Amber and then continued. "If I'm not being nosy, of course. You don't have to answer. I'm just curious."

What on earth do I say to that? Before I could come up with an answer, Mitch stepped in. Heaven love him.

"Oh, neither of us had been out of Chicago until now, so when this opportunity came up over the holidays, we couldn't turn it down. And we're both glad we decided to take a chance and come out this way. We had always heard about how beautiful New England was year-round and especially during the holidays, so it was a must."

"Well, we're glad you did," replied Laurel. "I think you're just what we needed here in the office. You, too, Chloe. Both of you are what we needed, and we're glad you're here. We're going to need it especially this year."

"Why this year, if you don't mind my asking?" said Mitch.

Amber and Laurel passed a look between themselves. There was something going on that we weren't yet privy to, but I was sure we were about to find out. Maybe this was another reason why we'd been sent down here.

Amber finally spoke.

"There's been some cutbacks in town budgets for next year. And that involves the Recreation Department. If we don't somehow find a way to raise funds this late in the year, Laurel will be out of a job next year and we certainly won't have any assistants. Also, we have the separate Rec Center building where we have always held events, but we can't afford to keep it, so it's being sold and torn down for a new building."

Laurel's face dropped. I realized she already knew the news, but the reminder of it probably stung. I glanced at Mitch, wondering if he was thinking the same thing I was—that Emerson may have had an extra motive in sending us down here. Sure, we were to see our charges but I think she also wanted us to help save the Rec Department and Rec Center before the end of the year.

"Oh my gosh, that's awful," I said. "I'm so sorry. With that said, we're going to put our heads together and come up with some ideas on how to raise the funds that are needed, so you'll still have a job next year."

"Whatever you can come up with would be great," replied Amber. "We're already charging a bit more for the sponsorship of the Christmas parade booklet than previous years, but that's still not going to make up the amount we need."

I felt a hand on my shoulder and turned suddenly to see who was there. No one. Ahh. Got it, Emerson. Message from above that yes, we are supposed to help. On it.

I turned back to the table to see Mitch looking at me with raised eyes. I'd tell him later what was up. Laurel and Amber were talking to each other, so they hadn't even noticed. Phew.

What to do to raise money? I thought about the events we'd talked about and things I'd seen from above.

"The kids' party that is happening… Are there any raffles with that? Like gift baskets that are donated by local people or businesses, and the proceeds could go towards our department?"

Amber cocked her head to the side in thought.

"I like it. I hadn't thought to ask about that because I know this time of year is tough for people. But it's worth looking into."

I didn't think that would provide the full amount, but maybe it would amount to something. There had to be other ideas, though.

Looking at Mitch, I saw that his attention had been drawn to the little potted Christmas trees that were sitting out in the courtyard with us. Since I knew him so well, I could tell his wheels were spinning.

"Along those lines, what about a Festival of Christmas trees?" he asked. "People and businesses could fully decorate and donate the trees and we'd put them in some big room, where visitors could view each one and buy raffle tickets to put into a container for each tree."

Laurel's face lit up.

"Yes! I love that. I actually remember going to something like that as a kid and it was the prettiest thing all lit up at night. Perfect selfie opportunities, too! I've heard of the prospect of winning a tree in other towns, but we've never done it here. We should!"

I pictured it in my head. Sparkling trees all aglow, in a room bustling with people, and strolling hand in hand with a handsome man whose face I couldn't see. It was a lovely thought, and I was glad Mitch thought of it. I smiled at him, silently signaling, "Well done."

"You two are fabulous!" said Amber. "And the two ideas could be combined, because the items that would go into a gift basket could instead go under or on the tree itself, including gift cards, etc. Or toys, which are sure to get the kids interested. Heck, my two little ones will totally want to go to see all the trees, and will want each one."

"Oh, kids!" I said. "What are their names?"

Amber grabbed her phone and showed us her background photo, which was of an Indian man and two young kids.

"This is my husband, Mohindra. He goes by Moe and runs an antique store in town—and yes, I'll be hitting him up to donate a tree. And these are our two little ones, Maxi and Toby."

"They're so sweet and they both have your eyes."

"Thank you. That they do. They have my eyes and Mohindra's lips, which is good because I've always thought mine was too thin. You'd never know it though because I use this lip plumping lipstick that works wonders."

I glanced at her mouth, because what else was I going to do after that statement? Yes, I wouldn't have thought she was born with thin lips.

"I'm going to have to look into that. And, Mitch, that is a wonderful idea about the tree festival. I love it."

"You've given us a little bit of hope," said Laurel. "Actually you've definitely given me a little bit of hope. So thank you."

"Thank you." I looked at Laurel and then Amber. "We really appreciate the opportunity and promise to not let you down. We're going to put in 110% effort to make sure that your department is fully funded for next year and hopefully figure out a way as well to stop the sale of the Rec Center building."

"We know that you will and can tell that already," said Amber. "You've already come up with the idea for the Letters to Santa mailbox and that gorgeous design, and Mitchell has installed a new reporting system that's going to cut down our reporting time by 50 percent. Plus, your fundraising ideas, so we're already thrilled. You may not be able to save the Rec Center, because that sale is already in the works, though."

"We're glad to help anyway we can. Now let's dig more into this divine pizza and then I need to get back to the office for that meeting with the dino volunteers."

"They're awesome," said Laurel. "Every person who's a part of that group is so secure in who they are, which I guess you have to be in order to dress up in an inflatable dinosaur costume and dance around."

"It's funny. When I tried on that costume, I felt more like me in it. I'm not sure if it was that I knew no one could see me in the costume. That was probably a part of it. What I was wearing didn't have to be the latest style or flattering, and I didn't have to worry about my makeup running from the heat, or my curls wilting. No one could see me, so I was free to act however I wanted. It was a bit of a shield in a sense but also the freedom at the same time to fully be me."

"I love that," said Amber. "What a great way of explaining it. I have no doubt you're going to fit right in with the volunteers."

She was right. As the afternoon proceeded, I met the volunteers, who ranged in age from 20s to 70s, and heard all of their stories about their volunteer work. Each person did so because they genuinely wanted to help people and give back, and this allowed them to do so.

One volunteer, Ruth, who was in her early 70s and was a short woman with close-cropped silver hair, had been involved since the beginning. I was drawn to her when I was speaking with her.

"What made you get involved, Ruth?" I asked when we were both grabbing some coffee that Laurel ran out to get after lunch from Daylight Donuts along with donut holes, which were delicious.

"Oh, I was newly retired from the secretarial position I'd had most of my life and didn't want to just sit home all day and watch TV. I wanted to do something."

"So, what about becoming a dancing dinosaur appealed to you?"

"This is going to sound silly…" Ruth stopped and looked like she wasn't sure if she should continue.

I placed my hand on her shoulder, sending her some angelic love and support.

"Ruth, there's nothing you could possibly say that I'd find silly. I'm sure of it. Every single human… person… has their own story that no one else knows and it makes them the glorious being that they are. I sincerely want to hear yours, if you want to tell me."

She softened her posture, so I took my hand away.

"When I was a young girl, I wanted to be a ballet dancer, and I even persuaded my parents to sign me up for classes, because I loved watching ballet. It was so elegant and lyrical and I wanted to be part of that. My mother was on board and signed me up at a local studio. But when I went in, the other students, who were all these thin girls in their leotards, snickered at me behind the teacher's back. All because I still had my baby fat and was short. Okay, so I guess it stopped being baby fat and started being fat fat at a certain age, but I felt so ridiculed and out of place that I stopped going after that first class, and lost my passion for listening to music or dancing at all. I decided I'd just hide so I wouldn't expose myself to that hurt again. And I did. For years and years. Decades even. I refused to date and instead preferred to keep to myself. It even affected my career. I'd always wanted to teach in a school but after that, I didn't want to put myself out there, so I went to secretarial school and stayed out of the spotlight completely. I made good money as an executive assistant, mind you, but my heart wasn't in it. I was happy to retire when I did."

My eyes teared up and I saw that Ruth's were as well. That was brutal.

"Oh, Ruth. How horribly insecure those other students must have been about their own bodies to take that out on you. I wish the teacher had noticed and stopped them. And I hope you know that it was entirely their own hurt that caused them to act out. It doesn't make it any less horrible, but I've learned over the years that hurt people hurt people."

"You're very wise for such a young age, my dear. And thank you. It took me quite a while to learn that, too, but I finally did. It came about from hearing about this group, actually. Only after I retired and was sitting at home flipping through the TV channels did I finally listen to ballet music again. Swan Lake was on PBS and I was entranced and mesmerized all over again at the beauty. I'm not ashamed to say that I cried over how much I'd given up by letting those people hurt me. But I started watching again and shortly I was able to do so without crying and instead just becoming one with the music. I even started dancing around the living room."

My heart went out to her. I could picture that catharsis and I was glad that she had found that bit of peace, but I still had questions.

"So, how did you get from listening and dancing to music, which I'm glad you did, to becoming a dinosaur?"

"I listened to my heart and signed up for the ballet class at the senior center through the Rec Center here. Let me tell you, I was so nervous walking into that class, but instead of being ridiculed for being there, it was the opposite. I was welcomed with open arms by the teacher and other students and felt at home. It was exactly what I needed. I finally felt safe and comfortable in my own skin."

I wiped the tears that were openly flowing from my eyes. Ruth noticed and she reached into her purse and discretely passed me a tissue. Turning my back to the rest of the room, I dabbed my eyes.

"Thank you, Ruth. I'm sorry. I'm just so happy for you and sad at the same time that it took so long for you to have that moment."

"Don't be sad. Be happy. I am. That ballet class changed my life. As I was leaving the class the first day, I saw a flyer in the center about the dinosaur volunteers and seeing it made my heart happy. Without thinking, I tore off the piece of paper with the email address. I went home that night, ordered an inflatable T-Rex costume, and sent an email saying I was interested.

"I heard back right away from Nadia, who as it turns out was my ballet teacher at the center. I hadn't realized she was the one that was organizing the T-Rexes, but it was kismet. She said I'd be a perfect fit because I had such a love for music and my movements were fluid.

"The first meeting was that next week. I showed up with everyone else. There were about five of us at first and we all brought our costumes and tried them on to rehearse. And I was happy and felt included and felt so much like me."

"I love that. When I first tried on my costume, I felt the same way. I felt free."

"Yes, exactly. That's the perfect word for it. I was free. After the first event at one of the elementary schools, we all went out for coffee. I started talking to one of the other volunteers, Charlie, who's also in his 70s."

Ruth pointed across the room to a tall fellow with a full head of white hair who was chatting with the other volunteers. He looked nice.

"Ooh, this sounds promising," I said to Ruth.

"Oh, it was and is. He asked me out for dinner that weekend and we've been seeing each other ever since. He started volunteering a year after his wife passed away when his children recommended that he find something to do. I'm glad they did. In fact, about a year after that, he proposed and we've been married for a year now."

She held up her hand showing her beautiful antique engagement ring and gleaming gold band.

"First, that's gorgeous, but what's even more lovely is the gleam of happiness and joy in your eyes. This is beautiful. Thank you for sharing this with me."

"You're welcome, my dear. I'm glad to. This group of inflatable dinosaurs is quite special."

"I feel that just from this first meeting and I'm so glad to be involved. So, is this how you spend your time now? Well, besides enjoying married life, obviously."

"Actually, after all these years, I'm a teacher."

"What? Tell me more."

"Nadia and I became friends through this group, and she asked me to be her backup teacher for the ballet class. I laughed when she first asked me, but she was serious. So I agreed and there were a few bumps the first day, but I survived. I kept at it."

"She didn't just keep at it. She rocked it," said Nadia, who had overheard and come over. She was a willowy brunette in her 30s who'd been part of the Boston Ballet and had many lead roles in the corps until she decided to start a family. When her children started school, she started teaching at the senior center.

"You're too kind," said Ruth, blushing.

"I mean it. You really have come into your own and I'm so glad you're up there teaching. What Ruth hasn't mentioned is that she's now teaching a tap class entirely on her own and has been substitute teaching at the elementary school for the past year."

I felt goosebumps line my arms. I'd always heard that term, but had never viscerally felt it until this very moment. What a sensation.

"Ruth! That's amazing," I exclaimed. "I'm so proud of you."

"Thank you. I have Nadia to thank for all of this because none of it would have happened without her class. She even recommended me to the elementary school principal, who's her husband."

"Oh, Ruth," Nadia said, gazing fondly at her friend. "I have faith that everything would have happened regardless of if it was my class or someone else's class that you took. You just needed to be back in a welcoming classroom to find your inner light. I'm just glad it was mine and that you happened to see my inflatable dinosaur flyer as well, because having you in my life is a blessing, and seeing you shine and find yourself has been one of the greatest gifts of my life."

Ruth and Nadia hugged, both clearly overcome with emotion. I excused myself to go talk to the rest of the group.

From those conversations, I could tell from what they were saying and not saying that they all felt the same way Ruth did, for various reasons. The costumes were their shield, too, because no one could make fun of them for being goofy or different when they were willingly and happily being silly in a goofy and different costume.

I had the feeling a lot of the volunteers had also been bullied or been through something in their lives that made them want to help others and provide joy, and this gave them the ability to do so. I loved that they found a way to overcome that hurt and find the good from it. These were all solidly good people who had found each other.

At that meeting, we finalized the plans to put on shows at the four local elementary schools, the senior center, and two nursing homes in the upcoming weeks. Each one would be about an hour long—any longer in the inflatable costumes was like being in a sauna from what I heard—and involved somewhat synchronized dancing to Christmas songs.

The rest of the volunteers knew the dances down pat but this was all new to me. I made a mental note to watch the videos of the past events and learn the moves so I wouldn't embarrass the group. Part of me knew that the allure of being in an inflatable outfit was goofiness, so messing up would just be seen as an element of that. And I also knew the volunteers wouldn't think any less of me if I did so, but I wanted to put my best foot forward with them and with the Rec Department overall.

Since they did this annually, the events were already on the calendars of the various organizations, so it was just a matter of me reaching out to each to confirm that we would be there and find out what time they wanted us, and convey that to the volunteers.

Our shows would also serve to promote our involvement in the Silverton Christmas Stroll and parade, which was held the week before Christmas.

The rest of the day sailed by and before I knew it, it was time to head home. I had the videos of the past events to watch and learn from, and wanted to get started. After we got back to the apartment, Mitch went out to pick up burgers, fries, and shakes from a local burger place that Laurel had told him about. I was intrigued to try it, but also wanted to get my video watching started, so he went to pick it up while I stayed back. However, when he opened the door to leave, I saw Grace coming home and needed to chat with her for a moment.

I hoped she had time to talk.

Twelve

Grace

Time seemed to be slipping away today.

At school, all of my students seemed like they were in another world. Probably that December pre-holiday fatigue was sneaking in and it was mid-week, but I still needed them to be at their best to keep their grades up.

When I saw how the morning went, and especially when I caught one student on their phone texting a friend rather than paying attention to me, I decided to call the day a bit of a loss and change things up.

During lunch, I swung by the AV department and asked for a favor.

When I started off the next class, I told my students we were going to delve into Vincent Van Gogh's life today. That didn't get quite the reaction I'd hoped for. Instead, I delivered the news to pretty bored faces.

One of my top senior students, Cassie, even yawned. Ouch. She must have caught the cringe on my face and saw immediately what she had done and spoke up.

"I'm sorry, Miss Webster. That yawn wasn't about you or Van Gogh. I promise. You know we all love your class. I'm just zonked today. Think it's my seasonal allergies kicking in with the dust coming up from the vents now that the heat's on in the classrooms."

"It's okay, Cassie. Allergies can be a beast. So I get it."

I continued speaking to the whole class.

"Look guys, I know this is a tough time of year to concentrate since we're getting closer to the winter break, and I'm sure you're all looking forward to the change in scenery. But, I still need you all to pay attention because I want your grades to stay up, and if you don't pay attention, they're going to plummet. No one wants that, right? I sure don't want to have to give any of you anything lower than a C as a grade right before Christmas. And honestly, y'all know I'd rather give you all As but you have to put in the work to deserve that. So let's make that happen, okay?"

I turned to my desk to feign grabbing my lecture notes when there was a knock on the door.

"Hmm, now who could that be? Come on in." I called out.

Every single student sat up a little straighter as the door opened and our AV whiz, Jerry, walked in the room. If we were in the 1980s, he would have been pushing a big ol' TV with a VCR on the AV cart into the room.

In this case, however, he came in and walked over to my laptop and entered the AV Department's login for a certain streaming service.

While he was busy doing that, I heard the rustling of whispers circulate through my classroom. My students sure were awake now.

Jerry gave me the thumbs up and walked out of the room, closing the door behind him. I grinned and faced my rapt class. Now I had their attention.

"So, I didn't fib when I said we were going to dive into Vincent Van Gogh's life. I just left out how we were going to do so."

At my laptop, I synced it to the screen projector and pulled down a large white screen in front of my whiteboard. Then, I flicked off the lights.

"Class, it is my pleasure to introduce you to one of my favorite moments in the illustrious sci-fi series, Doctor Who. An episode called 'Vincent and the Doctor,' where the 11th Doctor and his companion, Amy, travel back in time to meet Vincent Van Gogh. You'll learn quite a bit about his life that you may not have known from just seeing his famous paintings. The episode is 45 minutes long, so let's get started. Settle in."

As the episode progressed, I saw the interest and attention in each student's face, as well as some teary eyes at the terribly sad, and uplifting at the same time, ending. I knew that after today, they'd all see Van Gogh's work differently as being from the perspective of coping with his depression. At least I'd hoped they would.

When the credits came on, the students all clapped. Yes! Exactly how I wanted them to react.

"I'm going to go home and read more about Van Gogh," said Cassie.

"Yes! I want to see what else is out there about him," replied another student, Alex.

One of my quietest students, who was named Amy aptly enough, spoke up for the first time in a while.

"There's a movie my mom told me about called 'Loving Vincent,' which is about his final days and looking into his life. I wasn't interested when she told me but now I want to watch it."

"Wonderful!" I said. "I'm so glad you all are interested. There's a homework assignment about this, but it's slightly different from the norm. I want you all to write a paragraph or two about what you'd want that museum curator to say about you and your life's work after you're gone. I know you're not all planning on being artists, but pretend there's a museum about whatever you want to do in life and focus on that. Envision it. Make every detail evoke an emotion that you left a lasting impression on this world, because I have no doubt that all of you will leave one heck of a beautiful legacy with your work. Okay, class dismissed before I get all misty."

As the students filed out of the classroom to their last class of the day, I heard them chattering about Van Gogh and the Doctor. Some of them even said they were going to start watching "Doctor Who". Well, that warmed the cockles of my Whoivan heart.

I did the same in the last class of the day, minus Jerry coming into the classroom to enter in the username and password, of course. And those students were actually enthralled. Between both classes, my faith in my students was further restored.

After class, I headed straight home, anxious to change into comfy clothes, wash my face, and dive into the cheese pizza and breadsticks I'd picked up on the way. I had zero interest in cooking anything, but knew I needed something to eat while I was watching Hallmark Christmas movies.

Carrying the pizza and breadsticks to my apartment, I passed a tall man walking by who smiled nicely at me and said hello. He didn't look familiar, so I took a guess that he was Chloe's roommate, Mitch, although his hair was brownish blonde rather than icy white. Hmm, maybe it wasn't him. Whoever it was, the man smiled and said a quick "hi" in return.

Chloe's apartment door was open, so I went to peek my head in to make sure she was okay, just in case that man wasn't her roommate who had walked by. As I got to the door, I saw Chloe standing there. Okay, she was fine. Phew.

"Hi, Chloe. I noticed your door was open and wanted to make sure you hadn't left it open by mistake or anything."

"Thanks, Grace. All good. Mitch was just leaving to pick up dinner. I was going to ask if you wanted to join us, but I see you're all set." She nodded her head towards my pizza boxes.

"Oh, so that was Mitch in the hallway. I wasn't sure… But yup, all good for dinner, and looks like you're all set, too. Excellent. How are things going at the Rec Department, by the way?"

Chloe smacked her head lightly.

"Oh, man. I'm so glad you asked because I almost forgot that I was going to tell you something. My mind's focused on food."

My stomach grumbled. I understood that. I also hoped this wasn't going to be too long so my food didn't get cold.

"It's super quick, I promise," Chloe added. Okay, that was like she read my mind.

"What's up?"

"Making it short. Not sure if you know, but there were town budget cuts, and unless the Rec Department brings in some funds last-minute, the Department will just be Amber next year. Plus, they're going to lose the Rec Center itself because it's up for sale."

I was boggled. That's the first I heard about that. Poor Amber and poor Laurel. They were such a good team that I couldn't imagine them not working together. And the Rec Center was such an integral part of the town. I couldn't imagine Silverton without it.

"No. I'm so glad you told me. Do they have any ideas for raising the money?"

"We're going to do a Festival of Christmas trees the week of the kids' party, with fully decorated trees donated by local people and businesses. People will buy raffle tickets for a chance to win a tree. I've heard of it raising a lot of money elsewhere."

"Oh, I love that idea! I'll totally donate a tree — maybe one decorated with postcards of my favorite prints and a gift certificate to a free art class."

As I said that, I thought about my art gallery show coming up. When did I think I'd have time to decorate a tree? That wasn't important. I'd figure it out, but helping the rec center was important.

"That's wonderful, Grace. Thank you so much!"

"Wait. That's not all. I'll do that, of course. Sign me up for a tree. But I have my show coming up, as you know. I was having prints of my work made to sell at the show. The proceeds were going to be split between Dani's gallery and me, but I'd much rather put my part of the funds towards the Rec Department. I know Dani might even be okay with putting some part of hers towards it as well. Well, hopefully she will… I should ask her first before I say that."

"That is amazing. Yes! I love it. Thank you. Thank you. Thank you! Talk to Dani and let me know and you can tell Amber if you want, since it's your awesome idea."

Of course, this would only be an awesome idea if people actually showed up at the show and there were any sales. If not, it was going to be the most lame idea I've ever had.

"I'll definitely talk to Dani and then get in touch with Amber. Thank you, Chloe. Let me go eat and then I'll take care of that."

"Yes, absolutely! Sounds good. I'm excited! Have a great night!"

"You, too!"

Once I was inside my apartment, I kicked off my shoes, changed into a comfy gray sweatshirt and joggers and then dove headfirst into the pizza and breadsticks, which were thankfully still warm. After, I went to wash my face to rinse away the tough morning and get a clean start to the evening before visiting the Hallmark world.

As I dried my face off, I heard my phone buzzing around on the table. Shoot. Of course someone would call as I was busy elsewhere.

I ran out of the bathroom and grabbed the phone to see that Abigail was calling. I hit "accept".

"Hey, babe! Was going to text you in a few minutes to say hi. You must have known. Great minds! How are you?"

"Grace…" Abigail's voice was cracking. It sounded like she'd been crying for a while.

Oh, no.

She continued on. "He's gone."

Had she found out about Ethan/Nick and they'd broken up? Had he created that profile knowing he was going to break up with her? A wave of anger and protectiveness toward my friend swept over me.

"Wait. Who's gone? Ethan? No. I'm so sorry."

"What? No, not Ethan. My dad. He passed away tonight."

Thank heavens I hadn't said anything about that other profile thinking that the news was about Ethan. This was even worse, though, because Abigail and her dad were always so close.

"Oh, honey, I'm so sorry. What happened?"

"I was at his house right after work because we were going to watch the football game tonight, and he had a heart attack right there during dinner."

"That's awful. And so unexpected. Do you want me to come over? What can I do?"

"No, that's okay. Thanks for offering though. I called Ethan when I got home from the hospital. He came right over and is going to stay the night with me, so I'm good. But, Grace… I know we were going to go look at clothes this week. I'm sorry. I just can't. I've got so much to take care of right now like planning the wake and funeral and writing an obit, and ugh, this is all so difficult."

"Don't you worry about that for even a second more. I understand completely. No questioning that. I can get Dani, Jessie, or Joshykins to go with me instead. All good, hon. You take care of yourself, and let Ethan take care of you, and call me if you need anything at all. Promise me."

"Of course I will. Thanks, Grace. I'm just stunned right now. Oh, there is one thing you can do."

"Anything. What is it?"

"Speaking of Dani and Jessie, can you tell them? I'm trying to make as few calls tonight as possible because it's just too hard…"

Abigail stopped what she was saying and I could hear her softly crying. I felt awful and wanted nothing more than to be there to give her a huge hug. Not wanting to interrupt what she was saying, I remained silent to let her continue.

"Ugh. This sucks. What I was saying before I burst into tears was that it's just too hard making the calls to spread this awful news. I called my aunt and uncle and told them and they're going to tell my cousins, so that's good. And then I called you. I don't even know who else I need to tell. There's my dad's friends and his fellow eye doc in his practice. Shoot. I need to call her next, actually, and get the office assistant's number so she can let any patients know that are supposed to come in. They're all going to be devastated…"

"First, yes, of course I'll tell Dani and Jessie. You can take that off your list. Do you want me to call your dad's colleague? Just give me her number and I'll do so."

"No. That's okay. Thanks for asking, though. Naomi and Shelly should both hear it from me, as hard as the news is going to be, since I've known them for years. I'm not looking forward to it, but I'll be the one to make the calls."

"You're welcome. I want to do anything I can. And yes, they're going to be devastated because your dad, Peter, was just the kindest man. I always looked forward to getting my eyes checked as a kid since I knew I'd hear his latest dad jokes that he always put such a funny spin on. I hope you know how great of a guy he was and how much he loved you. I have no doubt about that."

"You're going to make me cry again," Abigail said and then sniffled.

Was that too much? It was all true. Her dad and my dad were both the kind of dads any child would be lucky to have. They were strict about us studying and making sure we got good grades and showed good behavior, but they were strict about it in a kind way. And all of that made us the people we were today. We owed everything to our parents. I certainly wasn't going to say that right then to remind Abigail of what she'd lost, especially since her mother had died when she was in high school and both my parents were still alive, but it was running through my head.

"Thank you for saying that," she continued. "My dad really was the best. I'm going to miss him so much."

"Of course you are. I'm glad you were with him when he passed. I know you and I know you'd be kicking yourself if you were anywhere else instead of there with him."

"That's so true. I almost didn't go over for our weekly Sunday football watching, and it would have been for the stupidest reason. Instead, I was going to stay home and watch a movie instead. I'm so glad I didn't do that. Can you imagine the guilt I would have felt over that? I didn't get to say goodbye because it happened so suddenly but at least I was there. It's a small comfort right now."

"I can guarantee there was no last statement you needed to make to him, because as much as you know he loved you, he knew how much you loved him. There's no doubt in my mind about that. I just realized I should let you go make the other calls, which I'm so sorry you have to do and know that I'm holding you in my heart."

"That I do. As much as I don't want to make those calls, I do. Ugh. But yes, I should get off the phone and get back on the phone."

"I love you, my friend, and I wish I could give you a huge hug right now, but know I'm sending you one and I'll hug the heck out of you the next time I see you. We'll talk soon, okay. I'll give you a call tomorrow to check in on you and find out the wake and funeral details to pass along if you have them then. Okay?"

"Sounds good. I love you, too, and I'll talk to you then. Good night."

"Night, Abigail."

Oh, poor Abigail. That's horrible. Her dad was such a great guy. Jovial and just always fun to be around. What a loss. Any loss was a loss, obviously, but that he was so wonderful made it worse.

I quickly called Dani, who picked right up.

"Hey, babe, you had better not be calling me to tell me you're canceling your show. I won't allow it and you know that. I'll suddenly feign deafness and pretend I didn't hear ya."

"Har har, very funny. No, no. I promise I'm not canceling, as much as I'm nervous about the whole thing. I do have some not so great news to share though, as well as something to ask you about the show."

"Oh, no. What happened? Are you okay?"

"I'm fine. I'm sad, but I'm fine. Abigail just called me. Her dad died unexpectedly tonight."

"That's awful! Poor Abigail. What happened?"

"She was over to watch tonight's football game with him and he had a heart attack right there during dinner and never recovered."

"Ghastly, but I'm glad she was there. Hold on…" Dani's voice grew a bit faint as she turned away from the phone to tell Jessie. I heard her say, "It's Grace. Abigail's dad died tonight. Heart attack. I know… awful."

After a brief moment, she came back to the phone.

"Please tell Abigail that Jessie and I both send our condolences and we're so sorry for her loss. Actually, no need to do that. I'll dash her a message. She knows you were telling us, right?"

"Yes, she asked if I could let you know so she didn't have to call everyone."

"I get that. When my mom passed those years back, I let my brother make most of the calls because I just couldn't. It's horrible. Ugh. Does she need anything?"

"I asked that and she said she didn't, but she'll let me know when the wake and funeral are and I'll pass the word along. I do need something though. A favor. Shoot. Actually two favors."

"Anything, babe. You know that. What's up?"

"Tomorrow after work at about 6, Abigail was going to meet me at the mall to go clothes shopping with me for the gallery show. See, I promise I'm not bailing on my art show. I'm planning an outfit specifically for it. I'm just kinda leaving it til the last minute. With that said, any chance either you or Jessie could go with me instead because I trust your sense of style far more than I trust my own."

Dani left the phone again for a moment and she must have placed her hand over the phone this time as I only heard vague mumbles instead of words while she conversed with Jessie. Shortly enough, she was back.

"Okay, we're set. I have a meeting at the gallery tomorrow night that I was going to move, but Jessie checked her schedule at the hair salon and she's only working til 4, so she can meet you there. Just text her what mall and the time and she'll be there. What's the other favor? You said two…"

Hopefully, she was going to take this okay. I wasn't honestly sure.

"It's about my show and the Rec Department. I just heard that they've lost a lot of their funding, to the point that if they don't make enough money this month, Amber will be the only employee in the department and Laurel will be out of a job. And the Rec Center itself is up for sale."

"Oh, that's awful. So, what does that have to do with the show?"

I thought quickly about how to frame this, because I didn't want to assume Dani would be fine with giving up any of her half of any proceeds from the small prints.

"You know those prints you're making of my art? I know we were going to split the proceeds, but I want to use my half of the money to put towards the Rec Department. It will be a bit of a fundraiser for it. You know, if anyone shows up and actually wants to buy my prints."

I stopped talking, giving Dani a moment to think about what I'd just said.

"Okay, first, missy, there will be a huge crowd and your work is so excellent that they'll be lining up to buy those prints. No question. And yes, of course you can put your half of the proceeds from the prints towards the Rec Department. But I'm going to do so as well."

"Are you sure? I don't want you to lose out on money you could be putting towards the gallery."

"All good, babe. I appreciate it, but your girl had a great year. Yes, I'm tooting my own horn, but it really was. I want to help them out as much as we can, so I'm all in."

"Perfect. You're an angel. Well, actually, Jessie's an angel. No question. But I'm not sure about you."

Thankfully, Dani knew I was joking because she chuckled before she replied.

"Oh, I'm no angel, my friend. We both know that. And we're all the better for that."

"Nah, you have your angelic ways at times. We all do. Half angel, half devil, right?"

"I like that thought better. Yes, let's go with that, although I'm pretty sure you're like 85% angel, 15% devil, but that 15% is hilarious. Okay, so yes, that's set for tomorrow, and I'm going to go message Abigail now. Jessie will see you tomorrow night."

"Awesome. Thanks, babe. Tell Jessie I appreciate it. I'll text her right now. And I appreciate both of you for the company and dinner the other night. I had a blast as always."

"You're welcome. Always great to see you. Okay, talk soon. Love ya."

"Love you, too."

That settled, I ended the call, and then texted Jessie with where to meet at the mall and the time.

After that, I put my phone down and then picked it back up. No new notifications.

Stupid lack of notifications.

Stupid phone.

Stupid me for thinking there would be a notification.

Why did I think that someone was suddenly going to text in that one minute? Clearly Jordan wasn't going to. That wasn't news and I would be a fool if I thought otherwise. And Wyatt hadn't either, which was kind of a bummer, but that wasn't unexpected at all. He had clearly said he was busy and didn't seem to be much of a texter when he was busy. Part of me wished he was so intrigued by me though that he'd want to text to keep in touch and stay top of mind for me. Silly.

I hoped I'd see him later this week at my show and that he wouldn't wind up being too busy to come. At least then we would have met in person and I'd have an inkling of if he was interested and if I was interested. That first texting conversation intrigued me enough to want to meet him anyway.

I guess I'd see what the rest of the week brought. For now, I should go get a good night's sleep.

Thirteen

Chloe

After a good night's sleep, I was bright eyed and bushy tailed for the next day, and was even ready before Mitch. He came out of his room dressed for the day as I was finishing up a bowl of Cheerios.

"Good morning!" I called out. "You have to see this cereal I found in the cabinet. They look like little mini halos."

Mitch walked over to our kitchen table and picked up the cereal box to take a look.

"I wonder if Emerson chose that as a reminder of our duties."

"Oh, gosh. Probably. Or maybe because they're quite tasty and healthy—they improve cholesterol, whatever that is, according to the label. Do we have to deal with cholesterol?"

"I don't think so. We've never had doctor's appointments because there's no real need for them, so I'm thinking that's one of those human things."

Talking about human things reminded me of dinner the past couple of nights. Not that we ate humans, of course, but that we had a very human meal of burgers, fries, and a delectable strawberry shake that first work night, and then Indian food last night.

"By the way, thanks again for running out to grab dinner the last two nights. I realize we didn't get much of a chance to chat after work either night as I've been lost in the world of inflatable dino videos before, during, and after dinner. But the food was delicious, and I enjoyed it. We'll have to go to either place again."

"You're welcome. I was glad to go. It's funny actually because Laurel wound up being at the Indian place at the same time I was to also pick up food. The food was a bit delayed so we had more of a chance to chat further. She's hilarious—I could have talked to her for hours."

I bristled a bit at that thought, since I was the one who always wound up talking with Mitch for hours. He was my best friend. My person. Hours flew by like minutes when I was talking to him.

"Oh, wow. That's certainly a coincidence. Had you told her you were going there last night? Maybe she decided to go at the same time?"

"No, no. Nothing like that. I had told her Monday when she recommended a bunch of restaurants that I'd check them all out eventually, but that it might not be for a few weeks. We both just happened to be there at the same time."

Ugh. That sounded quite a bit like something we'd make happen with a nudge. But I couldn't imagine Emerson or anyone else doing that. At least I hoped not.

"Huh. So strange." I turned over my phone to check the clock. We still had plenty of time before we had to be at work.

"Sit down," I continued, pulling out the chair next to mine at the table. "Want some Angel'Os? Hmm, yeah, no. Not what I'm going to call them. Want some Halos?"

Mitch stayed standing.

"No, thanks. We should probably get going, actually. I told Laurel that I'd swing by the coffee shop again and pick up coffee for her and Amber before we got to work if the machine was down."

"Oh. Sure. Of course."

I stood up and dumped the milk from my cereal bowl down the drain and then quickly rinsed out and cleaned the bowl and spoon, putting them in the strainer to dry. Turning from the sink, I grabbed my purse, phone, keys, and the fluffy pink Teddy Bear Sherpa coat from the kitchen closet to throw over my bright pink sweater, black and pink dotted skirt, and black boots. That closet was a fun find because it had an assortment of outerwear for us in all weather from rain to sunny but cold skies.

I turned and expected Mitch to make a statement about my furry coat, but he was out in the hallway, already having thrown on a long dark peacoat over his navy blue sweater and khakis. He looked both professional and like a dashing grown-up. There was something about that coat that made him just look different.

While I pondered that as we got into the car and headed to work, our phones chimed simultaneously. Mitch was driving, so he didn't look at his phone, which was currently hanging out in the cup holder. I reached into my purse and pulled out my phone, unlocking it to find a text from Amber, which I read out loud for his benefit.

Coffee machine still on the fritz. I picked up some coffee on the way in for me and

Laurel since I ran into her on the street, but if you want some, you might want to pick it up on the way.

"Do you want a coffee?" Mitch asked.

My mouth was actually salivating at the thought of another cup of coffee, but I felt like things were a bit off at the moment, so I didn't want to add to that by making it all about me.

"The one I had yesterday was enjoyable, but I don't want to make you swing by if you don't want one."

"Since I didn't eat breakfast, I'm hungry, and don't want to wait for lunch again. So I thought I'd pick up a bagel sandwich while there. Laurel was telling me about this bacon, egg, and cheese sandwich they have that sounds delicious. And, of course, I can get you a coffee, too."

Of course she did. Seemed like Mitch was trying out all the things that Laurel suggested.

It was good for him to try new things, but I was feeling a bit territorial. That was silly, though. It's not like I could suggest any Earth foods though since I didn't know about any of them either except from ones I'd seen on the cams. They didn't have smell-a-vision up there, although that should be a thing—just for tasty foods. There were many things that I had no interest in smelling, ever.

Light dawned that I hadn't replied to Mitch and instead was lost in my own thoughts.

"Sure, that sounds fine. Just a coffee is good since I had those Halos this morning."

"The what? Oh, right, those little circular pieces of cereal. Got it."

Okay, what was going on? This wasn't the Mitch I knew.

I opened my mouth to just ask but we pulled into the coffee shop right at that time. Timing is everything.

The rest of the day went by in a blur. I confirmed the dates and times for the dino volunteer visits with each school and senior center; met with Amber a few times; and spent a lot of the day organizing the flyer for the Silverton Christmas Stroll and Parade. After seeing my sketch of the Letters to Santa box, Amber wanted me to try my hand at designing the flyer and some of the ads for the sponsors.

I was nervous since I'd never used a design program before, but after a tutorial, I played around with it and found I picked it up quickly. A couple of the sponsors wanted to use their past ad with some minor revisions, and that was easy enough to implement. Others, including the local flower shop, Flirty Flowers, and toy store, Thomas' Toys, both wanted brand new ones featuring their newest offerings. They sent over photos to use as a basis and I first did a sketch of what the ads would look like by hand.

Once I had the sketches done, I ran them by Amber and then emailed them off to the owner of each store for review. The flower shop owner, Flora (I did wonder if that was her real name or not), called back immediately, gushing about how much she loved the look of the ad and she was approving it.

She also asked me if I ever thought about working as a graphic designer. I blushed when I heard that and I thanked Flora for being so sweet. Maybe I actually did have latent artistic skills.

Part of me wondered if that's why Grace was my charge. Did Emerson sense that I was talented in art before I knew it or it had even been tested? I did enjoy being creative and seeing something I'd envisioned in my mind come to life in front of my eyes.

There really wasn't work for a graphic designer up there though. It's not like we're putting together advertisements to join us or flyers about any events going on. Maybe we should? I made a mental note to ask Emerson about that when I was back up or next talked to her.

The toy store owner, Tom Tinker, showed up at the Rec Dept office right after lunch. Laurel greeted him by name when he came into the office, so I glanced up to see what he looked like. It was a jolt to my system.

Simply because he owned a toy store, I had pictured Tom as an old guy who looked a bit like Santa, but with just white hair instead of a long matching white beard. That wasn't what he looked like at all. Instead, he was a tall, muscular, young guy in his early 30s or so with wavy almost black hair and light brown skin.

He looked very fashion-savvy in a light gray suit complemented by a stark white button down shirt that was opened just enough at the top to show he was quite fit, and dark brown shoes. Tom might as well have stepped off a runway. Wow. Yeah, not at all what I had been expecting.

I wondered for a moment if he was gay and might be interested in Mitch. Looking over at Mitch, I saw that he was engrossed in his computer. How did he not notice the hot guy that walked into our office?

I glanced over at Tom again while he was chatting with Laurel with his back towards me. Yeah, he was hot. Yowza.

Hmm, forget Mitch. I hope Tom is straight and single. I know I'm only here for a few weeks, but that doesn't mean I can't date.

"Let me introduce you to Chloe," I heard Laurel say. She was walking over with Tom towards me. Aaaah. Okay, stay cool.

Should I stand up? Should I stay sitting? What was the protocol here? I decided standing made more sense, mainly because then I could further evaluate if he was taller than I was or not. Not that it mattered, but still.

Tom walked over to me and held out his hand, which I took. I was looking at his chin. Okay, he was taller than me. I took his hand, relishing his firm handshake.

"Hi, Chloe. It's a pleasure to meet you."

"It's great to meet you, too, Tom. Although I have to say you were not what I was expecting."

He let go of my hand, but not before running his thumb along the back of my hand. I expected to feel a jolt of electric chemistry when he did that, but no.

"So what were you expecting? If you don't mind me asking."

"No, it's fine. I wouldn't have mentioned it otherwise. Based on the fact that you own a toy store, I was picturing an older almost Santa type. You're not that." I said that last bit with a grin.

Tom chuckled. "I've never been called Santa. That's a new one. But I get it. My dad, Thomas, Senior, actually founded the store, but he also never looked like Santa. He stayed pretty lean his whole life."

I noted the past tense and the use of "whole life", and I visibly grimaced before speaking.

"Oh, I'm so sorry. Is he...?" I didn't know how to finish that sentence.

"Thank you. Yes, he passed on two years ago, which is when I took over the store. I'd spent my whole life growing up around that store, so it was an easy decision to keep the store going and help out my mom. Before that, I was a model but I gave it up to come back here."

I knew it! Of course he was a model.

"That doesn't surprise me at all. You have such a strong fashion sense."

Out of the corner of my eye, I saw Mitch look up from his computer. He glanced at Tom quickly and a frown came over his face. When his eyes then turned to me, he realized I was looking at him and glued his eyes back to his screen.

Okay, so I wouldn't be introducing them. Maybe he just wasn't Mitch's type, although with how often Mitch was talking to Laurel, I was starting to think I didn't really know Mitch's type at all.

"I appreciate that. Everything I know I learned from the stylists I worked with for shoots and shows. If it wasn't for them showing me what worked, I would probably wear whatever was clean."

"So, a typical guy then?"

"Pretty much. Shh, don't tell anyone. My model cred will be ruined."

"Your secret's safe with me. So, what brought you here today, by the way?"

"I wanted to chat with you, actually, about the ad. Do you mind if we sit down somewhere?"

Oh, no. He hated the ad and wants it completely redone. I steeled myself for what I was sure would be a rebuke, despite the smile on his face.

"Of course. Let's sit down over here." I grabbed the sketch of the ad off my desk along with a notepad and pencil so I could mark down changes. Then, I pointed to the conference table and we walked over and sat down.

Might as well just get it over with.

"About the ad…"

"I loved it," Tom said. "I just have two minor changes."

Relief flooded through me at his words. Phew.

"You know you could have just emailed me instead of freaking me out by coming in. Made me think you hated it."

"Oh, gosh, no. I'm so sorry. Nothing like that at all. I had to drop off the check to Laurel, and thought I'd meet the person who created this amazing ad while I had a chance. That's all. And I'm really glad I did so."

I blushed. Was he saying he was glad to meet me in person?

"I'm glad you liked it. Thank you. So what were the changes?"

I placed the ad in between us so we could look at it.

"If you could move the teddy bear up to the top left, and the doll down to the lower right, then it would be perfect. The reason is that the top left gets the most eye traffic usually in an ad, and that teddy bear is something we've sold since the store first opened, so it's what we're known for. The second is just to list the owner as Tom Tinker, Jr. instead of Sr."

"Both of those are quite easy enough. I can make them happen in about an hour or so and then email the new version over to you. Sound good?"

"Yes, definitely Sounds great. Thank you, Chloe."

Tom stood up as if to leave, and I stood up as well to say goodbye.

"You're welcome, It was a pleasure meeting you, Tom."

"You, too, Chloe. Umm, I wonder. Any chance you'd like to grab a coffee with me after work some night next week? I'd love to chat more and maybe show you the store and get your take on the layout."

Was this a professional ask or a personal one, or both? So confusing. But I wasn't about to pass that up.

"Absolutely. Before I send the new version over to you, I'll look at my calendar and see when I don't have an evening meeting next week and let you know."

He smiled, showing gleaming white teeth. My word, he was a dentist's dream.

"Fabulous. Can't wait to hear from you."

He started to head out and then turned and waved to Laurel.

"Good seeing you, Laurel."

"You, too." She waved back. "Thanks for bringing in the check."

I walked back to my desk like I was walking on a cloud, and I sure knew what that felt like.

As I sat down, Laurel came over to my desk with a sly grin on her face.

"I know… I know… No personal stuff. But I'm just going to say that we've been working with Tom for a few years now and he's never asked me out.

Clearly he hasn't asked out Amber since she's married. I'm kinda jealous that he asked you out. Lucky girl!"

"Did he, though? It sounded like he wanted to get my thoughts on his store layout."

Laurel rolled her eyes at me. "Dude, he was totally asking you out. The 'see my store' bit was just a little bit of professional courtesy and his way out in a sense in case you aren't interested. Trust me. I know when a guy is interested and when he isn't. The question is, are you interested?"

She glanced over at Mitch, who was still working away at his desk, either oblivious to our conversation or pretending not to be. Usually, I could read him like a book and knew how he was feeling. But this week was different. Was it because we were on Earth or was it something else?

"He's hot. How could I not be, I guess. Right?"

Yes, I was only going to be down here for a month so it wasn't going to go anywhere at all, but hanging out with Tom would be an enjoyable way to spend some of the days. Maybe we could go ice skating, and I'd fall into his arms when I was trying to skate.

"Of course, right. So, yes, you're going. Easy enough!"

Laurel winked at me and then walked back to her desk to get some work done. I looked over at Mitch, who still hadn't looked away from his computer. Whatever he was working on was engrossing. I wanted to ask his thoughts about Tom because Mitch was my buddy and that's what I'd always done— gone to him when I was questioning something or wanted to tell someone something. But this time, it felt wrong.

Did that mean going out with Tom also wasn't a good idea? I wasn't sure.

Right now, though, I needed to get that revised ad back to Tom and also look at my calendar to see when I was free.

The rest of the afternoon flew by. Amber was thrilled with the ads, and I loved the praise. We also started work on finalizing the annual Christmas concert put on by the school bands and choral groups at our Town Hall auditorium.

Before leaving work, I took a walk down to the auditorium to listen in on the rehearsals. I was used to hearing harps, so it was unique to hear other instruments.

As I sat in the back of the auditorium, I found my ears and eyes drawn to the harmonious, deep sounds of the cellos being played on stage. The students playing them were all in their teens, but I would have assumed they were older based simply on the music they were creating. It was melodic and struck this chord within me to the point that I teared up. I was grateful to be in the back so no one saw me.

On the drive home, Mitch was a bit silent. He wasn't usually a chatterbox or anything—that was all me—but typically, we weren't silent with each other. We almost never had quiet moments and instead there was a constant flow of speech. This was different. I sure didn't like it.

We silently entered the building. As we walked up the stairs to our floor and the hallway came into view, I saw Grace, who looked like she was on her way out. Maybe she'd make Mitch a bit more chatty?

Fourteen

Grace

Oh, shoot. I was hoping I wouldn't run into anyone since I didn't have time to really stop and chat, or I'd be late meeting Jessie.

I felt tension when I saw them. I hadn't had much of a chance to talk to Mitchell besides that one hello, but I had just assumed he was the male version of Chloe. This wasn't that in the slightest. He was very tall, like her, but his face looked like something had gone horribly wrong for him and he certainly wasn't as exuberant and outgoing as Chloe.

The last time I'd spoken with Amber — to finalize the classes and make sure supplies had been ordered — she said they were doing fabulous and she couldn't be happier. So I didn't think it was work.

As for Chloe, when I'd first met her, she was so chatty and seemed full of life. Of course she was wearing an inflatable T-Rex suit at that time and was bouncing up and down the hall, but still. She seemed different now — like she'd been deflated and the air was leaking out of her.

Great, now I'm imagining a deflating T-Rex costume and trying not to chuckle because that's such a bizarre thought — the T-Rex's head first tilting to one side as the neck deflates and then the whole costume just getting smaller and smaller as it falls to the ground into a pile of plastic or whatever they're made of. Knock it off, self. You're going to laugh out loud in a moment and look like a loon. And then you'll really have to talk and won't get to the mall on time.

I closed my eyes for just a second and distracted myself by envisioning a cute shaggy puppy running through a field. And now it's running away from a shrinking T-Rex.

Dammit. More laughter.

Okay, never mind.

I opened my eyes and decided to just say "hi" as they came into the hallway.

"Chloe! Hi there! How are you? And you must be Mitchell! I'm Grace, your across the hall neighbor. We said 'hi' in the hallway, but I didn't realize it was you. A pleasure to meet you. I'm running out to meet a friend at the mall and I'm running late, but hi! Sorry, that was a lot…"

Mitchell came over and shook my hand. His grasp was solid and he managed to put a polite smile on his face.

"Grace. Hi. Yes, I'm Mitchell, and it's a pleasure to meet you, too. Chloe has told me so much about you."

Chloe did? How would she know a lot about me as we'd only spoken a few times?

Chloe jumped into the conversation to save Mitchell, giving him an unfathomable look. "He means Amber, not me. She's been praising your classes and how great you are and your art skills and just everything about you. Mitch must feel like he knows you already."

Since Mitchell (or I guess Mitch?) seemed like he'd had a long day, I just went with that explanation. Heaven knows I sometimes mess up my students' names after a long day at school, or even on just a day ending in "y".

"Totally get it. It happens. Are you guys settling in okay at the apartment and at work? Amber's treating you okay, right?"

"Oh, yes," said Mitchell. "The apartment is great and Amber's been wonderful. No complaints in the slightest."

"She's fabulous," Chloe agreed. "Thanks to Amber, I found out that I can do sketches pretty well. She has me working on the sponsor program for the parade."

I smacked my head. I'd forgotten about the mailbox idea that Amber told me Chloe had and that sketch she'd sent me. I'd meant to mention it, but the week got away from me.

"Yes! I'm so sorry I haven't swung by about that. I meant to, but it's been a week. Chloe, you did such a great job on that. Seriously, if I didn't know better, I would have thought you'd been working as an artist up til now. You're that good. Trust me. I know."

"Gosh, thank you. That means a lot to me, especially coming from you."

Her grin was contagious and I could feel myself matching it. I glanced at Mitchell to see if he was going to share in the happiness or even praise his roommate a bit as well, but nothing.

Shoot. I really didn't have time for this. But I felt I needed to offer to help.

"I really do need to rush and meet a friend. Mitchell, it was nice meeting you. Chloe, I'd love to talk to you some more. I'll be home in a couple of hours or so after shopping. If you ever want to swing by for coffee or tea or even a glass of wine, just knock on my door and we can chat about anything. Anything at all. Okay?"

I gave her a meaningful glance with those last two statements to show I did mean she could chat about whatever was going on with Mitchell. Hopefully she understood and would take me up on it, because I could just sense that she needed to talk and I was great at listening and providing advice. I wasn't so great at taking advice but I was excellent at telling others what they should probably do, and then stepping back and letting them either do so or not. It was up to them.

"Thanks, Grace. I appreciate that. Have fun out."

Mitchell gave a brief wave before turning away to their apartment to unlock the door.

I reached out and patted Chloe on the upper arm.

"You're welcome, Chloe. Seriously. Any time."

Okay, now I really had to hit the road to make sure I got to the mall to meet Jessie there at 6. Ooof, hopefully I'd find something to wear to my show. Nothing like putting that off til the last moment.

I couldn't take the thought of not looking my best at the show.

Fifteen

Chloe

As we got inside the apartment, and closed the door behind us, I couldn't take it anymore.

I twirled towards Mitch after I hung up my coat, and let it out.

"What's going on, Mitch? Why are you being so quiet? Is it something to do with your charge, who you haven't even mentioned? Are you not enjoying the job? What is it? Please talk to me."

He was quiet again for a moment longer, but I could sense that he was battling with his thoughts about what he should say. Did I want to hear what he had to say? Was it something I did and didn't know about?

I closed my eyes, and took a deep breath to try and center myself. It didn't work, so I reopened my eyes. Mitch had sat down at the table and his shoulders were slumped.

"Mitch… What is it? Are you sick? You can't be sick. We don't get sick. Do we? What can I do? Should I yell for Emerson? Or just go back through this closet into her office if that works? Would that work? I don't even know. Please talk to me. I'm rambling here because I don't know what's going on and that's killing me."

"First, I haven't seen my charge yet. Hopefully later this week, but I've been keeping track of them. It's not you. It's me. Well, it's partially you. That's not fair. It's really me."

I froze, uncertain what to say. It was like time stopped.

What had I done? Was he mad at me because Tom had asked me out instead of him? I couldn't help it that Tom was straight.

But he'd been kind of quiet all week, even before I met Tom, so that couldn't be it. Or maybe that was the straw that broke the camel's back that I'd met someone.

When I spoke, my voice shook. I tried to keep steady, but my nerves were too high. I couldn't lose him.

"You're my best friend, Mitch, and I can't bear the thought of not having our friendship because you mean so much to me. Talk to me. Please. I want to fix this. Whatever it is. Whatever I have to do, I'll do it."

Mitch looked like I'd slapped him, which wasn't my intent. I thought back to what I had said. Nothing there was wrong or an insult. He was my best friend and I was offering to fix things.

"Never mind. Just forget it. I thought things would be different on Earth, but it's all still the same."

I wracked my brain wondering what might be different. We were living in the same apartment; working together; and essentially spending all of our time together. Just like we did up there.

"What should be different, Mitch? I'm confused. We're trying something new and you seem to be doing really well at work and getting along well with Amber and Laurel. At least I thought you were. Are you not enjoying it? Did something happen?"

"No. Amber and Laurel have been great. It's not work. It's here."

The apartment? What on earth was wrong with the apartment? It seemed perfect to me. Did he not like the location, or was it sharing an apartment with me that was the issue? Maybe he would have preferred a different part of town, or sharing an apartment with a guy.

"I'm lost. Do you not like your room? Would you rather have mine? We can switch."

Mitch shook his head, clearly exasperated that I wasn't getting it, but I had no clue what was going on.

"When we came down here, I figured we'd be spending more time together since we're staying in the same apartment after all. But instead, you've been shut up in your room most nights after we get home watching videos or planning things for work—and I'm glad you're doing that and getting so into your work. But I miss you and it leaves me just hanging out in the living room here watching TV and that's boring. And now it seems like you might be getting out of your room more, but to spend time with Tom."

Oh.

He had a point.

When we were talking about coming here, I had talked about all the Christmas things I wanted to do with Mitch, and we hadn't done a single one yet. And yes, I'd been busy with work stuff, but I figured he was fine or he would have said something. Maybe I didn't know Mitch as well as I thought I did. But at least he'd said something now.

I did need to fix this. Pronto.

"I'm sorry. You're right. I've been so focused on wanting to make a good impression at work, and finding this artistic talent I didn't know I had, that I've been sequestering way more than I planned to. How about we go out tonight? Just you and me? I seem to remember there's a Christmas tree lighting in the town center tonight? Can we go?"

A broad smile lit up Mitch's face. I hadn't seen that smile in a while. I'd missed it. Looks like I'd suggested the right thing.

"Yes, that sounds fun. Let's change out of these work clothes into some warm clothes since it might flurry tonight and we'll head over there. We can get some pizza before the tree lighting, if that works?"

That sounded perfect, and exactly what I wanted to do more than anything right then.

"Awesome. And maybe there'll be a hot apple cider or hot chocolate cart to keep us warm while we're outside. If it snows more than flurries, I can throw a snowball or two at you."

Neither of us had encountered snow yet, so I was looking forward to finding out what it was like. The snowball comment was added more because I'd always see people throwing snowballs at each other and it looked fun.

"Don't you dare. I'm now going to hope it only flurries because you can't throw a flurry ball at me."

I snort laughed as I pictured trying to throw a tiny little snow flurry at Mitch.

"Are flurry balls actually a thing? Hmm, I don't know… Maybe I could nudge the flurries to form into a ball. Don't test me."

"I'm going to pray for no flurries then. Okay, you. I'm off to change. See you back out here in just a few minutes and we can head out."

"Sounds great!"

I ran off to my room and looked through the clothes in my drawers and closets. I settled on a dark pink fluffy turtleneck tunic sweater and fleece-lined leggings. Oh, those are comfy!

I was pretty sure that I'd seen boots in the front closet, so I went and grabbed those and my pink coat. As I put on the coat, I reached into the pockets and found matching pink gloves that certainly weren't there before.

Looking up at the sky, I smiled and softly said, "Thanks, Emerson."

The night was perfect. Mitch and I laughed and talked away over pizza, and had plenty of time to walk around downtown Silverton before the tree lighting.

"Hey, look, it's the florist shop I did the ad for," I said as I noticed the Flirty Flower shop across the street. Making sure to look both ways, even though the street was blocked off for the tree lighting so there weren't any cars, I crossed to take a closer look at the shop window. Mitch followed closely behind me.

Stopping in front of the shop as "Rocking Around the Christmas Tree" started playing from the street speakers, I was entranced by the display.

The focal point of the display was a dwarf Alberta Spruce (according to the little white card in front of each floral element) shaped like a Christmas tree and decorated with mini ornaments. Surrounding it were brightly wrapped boxes and various floral arrangements, including potted poppy red Amaryllis; red Poinsettias; white Christmas roses; and sprigs of holly, ivy, and mistletoe.

There was a Santa doll off to the side sitting in a chair, and some penguins sitting on a faux ice rink on the other side.

"That's beautiful," said Mitch. "I had no idea there were so many plants and flowers affiliated with Christmas."

I badly wanted to sketch it all, but instead, I took a mental picture of it to hopefully remember later.

"I wish I had a piece of paper on me," I said. "I want to remember this. Not that a sketch would capture the sounds and the feelings, but that is a vision."

Mitch reached into his pocket and took out his phone. He stepped back a few paces, making sure he wasn't about to walk into anyone, and then held the phone up in front of the window. What was he doing?

After he looked at it, he punched a few buttons on the phone and turned to show me what he'd done. It was a picture of the display. I couldn't believe it.

"How? What? I didn't know phones could do that."

"That's something I've picked up from watching people on the cams. They all take pictures with their phones now to remember moments, so I thought I'd do the same. I emailed this picture to your work email so you can print it out there or sketch it from the picture before we leave. It's also now on your phone in your texts, too."

I pulled out my phone and opened up the text. There was the image of the Alberta Spruce tree. How beautiful.

"Could you show me how to do this?" I asked.

Mitch stood next to me and showed me where the camera was on my phone. When it opened, I chuckled because instead of the tree, it showed me and Mitch with our heads close together looking at the screen.

He reached over and clicked the big white button and suddenly our faces were frozen there on the screen looking back at us. It wasn't the best pic of either of us, but I loved seeing it because we were together and happy.

"Now that you've seen the front-facing camera that comes up, I'll show you how to take a pic from the back camera."

Mitch pointed to a circle with two arrows in the bottom right of the phone screen and I was no longer looking at us, but instead at what was in front of me. Since I already had the Alberta Spruce on my phone thanks to Mitch, I turned and took a picture of the town, wanting to remember the night forever.

I grinned. It was so thoughtful of Mitch to take the picture and teach me about the phone's camera, which was him to a tee. I hugged him, overcome with emotion.

"Thank you. Seriously. I didn't know about that, and I'm forever grateful that you did."

Mitch hugged me back. Being in his arms and being around him always felt like home. I closed my eyes for a moment, wishing I could take a picture of this moment as well.

When I opened my eyes, something caught my attention and I yelped.

"Ooh, look!" I jumped out of Mitch's arms and pointed. Right there two buildings down was a hot chocolate stand. "Let's go!!"

The stand offered regular hot chocolate and peppermint hot chocolate, which caught my eye. It was just as delicious as I thought it would be, complete with mini marshmallows and shavings of candy canes as a garnish.

As everyone gathered around the Christmas tree counted down to the tree being lit, Mitch put his arm around my shoulder and drew me close to him. I rested my head on his shoulder and grinned up at him, feeling safe and comfortable.

I only realized the lights on the tree had come on when his eyes sparkled even more than they usually did, thanks to the lights. Oops. I'd missed the actual lighting, but seeing it in his eyes was good enough.

Glancing down at me, Mitch squeezed my shoulder.

"Thanks for coming out with me tonight. This was great."

"You're welcome. I'm glad I remembered it. I enjoyed myself, as I always do with you."

We headed back to the apartment, and this time, when Mitch was watching TV that night, I was sitting on the couch with him to watch Rudolph the Red-Nosed Reindeer. It was adorable, but I felt bad for Rudolph being bullied. Mitch agreed with me, but we both loved the end.

I had my buddy back and it was wonderful.

Sixteen

Grace

This is wonderful.

I looked around at my paintings up on the red brick walls of Dani's gallery, the Center Space Gallery, which was located on the first floor of an old mill building. The 14-foot tall pine ceilings were offset by rigged spotlights and white drapery at nine feet to focus attention on the artwork.

Surrounding me were my paintings of a tulip field; my cottage on a beach; a lake; an owl (the one foray I took into painting an animal); a stone wall; an arching gate into a cemetery; and the moon setting over the ocean, among others.

"I can't believe this is really happening," I said out loud. "Pinch me!"

I shouldn't have been surprised when Dani took the opportunity to pinch me, but I was.

"Ow!" I rubbed my arm.

"Hey. You said to pinch you. Wanted to make sure you knew this was reality. What are friends for?"

"Not that! But in all seriousness, you are such a good friend. Thank you, thank you, thank you for talking me into doing this show."

"You're welcome. It's time for everyone else to see how talented you are, and if the RSVP numbers are any indication, there will be a lot of people who'll learn that tonight."

"Ack. Okay, now I'm nervous. What if I bomb? What if no one actually shows? What if no one buys any of the prints and we don't raise any money for the Rec Department? What if I trip and throw red wine onto one of my paintings and then someone sees it and thinks that was intentional but instead it's that I'm a huge klutz?"

"Okay, breathe, my friend. First, your paintings rock and if you don't know that, you're blind. The second I saw the cottage painting, it brought me straight back to our girls' weekend. I knew you were talented, but I hope you know just how talented you are. I feel like I'm there in front of that cottage, babe"

"Thank you. I'm glad you liked it. That's the painting that really does mean the most to me. I don't know why, but it has just stuck with me like no other. Don't get me wrong. I love all of my paintings, but I knew I had to paint that cottage when I saw it. Oh, I hope people do love the paintings…"

Dani squeezed my forearm before responding.

"The doors open in 10 minutes and you need to breathe. You will not bomb. People will show. There are already people waiting outside. Will people buy? That we don't know, but I'm glad you let me make copies of each painting in print form as well, since people sometimes have an easier time buying prints.

And that way, if… nope, when your paintings sell, you will still have the print of how it looked. Now that last part… that might actually happen knowing you, which is why you can have a beer or white wine tonight and no red. My floors were just cleaned and you don't want to ruin that amazing dress."

I had the amazing dress thanks to Jessie. She was the one that had found this emerald green off the shoulder velvet sheath dress by Calvin Klein when we were at the mall. I wasn't sure at all, but when I tried it on, I fell in love.

"Thank you! At least it's dark so if I spill anything, it won't show too much."

"You're not going to spill anything. That dress makes your eyes sparkle. You should seriously wear that color more often."

"So, it'll be my signature color like you have?"

"Yes! Makes dressing so much easier. Let me tell you."

"I know, but I like being able to wear any color. Plus, it keeps the kids' attention at school if I show up in different colors and prints. Otherwise they'd get bored."

"You're their teacher, Grace. How could they ever get bored? You're so passionate about painting and helping others learn that it just exudes from you."

"Thanks, babe. I wonder who's going to be here. I know Abigail can't make it, which is a bummer, but with her dad's death, she wasn't feeling like going out. I completely understand and I wish I could be with her, but I've called every day this week and I'll be there for the wake and funeral. And I know that Ethan is taking care of her, so she's not alone."

"It's brutal that she can't be here," Dani said. "I know how close she was with her dad, and that heart attack didn't give her a chance to say goodbye, which must be killing her. You're a good friend and she knows that. If you'd wanted to cancel, I would have let you, of course, because I love you, but the people waiting outside would have been disappointed."

"I love you, too. And of course I wouldn't let you down by canceling, but thanks for saying that. I'm just wondering if Wyatt is going to show up, or Jordan, or anyone from work."

"If Jordan tries to come in, and especially if he has a date with him, I'm going to grab him by the ear, even if another part of his anatomy would be easier to reach from my chair, and show him the door."

That visual gave me quite a chuckle, since I had no doubt Dani would indeed so.

"Thanks, babe. Okay, so let's hope Jordan doesn't show. I'm still nervous, though, as to how this is going to go."

"I'm going to offer you the advice I offer every artist who has a show here," said Dani. "Those doors are going to open in a minute. But for right now, this is your moment. I'm going to walk over there near the entrance, and you, my dear, are going to look around and soak all of this in. This is all for you and because of you and your talent. So, take a deep breath, close your eyes, and then open them and look around and see what you've created and made happen here. I love you and I'm proud of you."

"I love you, too," I said, getting a bit choked up. "Please don't make me ruin my makeup."

"There are only happy tears allowed here, girl."

Dani gave me a huge hug, patted me on the back, and then wheeled off to give me that moment.

I did as my friend requested and shut my eyes and took a deep breath. When I opened them and looked around to take everything in, everything seemed amplified in that moment and intensely quiet at the same time.

How did I do this? How was it real life that my paintings were up on the walls of an art gallery to be seen by others? That had been a dream of mine for a while that I never thought would happen, and for it to be in Dani's gallery made it all the better.

Behind me, I heard the doors open and turned to see so many people entering the gallery. They were all there to see my paintings. That thought was just crazy.

The evening flew by in a bit of a blur. Joshykins and Zack were there; a bunch of my fellow teachers came out; and people from the rec center, including Amber and her husband, Moe; and Laurel. It was great to see them all, but I felt like the second I had a moment to actually talk with someone, I was pulled away somewhere else.

Halfway through the event, I found myself alone standing in front of my beach cottage painting for the first time that night.

"Wow. The house in that painting looks just like my grandparents' summer home."

Gosh, I hope that's Wyatt when I turn around because I really like that voice. It sounded deep and strong and assured. I hadn't counted on him actually showing up though if it was him. Shoot. I wonder if he matches his profile pics, or if those are years old and he looks completely different.

Oh, now I don't want to turn around in case I'm disappointed. I grimaced internally but kept my resting smile face on, which was one of my known qualities, and critical for teaching and in this case interacting with a crowd.

I slowly turned away from my painting towards the voice.

Ohh, wow.

It sure was Wyatt and he was even better looking than his pictures and wearing a three-piece suit complete with a vest. Did he remember that from our conversation or did he always wear them?

"Wyatt, I'm assuming," I said, collecting myself. "Are you serious, or was that one hell of a pick-up line? If so, well done on the originality, sir, because I've never heard that one before."

Wyatt chuckled. "I have my clever moments, but I'm not that clever, Grace. And yes, it's me. It's really nice to meet you in person and see that your pics were current ones. As for the painting, that really does look like my parents' cottage on the beach in West Harbor."

"Funny, I was thinking the same thing about the pics, and it's great to meet you, too. When I told you about this event, I honestly didn't think you'd be able to make it. But I'm glad you did. Kind of a low key way to first meet. Well, minus that the entire event is focused on me, and if it had bombed and no one had shown up, that would have been pretty embarrassing."

"This certainly wasn't a bomb. I couldn't find parking right outside, but I parked down further in the warehouse lot by the restaurants there. So, tell me about that cottage?"

"Oh, right. It wasn't West Harbor. I saw it when I was down in Seatown for a getaway weekend with my college girls and I had to sketch it, which led to this painting. Did you come here by yourself?"

Why did I just ask that? My face flushed.

I know he's single because we met on Connect, and hopefully he's not the kind of guy who would bring a date to the first time meeting someone. He's going to think I'm an idiot.

"I managed to drag a few of my co-worker friends along. They're those guys over at the bar who are staring at us and not being obvious about it at all, by the way. Ugh. Good job, guys. They heard art galleries are a great place to meet women. Okay, so I might have told them that in order to get them to come along with me as I didn't want to just show up by myself in case you were busy and we didn't get a chance to talk."

I glanced over at the bar and saw three guys standing there, also in suits, who looked like they'd stepped off Wall Street and had probably never looked at a painting in their life. Yeah, they're a bit out of their usual element, but they thankfully don't look like jerks.

"Have they also worked at the law firm for a while?"

"They haven't been there as long as I have, but yes, it's been a while. I know you're a teacher, but based on what I see here, I'm surprised you're not a full-time painter."

"Oh, this is something I've always enjoyed doing, but no, painting full-time doesn't pay the bills, you know? Plus, I like helping others find their creative side by teaching. And for relaxation, I'm a licensed Reiki practitioner, but I only did it for my own stress. You probably have no idea what that is…"

"I've heard of it. Reiki, obviously. Stress is something we all know. A buddy of mine actually received Reiki as part of his sports therapy for a busted knee and it really helped him."

I'm so glad he didn't make the usual joke about how I must be good with my hands if I do Reiki. Shoot. Did I just jinx it and he's about to say that next? This started out so well.

"I've gotta say…" said Wyatt.

Shoot. Here it comes.

"I'm really glad I came out tonight, and got my coworkers to come with me," said Wyatt. "I was nervous to do so since I'd be meeting you for the first time and I wasn't sure how I'd feel about an art show, but your work is great, and talking with you has been easy. How many shows have you done?"

"This is my first real one," I replied. "My friend, Dani, runs the gallery and has been trying to have me do a show forever. I did one for her as part of a group back in college, but this is my first solo show. She's that hottie over there in the black and gray jumpsuit."

I pointed at Dani, who was by the door greeting visitors as they came in.

"Well, congratulations on your debut," said Wyatt. "That's quite an accomplishment. Plus, you have one heck of a turnout here."

I looked around and fully took in the throng of people attending my show. They all seemed to be enjoying my paintings—and if that was a side result of the flowing alcohol, I didn't care, because I loved seeing everyone responding so well to my work.

Flushed with joy, I turned back to Wyatt, stepping closer to him in the process. As I did, I realized he was wearing something akin to Drakkar Noir, which was my personal kryptonite from my college days.

Uh oh. Danger, Will Robinson…

"Thank you, Wyatt," I said. "That's nice of you to say and I'm really glad you did come out to my show, because I've also enjoyed talking to you. As much as I don't want to drag myself away right now, I should really mingle some more before Dani kills me…"

"Of course. I understand completely, and was wondering something… Is there any chance we could grab dinner nearby when the show ends to continue talking and get to know each other more?"

Yes! He liked me enough in person to ask me out on a date. Okay, be cool…

"I'd like that a lot. Yes, let's do dinner after this. The show ends at 8, which you probably know."

Wyatt grinned. "I do indeed. Awesome. How about I go chat up my coworkers so they stop feeling abandoned and they can stop staring at us. Who am I kidding? They're staring at you and probably are quite jealous that I'm the one talking to you. I'll let them know they can head off to a bar without me when your show ends and then you and I can meet for dinner. I saw a little Italian place a few doors down, if that works? Do you even like Italian? If so, I'll meet you there."

"Italian is perfect. That's my favorite type of food."

Wyatt's phone buzzed with a notification, so he turned it in his hand to glance at it. Since we were standing so close, I caught that it was a call coming in from someone named Sally. Did I have competition? And why had I even looked? That was nosy.

He grimaced, but that could have been from not wanting to talk to whoever Sally was or being embarrassed that the call came in while he was talking to me.

"Need to take that?" I asked. Hopefully, the tone of my voice came across lighter than I felt.

"Nah, it's okay. I can call back later on my way over to the restaurant."

I pulled out my phone and glanced at the time.

"There's about 20 minutes left, so we'll talk more soon. I'm off to make the rounds, but first, put your number in my phone in case anything comes up, so I don't have to message you through Connect."

Wyatt took my phone and put in his number.

When I got my phone back, I saw his full name was Wyatt Armstrong. Ahh, that's his last name. I like it. Strong.

I dashed him a quick text:

Hey. It's Grace. See ya in a few.

Wyatt's phone vibrated immediately. Okay, phew, he gave me his actual number. He smiled as he glanced at the phone to read my text.

"Arriverderci," replied Wyatt. "Sorry, couldn't resist since you said Italian's your favorite and that's the one Italian word I know."

I grinned and somehow managed to pull myself away to walk through the crowd and answer questions about my paintings.

25 minutes later, the last of the attendees had exited the gallery, leaving me and Dani to finally take a breather, talk just between us again, and celebrate a successful debut while I let my feet rest out of my heels for a moment.

"Babe, you killed it," said Dani, holding up the sales receipts. "Every single one of your paintings sold, except for that beach one you asked me not to sell. But I did sell ten of the prints of that painting, so there's that. Along with a slew of the postcard-sized prints and 50 of the 8x10 sized prints. I did keep two postcards of each print for you to put on the tree you're donating and one for you to keep of each, so you're all set there. And we raised close to $10K towards the Rec Department, thanks to a few generous donors that wanted to remain anonymous."

"I can't believe it," I replied. "Oh my gosh. That's unreal. How did my show generate $10,000?? Back when we met in college, did you ever think one day I'd be holding a show of my own at your art gallery. I know I had dreams about it, but it's crazy when I think about how this is now real. This is the art gallery of your dreams."

"It really is," said Dani, looking around her studio. "But look at us, girl. We did it! And now, you have to tell me about that hottie you were talking to earlier. He looks familiar, but I can't place him. I know what a sucker you are for a guy in a good vested suit and he rocked it. So spill. What's his info?"

"That's Wyatt. Remember when we had dinner and I was swiping through Connect and saw the guy in the Halloween costume there. That's him. We started messaging through the app that night and this is the first time we've met in person. I like him and I'm relieved as heck that he's just as handsome in person as he was in his pics. We're meeting up for dinner at that Italian restaurant a few doors down in a few minutes, but I wanted to chat with you first."

Dani looked aghast and quickly wheeled herself over to the gallery entrance and opened the door.

"Wait a minute!" she said. "There's a guy you like who's waiting for you and you're sitting here talking to me. Shut the front door! If there was a woman I liked waiting for me at the restaurant, you and I would not be talking because I would be at the restaurant already. We can catch up tomorrow, so shoo! Seriously."

I laughed, put my heels back on, and stood up.

"Hey, you have Jessie, so shush. I'll go. I promise. I'm nervous since this is the first legit date I've been on since Jordan. But, first, thank you, Dani, for having faith in me to have my own show here. I love you, my friend."

"You know I love you, too, babe. I was honored to host your first show and this is going to be the start of something so huge for you. I'm going to drop that check off to Amber or Laurel after all the funds get sorted through the bank."

"You're amazing. Thank you, Dani!"

"You're welcome, my friend. Oh, also, your hottie bought one of your prints."

"He did? Oh, wow. That's sweet of him. Thanks for telling me."

I reached down and gave my friend a huge hug. My gratitude level was off the charts for this event. Dani hugged me back and then pointed towards the door so she could ferry me on my way to my date.

"Get out of here, and don't do anything I wouldn't do."

"Hmm, that leaves out a lot since Wyatt is, you know, a guy."

I winked at Dani with that statement.

"You know what I meant, you goof. And text me when you get home so I don't have to send out the SWAT team on Mister Halloween Fan Wyatt."

"Of course I will," I said. "I'd say text me when you get home, too, but since you live above the gallery, I'd be hearing from you in two seconds the second the elevator door opens into your apartment."

"Okay, true. But I will be listening for the chime of your text, missy."

"Have fun," I said as I opened the glass door of the gallery and stepped outside. "Tell Jessie I'm out on a date with a woman just to freak her out."

"She knows you're strictly into guys," said Alex, "so there's no way she'll believe that. And we all know that up until now, you've been mainly into guys who like to play games or mess with your head. Let's hope Wyatt is the exception or maybe you will start dating women."

"Now why haven't I made THAT my Connect profile headline?" I replied. "I love guys who like to play games with my mind and heart. That would get all the guys swiping right. Forget this date. I'm off to go change my information..."

As the door closed behind me on that statement, I chuckled and turned to walk down past the other warehouse shopfronts to the Italian restaurant. The street lights spilled across the pavement on this balmy night, guiding me through the people milling around outside.

Seventeen

Grace

Glancing around the restaurant, Vecchia Nonna, from the entryway, I appreciated the typical Italian restaurant decor of tan marble walls and Italian white bistro lights strewn across the ceiling. The tantalizing aroma of garlic and tomatoes permeated the air, prompting me to take a deep breath in. It didn't come close to the smell of Subtle Savors, but it was still making my mouth water.

Well. Props for a decent restaurant choice. Better than my first ever date in college, which was drinks at a cheap bar and really shouldn't even be called a date.

As I looked around, I noticed that the white bistro lights made it look like the room was shimmering, as if fog kept settling over the room and then dispersing to bring the room back into focus.

I haven't even had a glass of wine yet, so it wasn't from that, but I really liked that ethereal effect… Hmm, maybe I'll paint that later.

Putting that thought aside, I headed towards the hostess stand where a number of people were standing in a group to see if Wyatt was waiting there.

Oh, please let him be here. This was the place, right? There wasn't another Italian restaurant here, I don't think. Ugh, maybe he got a better offer from whoever that Sally was that called him…

Wyatt wasn't standing at the hostess stand. To pass the time and look busy, I pulled out my phone by reflex to scroll through my social media feeds. I promised myself to not text Wyatt to see if he was on the way or got waylaid somewhere between the gallery and here.

No. Be cool.

We only just met in person, so maybe he actually wasn't as attracted to me in person as he was by my pictures and our texts, or his friends didn't think I was hot enough for him and they went off to a bar instead. It happens.

He bails, he bails. It wouldn't be a big loss. I'm not going to check in to this restaurant online in case this doesn't work out and he doesn't show. Don't need people asking me how a restaurant is that I never got a chance to try.

If he doesn't show in five minutes, I'll text Dani and tell her I'm coming over and she should open a bottle of wine.

"Hey, Grace," I heard Wyatt say.

He walked over to me from the bar area off to the right of the hostess stand. "Phew. I gotta say I'm glad you're here because I was nervous you had second thoughts about our date after meeting me in person and decided to not show up."

I looked him up and down surreptitiously (or hopefully without him noticing), appreciating the fit of his suit and his great eyes and smile. He was holding a bag from Dani's gallery with a rolled-up print inside. Made me wonder which one of my prints he'd bought, but I'd wait until he told me. Still cute. It wasn't just the lights in the art gallery, although the lights here are certainly funky. What a relief!

"Sorry I'm running a little late," I replied. "I got caught up after talking to Dani about how the show went."

"No worries. I was able to catch some of the game while waiting and the Pats are winning against the Bills, which bodes well for me."

I looked over at the bar area for the first time, noticing the large flat-screen TV that flanked the wall behind the bartenders. And wondered why the winning team boded well for him.

Oh, please don't be a gambling addict. Wow, brain. Stop that. Why did my mind just go there? Next I'll have him being an ex-con despite that he was a lawyer.

"How does it bode well for you?"

"One of my buddies at work, Jim, is from Buffalo, so any time these teams play each other, the one who roots for the losing team buys the other lunch the next day. With how the game's going, I'm pretty sure I'm getting a free lunch tomorrow. Otherwise, I'll be buying him lunch when we meet up to shoot hoops."

Guess I'll get to take his leftovers home then either way since he won't need them tomorrow. Sweet.

"Well, then I can just take you home tonight. That works out well for me."

As those words came out of my mouth, I flushed in embarrassment and horror.

What the heck made me change "your leftovers" to "you" in that sentence. He's going to think I'm a perv or easy. Embarrassing.

Okay, Apocalypse, you can start right this second to end this conversation here.

"Ummm…" said Wyatt, looking anywhere but at me.

At the same time, I managed to say "Oh, gosh. Sorry. I was trying to joke that I'd take your leftovers home tonight since you get a free lunch and that attempt went horribly wrong because of course it did. And did I mention I tend to ramble when I'm nervous or feeling embarrassed, which I totally am right now."

Wyatt laughed nicely, making me feel a bit more at ease.

"Don't worry," he said. "I'm a bit old-fashioned and take things a little slower than that."

"That's a relief. Thanks for understanding, because, oy, that was a bad one."

"Seriously. It's okay. I got a good laugh out of it and I knew what you were trying to say. Was just messing with you with the ummm."

I reached over and smacked him lightly on the shoulder.

"How dare you! I thought for sure you thought I was blatantly hitting on you, which so isn't me."

"How about we get to our table, and we can see what those leftovers will be that you're taking home tonight, instead of me."

I put my left hand up to my cheek and shook my head, laughing.

"You're so not going to let me live that one down, are you, mister?"

"Probably not right away," replied Wyatt. "Can't let that moment slide. Plus, usually I'm the one with the words coming out wrong."

"I don't believe that for a second. Not possible. No one screws up words more than I do, which is why I paint instead of, say, act or write."

"But you're a teacher. You have to talk all the time."

"It's different there, for some reason." I thought about that for a moment and continued.

"When I'm teaching, I'm providing knowledge and thoughts about art and art techniques that I've had for years. That's all ingrained in me, so it comes out naturally and I know my stuff, so I'm not nervous at all talking in front of students. But get me on a first date when I want to make a good impression because I like the guy and I'm a rambling fool."

"Hey, you like me," said Wyatt. "Well, that's good to know from the start because I like you, too, Grace, and I'm glad to be here to spend some time with you. And I get it. I do. I may look smooth and debonair in this suit, but it's all an act."

"Well, it's a good act. Because looking at you, I just see a super confident self-assured lawyer man."

"Lawyer man? Hmm, I think I'd prefer being Superman or hell, even Aquaman. Lawyer man sounds like the dude that has to have the superhero protect him or like Frozen Caveman Lawyer."

"That was a great skit. But no, I don't think you've ever needed someone to protect you, Wyatt."

"Maybe when I was little, but every kid does, right?"

The hostess arrived back at the stand, and promptly found us a table, leading us through the crowded restaurant of diners seated at tables with white tablecloths. Our destination was a secluded table for two in the back corner of the restaurant.

"This is perfect," said Wyatt to the hostess, handing her a twenty as thanks for getting the table. As the hostess departed, Wyatt took the back of the seat in front of him and held it out for me to sit down.

Wow. He has manners. Haven't seen that in a while. I could get used to this.

"Thank you," I said. Wyatt took the other seat and we picked up the thick menus with rich red padded covers at our plates.

"So, what will it be?" he said. "Bottle of red? Bottle of white?"

I couldn't help but burst out laughing.

"You didn't just quote that Billy Joel song to me in an actual Italian restaurant? Oh my god. Maybe you're right and you really aren't all that smooth."

"I had to do it," said Wyatt. "Was looking at the wine list and it just came to me."

"I'll admit it was funny. Okay, so seriously. Are you a red fan or white?"

"Typically, I prefer a good beer, but wine seems more like the fare here, right?"

"I'm sure they do have beer, but you're right. At an Italian restaurant, you just kinda have to have wine with your meal. Think you get kicked out otherwise."

"Wouldn't want to risk that. Then you won't have leftovers to take home."

Okay, he's a joker. I liked that.

"So, answer my question, silly. Red or white?"

"My mama raised me to let the lady choose, so it's your choice."

"Your mother sounds like a very smart woman. My choice is red. I used to drink white but then tried red once in a sangria and haven't looked back since."

"She was quite a smart woman..."

Shoot. That word "was" said it all right there.

"Oh, no. There I go putting my foot in my mouth again. I take it your mother passed. If so, I'm sorry."

"Thank you. It's okay. She died when I was young. It was rough and we still miss her quite a bit. She was indeed amazing. I learned a lot from her."

I watched Wyatt's face closely while he was talking about his mother, and noticed the warmth that lit up his deep brown eyes.

Awww. He really loved her. She must have been something very special.

"Even though it was a while ago, my condolences."

"Thanks. My dad remarried two years ago, and my stepmother is thankfully great for him. Okay, lighter topic. Red it is. Did you want sangria or no fruit?"

"Just like I've moved from tons of cream in my coffee to just black, I've also moved from fruit-laden wine to just red wine itself. That okay?"

"Of course. I don't consider myself a wine buff, so I'm open to suggestions."

"Honestly, I tend to buy wines based on if I like the design on the label or not, so I'm not actually any help there. Shhh, keep that a secret. Wouldn't want to give up my wine cred."

He mock locked his lips and threw away the key.

"Your secret's safe with me. Okay, so neither of us knows much about wine. How about we go with the house red?"

"Easy enough. Okay, so that's decided. Now, I'm going to be a nosy artist and ask which one of my paintings you bought, since I recognize that bag."

He glanced down at the bag and then grinned up at me.

"First, don't let me forget that. I don't want to leave it here. Second, it was the beach print. That was the one that caught my eye, so I had to have it. The gallery owner said I couldn't buy the painting itself, but the print was the next best thing."

Oh, how sweet. That was the one we met in person in front of. I liked that he really was interested in the print and that it wasn't just a line, unless buying the print was also part of the act. Stop it, self. Be grateful.

"Thank you. That really is one of my favorites. It's the sole print I told Dani that she couldn't sell, but I'm glad I had the postcards and prints made up. Plus, it's going to a great cause."

"Oh? How's that?"

"I do a lot of work with the Recreation Department in Silverton—art classes for them and the like. Recently, I learned that they lost their full funding in budget cuts for next year, and the department will be slashed in half if that's the case, causing their assistant manager to lose her job, which would be awful."

Wyatt shook his head at the news.

"That's horrible. It's never a good time to lose your job, of course, but knowing that you are right before Christmas makes it even worse."

I agreed. Plus, Laurel was such a good person. I couldn't bear the thought of her losing her job.

"Right? And it's even worse for them because at the same time, the Rec Center is about to be sold out from underneath them to some company that wants to raze it and build on the site. It hurts my heart to think about that center not being there as I have so many fond memories of attending events there over the years, and it's where a lot of kids have met Santa for the first time. So I want to do anything I can to stop that from happening."

Wyatt looked like he was about to say something, but I kept talking before he could.

"So, I thought about my show and had Dani make up the postcards and prints to sell along with the rest of the paintings, besides that beach one, and all the sales are going to the Recreation Department. I don't know if any of it will help keep Laurel's job or help us keep the Rec Center from being sold, but I have to try. It means too much to not try."

Wyatt's jaw dropped. Realizing what he had done, he closed his mouth, but he still looked surprised. He looked closely at me as if he was reassessing me.

"That's wonderful of you to do. Seriously, you're doing a really sweet thing to donate the proceeds to them instead of taking it yourself."

I blushed. This is why I didn't like talking about myself much, because it put the spotlight on me. I also didn't want to wind up on a pedestal he created for me, as that's a long fall when reality hits.

"Thank you. I appreciate that. It's nothing. Really. We were able to donate quite a good chunk of money, and thank you for the purchase of the print as help towards that, but just that alone isn't going to save the department. I want to help them by thinking of other ideas. They're doing a Festival of Trees fundraiser at the Rec Center and I'm donating a tree to that, but I want to do more."

"That sounds fun. Maybe we could go check out the Festival of Trees together, if you're interested."

He wanted to see me again. Yes! I stopped myself from cheering, but instead made a little fist of cheer motion out of sight under the table."

"I'd like that, Wyatt," I replied.

"Good. So we will see each other again. Awesome. Now let's check out the food."

Out of the corner of my eye, I saw two tall people walking over to our table. They looked familiar but I couldn't place them at first. As they came closer, I realized it was Chloe and Mitchell.

"Grace, hi!" said Chloe, coming up to the table. "We're so sorry. Mitch and I wanted to make it to your gallery show, but I got stuck in meeting with the dinosaur volunteers for the Christmas events that went longer than planned. When we got to the gallery, we saw the closed sign and realized we'd missed it, so we stumbled in here for some dinner."

"No worries at all," I replied. "I understand and I hope the planning is going well. The T-Rex costume is still working okay?"

"Oh, yes, Pinky T-Rexadero and I are now good friends. I guess we must be since I've given her a name. I can stomp around like any other inflatable dinosaur."

I noticed a look of bemusement at the conversation on Wyatt's face and realized I should introduce him. But before I could, Chloe spoke up.

"I'm so sorry for interrupting your dinner, but just wanted to apologize for not making the show. And now I'm apologizing for not introducing myself. I'm Chloe and this is Mitch, and you must be Jordan. It's nice to meet you."

Aaah. No, Chloe.

No, no, no.

When the heck had I mentioned Jordan's name to her? It's possible I had during our first meeting, but yikes. Of all the details for her to remember and assumptions to make.

"No, Chloe," I said. "This is Wyatt. We met online, he came to my gallery show, and we're grabbing dinner now…"

And it would maybe be our first and last date after that statement. Ugh.

"So sorry! I'm an idiot," said Chloe. Mitch looked horrified by her botch up, and I'm sure that was also showing on my face.

Mitch stepped up and held out his hand to Wyatt with a look of chagrin.

"Wyatt. It's a pleasure to meet you. I'm Mitch."

Wyatt glanced at him curiously.

"Have we met before? You look so familiar, but I can't place it."

Mitch cocked his head to the side in thought before replying.

"No, I don't think we've met. Chloe and I have only been here for a little while. But maybe you saw me somewhere in town. I've been trying out a lot of restaurants."

"That could be it. I do tend to eat out a lot. Well, nice meeting you, Mitch."

I noticed he left Chloe off that statement, and wondered if that was just a slip or intentional for her calling him by my ex's name.

Chloe seemed to be wondering the same thing. I saw a flash of irritation across her face, but it was quickly replaced by a warm smile.

"So, we're going to get going," said Chloe, grabbing Mitchell by the hand. "I just realized I might want a hamburger instead. Mitch, let's go hit that place called Four Dudes that I saw. Have a good night, guys. Nice to meet you, Wyatt."

Great. Thanks for doing that and then dashing, Chloe. But there really wasn't anything she could add to make that better. The conversation was now all on me.

I turned to Wyatt, trying to figure out some way to explain this one that didn't make him think I was involved with someone else.

"So…" said Wyatt. "I didn't even think to ask, but tell me you are single and not married to some guy named Jordan. I'm not into getting involved in open marriages or anything like that."

"No, it's not that at all. Ugh. I'm so sorry that happened. Jordan is the guy I last dated. We broke up before I joined Connect."

"That's a relief. I mean, if you're dating other people, I can't say anything because we're on our first date. I know people tend to date around for a while before figuring things out and settling down. I'm okay with that. I just wanted to make sure you weren't married."

Dammit. Does that mean he's dating other people? Would that Sally be one of them? Stop it, self.

"I promise I'm not married. I'm single. And I honestly don't remember even mentioning Jordan to Chloe when she and I met. She and Mitchell are my neighbors, but I guess I got a text from him or something while we were talking and she just assumed. I'm embarrassed."

"Hey, we all have a past. It's okay. All good. Now let's take a look at the menu and we can talk about what we're going to get instead of exes or anyone else."

Wyatt glanced at his phone as a notification came up, and I couldn't help but wonder if it was from Sally.

"Excuse me for a second," Wyatt said. "Nature calls."

I noted that he did bring his phone with him when he left the table for a moment. Surely to reply to the notification that had popped up. I should give him credit for not replying to whoever it was in front of me, but I was still annoyed.

Like Wyatt said, we were on a first date and certainly not exclusive, but my gut twisted at the thought of him dating other people.

I guess that was a good sign, but I sure didn't like it. Jordan had already decided I wasn't enough and chose other people over me. Didn't really need nor want another version of that.

Maybe it was me and I just wasn't enough.

Okay, I should really stop thinking about that. I wasn't being fair to Wyatt. For all I knew, he wasn't replying to anyone and really had just gone to use the facilities.

I picked up the menu to focus on the food instead, and was doing so when Wyatt came back to the table.

"Sorry about that."

"Oh, no worries. I ordered for both of us. Vegan platter for the whole table."

He looked at me in horror, which caused me to break the straight face I was showing and laugh out loud.

"Your face. I'm sorry. I couldn't resist. I certainly haven't ordered, and I'm not vegan."

Wyatt chuckled, realizing that I had indeed been joking. Phew. He was a good sport and could take a joke as well as dish them out.

"So what did you order? Dare I ask?"

"I haven't ordered at all yet. Promise. Only just opened the menu. How about we take a look at it and see what we want to get."

I was impressed with the offerings I saw. This restaurant wasn't the standard Italian fare I was used to of pasta with red sauce and pizza. Not that there was anything wrong with either, since I could easily live on both. Especially pizza.

"Ooh, Caprese salad," I said. "Yum! One of my favorites. I think I'm going to get that with the veal tortellini."

"That does sound good. I'm eyeing the lobster ravioli and some bruschetta."

"That will make for great leftovers tomorrow," I replied with a wink.

"Good one! And here comes our waiter. How do they have such great timing?"

Conversation flowed easily. We talked about our jobs, growing up, and favorite movies and he asked me just as many questions as I asked him, instead of being a one-way conversation of me asking all the questions. It felt good.

When the check came, we both reached for it at the same time. For me, it was more out of habit because when I was out with girlfriends we just paid our own share.

With Jordan, he'd paid at the beginning but then I had offered to pay once out of courtesy. After that, it seemed we switched off who paid each time, no matter where we went. So, picking up the check was something I did subconsciously.

I wonder if he's still paying all the time with whoever it is he's dating now. And that train of thought wasn't going to help in the slightest.

"Thanks for even reaching for the check, but you're not paying," said Wyatt. "I asked you out for dinner, which means I'll pay."

I took my hand away from the check, happy that he'd offered.

"Thank you. I appreciate that and it's sweet and gentlemanly of you to do so. But I don't want you to feel like you have to each time. If there is another time, perhaps I can pick up the check then?"

Should I have said that? Ugh.

This part of a date was the worst, when you didn't know if the other person was interested. We had seemed to have a great conversation that flowed easily, and he had mentioned checking out the Christmas Tree Festival together, but it was still a first date, and may not have gone as well as I'd thought. Heaven knew I'd had plenty of first dates before that didn't result in second ones.

"I sure hope there is another time," said Wyatt. "Maybe we could grab dinner again or coffee tomorrow, if that's not too soon?"

I was relieved and quite pleased that he wanted to see me again so soon. I'd enjoyed myself and I liked him, but I knew he could be dating other people.

As I thought about that, my phone buzzed. Without thinking, I glanced down at it, wondering if it was Abigail needing something before her dad's wake the next day. It was Joshykins. The message preview simply said:

Dani told me about your hot date. Details now.

I stifled a chuckle and suddenly felt guilty for looking at my phone when I didn't normally do that while I was out. But this was different since Abigail might have needed me. Wasn't fair to Wyatt though, especially since he didn't know that. And I just realized I hadn't replied to him yet. Great. I was just sitting there ignoring him like an idiot.

"I'm sorry. That was horrible of me. First, yes, I would love to see you again."

Wyatt smiled. Okay, he wasn't mad. Good. I continued on.

"But, tomorrow's no good. I glanced at my phone because I thought it might be my friend Abigail. Her dad passed away suddenly and his wake's tomorrow, so I thought she might need something. Who it was instead was my buddy, Joshykins, who heard about this dinner and anxiously wanted details on how it went."

"I'm sorry about your friend's dad. That's awful. As for Joshykins, what are you going to tell him?"

I thought about that for a moment. What was I going to tell him?

"That the date went great and I plan on seeing you again. How about Sunday for coffee instead? I have my friend's dad's funeral in the morning, but I'll be back this way in the afternoon and could meet up after that in town?"

"I'm glad to hear that. And yes, Sunday sounds good. I have brunch plans with my dad and step-mom that morning, so coffee that afternoon works well. I'll look forward to it."

I was looking forward to it, too, I realized.

"Awesome. Then yes, Sunday it is. I'll text you with a time that might work once I see what time I'm leaving the post-funeral reception. As for a place, there's Coffee Colony if that sounds okay?"

"Sounds perfect. Okay, how about I pay for this check now that we have that settled?"

He called our waitress over and settled the bill, for which I thanked him again.

As we stepped outside to go to our cars, we stopped in the parking lot. Was he going to kiss me? Did I want him to kiss me?

"I had a wonderful time tonight and I'm glad I did come out to your show, so we could meet and then get dinner. Thanks, Grace."

Wyatt held out his hand. Huh. Not even a hug? Okay, maybe he really was old-fashioned or he wasn't as interested as I thought. I shook his hand, struggling to keep a smile on my face.

"It was great meeting you, too, Wyatt. I'll look forward to coffee on Sunday."

"Me, too. Safe travels home and we'll talk soon."

Honestly, I felt a bit deflated. He liked me enough to want to see me again, but no kiss? Did he think I wasn't a first date kiss type of person? He had said he was old-fashioned, so maybe he really was.

Once I was in the car and safely out of earshot, I called Joshykins to spill on the details of the date, making sure to include the bit where Chloe called Wyatt 'Jordan' because I knew he'd relish that bizarre part. Sure enough, he did.

My thoughts swirled on the way home, going around in circles.

Eighteen

Chloe

"Circles are fun!" I said, as I drove the car around in circles in the empty elementary school parking lot Saturday morning, with Mitch in the passenger seat.

I had my first dinosaur show later that day, so as soon as Mitch had woken up, I'd asked him if we could try driving since it was a clear sunny day. The thought of my first attempt driving on a snowy or rainy day didn't sound at all appealing, and I wanted to at least try driving once before we went back up.

Thankfully, he had agreed. When we got back to the apartment last night after seeing Grace and Wyatt at dinner, I assumed we'd sit and watch TV again. Instead, Mitch had said he was feeling tired and was just going to go to bed.

Once again, I watched dinosaur dance move videos in my room, but that time, I found myself thinking of Mitch and wondering if things were okay rather than paying attention to the dances.

He seemed in better spirits this morning, and I hoped it would stay that way because I didn't like feeling like I'd disappointed him at all. But at the same time, I knew that I shouldn't have said Jordan's name instead of Wyatt's and that he was probably disappointed in me for that. I was surprised he hadn't said anything the prior night actually.

When we got to the parking lot, he had pulled into a space and we exchanged seats. Sliding behind the wheel of a car was such a strange sensation. I was the one in control of the wheel and the brakes and all the things.

Mitch showed me how to back up and to look behind me as I did so, which was trickier than I thought it would be. Putting the car in reverse was very clunky and I slammed my foot on the brake the moment the car moved because it was so bizarre.

When I rode in the car with Mitch, he made driving look so easy. I had assumed it would be the same for me, but I was quickly seeing that wasn't the case.

Going forward was smoother, and Mitch suggested making some circles because that involved learning how lightly you needed to move the wheel to get it to turn. Circles were a blast.

"Can't I just drive in circles forever?" I jokingly said to Mitch.

He didn't say anything, so I quickly glanced at him, and noticed his hand was tightly gripping the hand hold of the car and he was a light shade of green. I was so startled by this that I pressed down on the brake again, causing the car to jerk to a stop.

Mitch reached over and put the car into park. "Chloe, please keep your foot on the brake, and turn the key to turn the car off. Once you've done that, we can switch seats again. It'll be good for me to get out of the car for a moment anyway since I need some air."

Did I make him sick with the circles? I guess that was possible because I was the one driving so I had that to focus on while it probably felt like he was spinning out of control. A wave of guilt washed over me.

I got out of the car and stood face to face with him in front of the car.

"Mitch, I'm sorry. I was having so much fun that I didn't think that it might be making you feel sick…"

"Yes, I feel like I'm going to puke, which isn't the best feeling, because it's certainly a new one to me. I thought you'd notice it but you were thinking about anything else but me."

Where on earth did that come from? I felt like he'd slapped me. But when I thought about it, he was right. I'd been enjoying myself and just didn't think about it affecting Mitch.

"I'm sorry. I said I was sorry. I really am."

"Sometimes sorry isn't enough, Chloe. You can't just do whatever you want and say whatever you want and not think about the consequences."

"Say whatever I want? Why do I think this has nothing to do with this car ride now? And I do think about the consequences. Sometimes. But a lot of the time, I just go with what feels right. What's wrong with that? I'd rather do that than overthink everything and never act at all."

Mitch shook his head in frustration.

"There are moments when I realize we're completely different people, and this is one of them. Yes, I overthink because I have to. I'm fully aware of the consequences of everything and anything I do, and I wish you were more like that sometimes. Like last night…"

Okay, we were getting to whatever was annoying him. I really didn't want to hear what he had to say if it was going to be more of a rebuke of my actions, but I guess I had to listen.

"What about last night? I'm sorry we were late and didn't make it to the gallery, but we saw Grace for a moment at the restaurant."

"Yes, and you called her date Jordan when you knew full well that that wasn't Jordan she was with. She was with Wyatt, who is a very decent fellow. While Jordan…"

I was flabbergasted.

"I called him Jordan because I wanted her to remember Jordan even though she was with someone else. Jordan is who she belongs with. Not this other guy. He's a blip."

"Are you sure about that? Are you really sure? Because I think you're so blinded by what you think you know about Jordan and Grace that you're not really seeing them. She could be meant to be with Wyatt instead. Or someone else entirely. But you could have thrown a wrench in them dating with your little antics last night."

He was making me sound like a frivolous child, and that grated. Mitch may have been my best friend, but he was taking that a bit too far at this moment.

"You clearly don't know either based on what you just said. So maybe what I did helped instead of hurt things last night, by keeping Grace thinking about Jordan and not that guy."

"That guy. Ugh. Chloe. I don't know what to say to you sometimes when you get so obsessed over something and this is one of them. Let's go back to the apartment and consider this driving lesson over. You're my best friend and I adore you, but I really don't want to talk to you anymore right now."

Ouch.

"I understand," I said, a bit colder than I intended it to come out. "Let's go. I have to get ready for the dinosaur show anyway."

We each got into the car silently, and sat there for a moment, until Mitch spoke.

"Right. Do you need a ride over to that?"

Typical Mitch. Even when he was mad at me, he still thought about my needs and what was best for me. I softened a bit.

"No. Nadia's going to pick me up on the way. Thank you, though, and Mitch?"

He turned his head to me slowly, as if he thought I was going to yell at him. Ugh.

"Yes?"

"Thank you for asking if I needed a ride to the show. I appreciate you. You really are my best friend and I adore you, too. We've known each other forever so we've seen the good and bad sides of each other, and sometimes that means hearing things we don't want to hear, but we need to."

I saw Mitch about to speak, but I stopped him.

"Let me get this out, because I don't want it to linger out there. You were right. I do need to think before I act more often, and you're right, I shouldn't have called Wyatt by Jordan's name. That was petty of me, which is why I bristled when you mentioned it. I don't want to be that way, but I know I can be. Usually I reign it in, but I feel so strongly that Grace belongs with Jordan that I needed to do something when I saw her with someone else. That wasn't what I should have done though. And I'm sorry I didn't notice you weren't feeling well from the circles. I was focusing on driving and the exhilaration of driving for the first time. Forgive me?"

Mitch sunk into his seat a little bit. I hadn't realized until then that he was sitting ramrod straight like he had to prepare for battle until he wasn't doing so anymore.

"Thank you. I appreciate that and I can tell that you thought about it before you said any of that instead of just reacting, so thank you for that, too."

"Thank you for being the one who calls me out when I do something I shouldn't. That's what friends are for, right."

I reached over and patted him on the arm as if to reaffirm our friendship.

"Yes, Chloe, that's what friends are for."

Nineteen

Grace

This is what friends are for… to be there for you when they need you, like at your parent's wake.

I found the funeral home for Abigail's dad's wake easily enough, but parking was going to be an issue. As the GPS announced I'd arrived, I saw there wasn't a parking lot like I thought there would be. If there was, it was around the back of the building down a dark driveway and I sure wasn't going to pull in and then have to back out onto a busy street if it wasn't there.

Continuing down the street, I found a church on my right with a well-lit and vacant parking lot. Okay, that works.

Nerves hit as I approached the funeral home door. I don't want to go to this by myself. Why do I always have to go to events on my own instead of with someone? Could I just turn around and leave? I hadn't gone in yet.

Nope. I needed to go in. I was doing it for Abigail.

Taking a deep breath, I opened the door. Okay, no one was standing there so I didn't have to do small talk with anyone right away. I saw the memory book to my left and went over to sign it before walking in.

Once that was done, I walked into the parlor and looked around a bit more. The casket containing Abigail's father was over to the left without anyone standing in front of it but a few people were seated there. I didn't see Abigail but that didn't mean she wasn't there yet. Looking to the right of the hall I saw a priest and some military men, who must have served in the Army with Abigail's dad, standing in the other room.

I turned left, walked up to her father Peter's casket, crossed myself, and knelt down before the casket on the padded red velvet kneeler. Looking at Peter, I didn't see the body that was lying there. Instead, all I could see was how he was in the pictures Abigail had emailed to me of her dad over the recent years. Images flitted through my head of Peter riding a bike at age 80 and of holding a can of jam that they'd made together. In every one, he was smiling and had the kindest eyes, and Abigail had the same happiness in the pics that I knew Peter had taken of her. I knew how close they were, especially after Abigail's mom died when Abigail was 15, and how lost Abigail must be feeling. Tears threatened to spill as I thought about that.

Trying to get those thoughts out of my head, I let an "Our Father" go through my head instead and a prayer for Peter to be well in Heaven and to watch over his daughter. I crossed myself again, stood up, and turned, and there she was standing there.

"Hey," I said. So eloquent, self…

As we hugged, I glanced at the door, wondering if Ethan was going to show up soon or if I should offer to sit with Abigail. I didn't want to leave her hanging by herself.

Pulling back from the hug after a moment, I started to talk, and Abigail did at the same time.

"I'm sorry…"

"Thanks for…"

I chuckled, and then said, "You first."

"Thanks for coming," said Abigail. "I know it was a long drive for you and you didn't have to do so."

"I wouldn't have been anywhere else. You're one of my best friends. Traffic was, surprisingly, a breeze through the city to get down here, so all good. How are you, by the way? Okay that's a stupid question, I know…"

"Right now, I'm just getting by and getting things taken care of. It still honestly feels a bit unreal and just so sudden. One minute, we were watching TV, and the next he was clutching his chest. I hoped that he'd just recover from it or need surgery. I don't know. I'm glad I was there, but it sucks that I didn't get to say goodbye because he was just gone."

I reached over and hugged Abigail, clutching her close to me. My friend was hurting. This is exactly where I should be right now. I cringed thinking about how close I came to not being here for her because of my own anxiety about having to walk in the door myself.

"You can still say your goodbyes to him, hon. I am sure he's still with you and watching over you. So anytime you want to, it'll be the right time to say what you want to say. He'll hear it. And even if you don't say anything, he knows how much you loved him and love him. It was clear from every time you spoke about him."

"Thanks, Grace. I appreciate it. I hope you're going to stay for the mini-service.

Father Doherty will be speaking soon."

I started to say that of course I would, but noticed a man and woman had entered the funeral home and were waiting to speak to Abigail. Excusing myself, I slipped away to go find a seat, choosing to sit in the middle of the rows on the right side.

As I did, people who were seated on the left side of the room started moving over to the right to make way for a military procession with Father Doherty at the front. An elderly man came over and sat next to me, asking if that seat was taken. He didn't look familiar, but he was probably Abigail's great-uncle or something.

"All good. You can sit there, of course."

As Father Doherty and the servicemen stood at the front, Ethan rushed in and sat down next to Abigail, taking her hand.

Thank God he's here for her. It's where he should be and I'm glad she has him.

Father Doherty spoke fondly of Peter, reminiscing about their days in Catholic school together, Peter's time in the Army, and what a devoted dad he'd been to Abigail. The personal memories made me tear up and especially hearing how Father Doherty served in the Vietnam War with Peter when Father Doherty was a chaplain, and how many people Peter had helped to save over there.

I wondered how much of this Abigail already knew and how much she was hearing for the first time. I appreciated the eulogy of sorts more because it was being given by someone that actually knew Peter. There was always something a bit more heart-wrenching when it wasn't the standard rote statement about how much someone would be missed without anything personal included.

Father Doherty ended on a prayer and walked back into the other room leading the recessional of the men Peter had served with in the Army, stopping for a moment to lay a hand on Abigail's shoulder. She collapsed in tears onto Ethan's shoulder, and I thought about going to the front to further console my friend.

"So, how do you know Abigail?"

I looked to my right, having forgotten that the elderly man was seated next to me.

"Oh, we went to college together."

"Sorry, can you say that again?"

Oh, gosh. I don't particularly want to raise my voice while the recessional is going by… I spoke again in just a slightly louder tone than my previous whisper.

"We're friends from college. How do you know her?"

"I used to work with Peter. I'm Larry, by the way."

"Nice to meet you, Larry." I reached over and shook his hand, taking in the age spots on his hands and face, his very white hair, and what seemed like kind eyes that had crinkled up with laughter quite a bit over his lifetime.

"Where are you from?"

"I'm from up north in Silverton, on the border of New Hampshire. You?"

"Wow, that's a heck of a drive," Larry replied. "I live here in town. Moved here shortly after I married my first wife and we raised our kids here. Then, when Claire died a decade ago, I stayed because I couldn't bear leaving where all my memories were of her. I didn't think I'd ever find love again, but then I met Janet in a restaurant one day and I realized love could hit twice."

"Oh my goodness. Condolences on your first wife. I'm sure that was difficult. But how wonderful that you found love again."

"Thank you. I certainly did. Claire was the first love of my life. She was someone who always made things better and she supported my dreams and helped me turn them into reality. I've written dittys for decades now, and one of the tunes I wrote made its way into a movie. The producers I've met—let me tell you. When Claire died, I thought she took my interest in creating melodies away with her, but one day I was thinking of her and started humming and had to get my sheet music to write it down. That song was just used in a Broadway production. And then I met Janet and she reminded me so much of Vivien Leigh. Her beauty was just timeless."

Wow. Wait, am I having my *The Holiday* moment here, when Kate Winslet's character meets the adorable old man played by Eli Wallach, who was a famous screenwriter and tells her all about the world of old Hollywood and bolsters her self-esteem in the process? I've always felt an affinity for her character. That would just be perfect.

"Did you wind up writing melodies about Janet, too, Larry?"

"I sure did. I wrote ones that reminded me of our honeymoon in the Caribbean and I'm actually talking to their tourism board tomorrow about using one of those in their ads."

"That is amazing. She must be so proud."

"She would be, but she passed away five years ago."

Larry reached into his wallet and pulled out pictures of two gorgeous women, one blonde and one with dark hair. He showed me the blonde first.

"Here's my Claire. Isn't she beautiful? And this was Janet."

"They're both stunning women, with such wonderful smiles."

"Thank you. Yes, they both just had this energy that took over a room any time they entered. You wanted to be around them. I can feel that same energy off of you."

"That's very sweet of you, Larry. Thank you."

"I was lucky that I had two loves of my life. Some people don't even get one. Tell me, do you have someone that loves you? You must because you're so sweet and just beautiful."

Ack. This is feeling far less like "The Holiday". Time to make this guy go away, even if it meant I had to lie.

"I do, yes. I definitely do."

"Good, good. Someone like you should be loved and taken care of. All good women should. My kids don't understand that."

Oh, where on earth is this going?

"What do you mean, Larry?"

"They're not talking to me right now because of my girlfriend. She's in her 30s and they think that's gross because she's 10 to 20 years younger than them. But love is love, right? My doctor tells me I'm still virile and like a man who's in his 50s. I tried dating women my own age, but they're just all so old, dried up, and wrinkly. I like younger women because they're still perky. Like you."

Out of the corner of my eye, I saw one of Abigail's cousins who had been sitting in front of us look aghast at those statements. He then stood up and left the row to go into another room. Possibly to puke, which is exactly what I wanted to do.

Perky? Yes, it's a compliment, but not okay! So definitely NOT my "The Holiday". Ugh.

"I'm sure your children want you to be happy and hopefully they'll see that you are."

"Just because I treat her great and I'm paying for the clothing business she is opening, they think she's taking advantage of me. But she entertains me and I want to make her happy, so of course I will. Plus, she says I'm better than any other guy she's ever been with."

Also didn't need to know that tidbit of info. She's got to be in it for the money. I'm certainly not going to be the one to tell him. How can I get out of this convo?

I picked my purse up from underneath my seat, hoping he'd get the hint that it was time to go.

Larry glanced at his watch and said, "It's later than I thought. Hopefully my girlfriend is still up when I get home. Thanks for talking with me, miss."

"You're welcome. I hope life treats you well."

Larry got up and went over to Abigail and said his goodbyes. After he left, Abigail came over to stand and talk with me as the crowd had thinned out a bit.

"Sit down," I said, patting the seat next to me that Larry had just vacated. "You could probably use the moment of rest after all of this. Plus, I have one heck of an entertaining story for you."

Abigail took the seat and leaned back with a half quizzical look, half grin on her face.

"Okay, what's the story?"

I glanced around to make sure no one was standing right there or within earshot before I told her.

"Your dad's friend, Larry, who I was just talking to? He was just telling me about the sweet story about his first two wives and then veered into how his kids aren't talking to him because of some 30 year old he's dating at age 80 and he's funding her business. And how virile he still is according to his doc. Well, and him."

"Larry?" Abigail started laughing. "Oh, gross! He's loaded, from what I remember. When he and my dad worked together, Larry was one of the top performing sales guys."

"That explains it. She's totally dating him just because of the moolah then and not because he's the love of her life. And I know I'm making assumptions because she could be the sweetest woman in the world and isn't a gold-digger, but c'mon..."

"Yeah, no. You're most likely right. I'm glad he didn't bring her, although now I'm curious as to see just how sleazy looking she is, because I'm picturing Ana Nicole Smith."

I put my hand up to my mouth to stop myself from laughing out loud at that, since it would be just like me to do that at a wake of all things. With the other hand, I smacked Abigail lightly on the shoulder.

"I almost snort laughed… Would have been worth it, though. How are you holding up, by the way? Father Doherty's eulogy was lovely."

"It really was. I'm glad you got to hear it. I'm okay. Surprisingly so."

Looking around, I saw that only a few of Abigail's cousins and Ethan remained while everyone else had gone. Glancing at my phone, I saw it was 7:40. Part of me wanted to ask Abigail if she wanted me to stick around, while the other part of me just wanted to head to my hotel and grab something to eat since I'd had a long drive and was starving.

"I didn't realize it had gotten so late. I should probably head out."

I stood up and Abigail followed my lead.

"Thanks for coming, Grace. Really. It meant a lot to me that you did, especially since it's such a long drive."

"No worries in the slightest. I grabbed a hotel room in the next town over for the night, so I'm going to be nearby to get to the funeral tomorrow. Glad to be here, but now I'm going to go grab some food and then get some sleep."

I hugged Abigail goodbye.

"I'll see you at the funeral tomorrow morning, babe, and know I'm thinking about you tonight. May everything go as well as it can," I said as I stepped back from our hug.

"Thank you. Drive safely please."

"I will. Promise."

Walking out of the funeral home into the dark night, I was grateful that the street lights were all ablaze as I headed up the street back to my car in the church parking lot.

Yawning, I knew leaving was the right answer because I was tired and knew I'd sleep soundly tonight.

I'm so glad Ethan's there for Abigail and would be at the funeral tomorrow.

As I walked down the street back towards my car, my phone lit up. Glancing at it, I saw that it was a text from Jordan. My heart jumped more than it should have with that notification. Why did he still have that impact on me?

I opened the message.

LOL That was funny. Hope your week's been good. Busy one here. Could use a drink...

Shoot. I had no idea what I'd said or sent that was funny, because I had deleted the thread of any message I sent Jordan immediately after I sent it, so I wouldn't have a "read" mocking me without a reply. The things we do for self-preservation.

The last message I had sent him was about a week or so back, which was pretty on par for getting a response from him now. What had I sent? Probably some random story of something that had happened to me that day. Guess it wasn't all that important to me any more.

The timing of his message, though, was funny considering I'd just been thinking of Abigail and Ethan. Was this fate telling me I should give Jordan another (or a 50th) chance?

I got into my car, plugged my phone into the charger so it wouldn't die on the way to the hotel while I was using the GPS, and felt compelled to type back to Jordan. I always told myself that I wouldn't text him back right away when I heard from him, but I guess I just didn't want to play the same games he did.

I started typing…

Hey, just leaving Abigail's dad's wake, so the week's been mixed... Glad...

As I wondered what I really wanted to say, or if I actually wanted to reply at all, another notification came in. I went to open it, thinking it might be Abigail telling me I'd accidentally left something there.

Instead, it was a message from Wyatt:

Stumbled across 'Singles' on TV and thought of our talk of that movie. Look forward to grabbing coffee tomorrow. Gesundheit.

I bit my lower lip, grinning at the words and the confirmation of our coffee date.

Great movie. Looking forward to it. Hope I don't get stuck in traffic so it won't take me so long. Getting in my car now to head out from the wake. See you tomorrow for coffee.

After I texted Wyatt, replying to Jordan didn't seem as interesting to me, so I got rid of the start of that reply and closed the text window. No need to reply.

I couldn't wait to see Wyatt tomorrow for coffee.

Twenty

Grace

This hotel coffee and breakfast was just what I needed. I'd slept fine, but knew I'd want to eat before the funeral, since otherwise my stomach would be certain to growl during a quiet moment. To my delight, the hotel breakfast hadn't been just some bagels but was instead a full spread with pancakes, scrambled eggs, and bacon. Yum! And it was all delicious.

Abigail's dad's funeral, held in St. Andrew's, which was a stunning Gothic church, was well attended. The stained glass windows went from floor to ceiling before the pointed vaulted arches, allowing brightly colored streams of sun to dance along the packed pews.

I'd arrived at the church somewhat early, so I was able to sit a few rows back from the front. Quickly, the seats around me were taken and I was glad to see that Larry wasn't one of the people right there, since I wasn't relishing a further conversation with him.

The funeral service was lovely, and it was clear that the priest knew Abigail's dad well from the eulogy. Near the end, they sang "Amazing Grace" and "How Great Thou Art". Both of those songs make me cry, so I was glad I had thought to bring tissues. They were needed.

After the funeral, there was a brunch at the Elks Hall down the street, which also had a solid turnout. Instead of branching out to talk to new people, considering how well that had gone with Larry, I sat with some of our college friends and caught up.

When the food was served, I headed over to the buffet line with the girls. My eyes scanned the crowd as I walked to make sure I was avoiding Larry, and then I noticed Ethan standing against the wall by himself. We locked eyes and he looked straight back at me with a flirty grin as he adjusted his dark red tie that matched nicely with his black suit.

In reply to his grin, I scowled at him, and he looked confused.

What the heck? Okay, this was not the place at all to tell Abigail about possibly seeing him on Connect, but it also wasn't the place for him to be flirting with another woman. It was his girlfriend's dad's funeral for heaven's sake.

Forget the food and sticking around for a while. I had to get out of here. Now. Where was Abigail?

My eyes scanned the crowd and I saw her standing with a small group of people. Perfect. I'd say bye, feigning an excuse, and figure out what to say to her about Ethan at a different time.

I walked up to her and waited a moment for the other people to walk away. She turned to me.

"Hey, sorry we haven't had much time to talk."

"Oh my gosh. No apologies at all. I know you've been busy talking to everyone. I'm going to head out soon. Just wanted to say bye first."

Abigail cocked her head to the side.

"So soon? Have you eaten? I figured you'd be catching up with the girls for a while and we'd talk later when the crowds quieted down."

"I..."

Before I could say whatever I was going to say, Ethan came over and put his arm around Abigail's shoulder.

"Hey, Grace," he said. "Glad you could make it. What a turnout, huh?"

I was baffled. He was acting like he hadn't just been flirting with me across the room. He really was a cad standing there in that black suit and red...

Wait.

He'd been wearing a red tie previously, hadn't he? The one he was wearing now was a light gray tie. When and why did he change ties?

Ethan caught me looking at his tie, so he glanced down. When he didn't find anything there, he looked back up.

"Is there something wrong with my tie?"

"No, no." I hastily said. "I thought at first you'd spilled something on it, but it must have just been the light."

Was I losing my mind? People didn't normally carry spare ties around with them to change.

Abigail looked at me quizzically.

"You okay, Grace? You look confused. You were going to say something."

"No, Whatever it was, it can wait. We'll talk another time. In fact, let's make sure we have a girls' night — just us — very soon."

"Of course. We have those New Year's Eve plans set, but before that works, too."

She looked over my shoulder at someone approaching.

"Hey!" Abigail called out to the person I couldn't see. "Grace, I just realized you haven't yet met Ethan's brother."

"You're right. I haven't. Will be good to meet him."

I turned with a welcoming smile on my face, expecting to see a younger or older version of Ethan. My smile faltered when I realized the brother was instead a dead ringer for Ethan. And he was wearing that red tie.

Oh.

I looked back and forth between Ethan and his brother a few times.

I chuckled, which probably looked ridiculous, but I was so relieved.

"Yes," he said as he approached. "I'm Nick. Ethan's twin brother. And you are?"

"Grace, Abigail's dear friend from college, who didn't know Ethan was a twin until just this moment."

Abigail looked back and forth between us.

"Did I forget to mention Ethan was a twin? I'm sure I told you."

No, that she had not. Now the Connect profile made sense. It was actually Nick, not Ethan using a different name. Ooof.

"No, you hadn't, missy. This guy was smiling at me earlier from across the room and I may have growled at him because I thought it was Ethan flirting and was ready to kill him. And I was also swiping and saw Ethan's pic come up but with the name of Nick. So I thought he had been catfished, but didn't know how to tell you."

Didn't mean to reveal that last bit, because she was going to wonder why I hadn't mentioned that. I know I'd be wondering.

Ethan held his hands up. "I promise it wasn't me flirting, and I closed down all my dating accounts a week after I met Abigail."

Nick started laughing. "Aha, that explains it. I almost didn't come over here because of that death glare you gave me. Now that you know that I'm not Ethan, how about grabbing a drink with me?"

"Down boy," said Abigail. "Unless you're interested, Grace. I mean he is indeed single, and that would be a fun double date."

Oh, no, that would be way too confusing. My brain was already muddled enough with the twins.

"Thanks. I'm flattered, Nick, but I'm actually leaving for a coffee date with someone else, so I'll have to pass, but thank you. Really."

"He's a lucky guy. If it doesn't work out, though, reach out to me through Abigail."

I grinned. It was nice to have someone interested in me, and if he was anything like Ethan, he was a great guy. But I didn't want to risk the potential with Wyatt. Plus, I wasn't the type at all to date multiple people. I knew Jordan was and it was possible that Wyatt might be, but I wasn't.

"Okay, Romeo," said Abigail. "That's enough of that."

She reached over and hugged me, and whispered "Thanks for glaring at him, but I'm glad it wasn't Ethan flirting with you. That would have sucked. You're a good friend for glaring, though and thanks for wondering when you saw what you thought was Ethan on an app. When was that?"

I couldn't say it was weeks ago, right? That would make me a crappy friend for not mentioning it, although hell, maybe I was, since I should have gone straight to her.

"You're welcome, and oh, it was right before your Dad passed. I wasn't about to tell you when you called me with that news, and then no time seemed right while you were grieving. I didn't want to add to it, especially since I figured that it was a catfish until I saw Nick looking at me today."

Okay, so that was kind of the truth. I felt guilty, but I'd get over it, and it turned out okay because it was Nick, not Ethan. Maybe if I said that to myself a few times, I'd start believing it. Anyway, I really did have to go.

Pulling back from the embrace, I said my goodbyes and made my way out to coffee with Wyatt.

Twenty-One

Chloe

It's only a coffee… and to see his toy store. There's nothing to be nervous about.

Who was I trying to kid? If it was just coffee, why was I so nervous walking over to Coffee Colony?

I now had two dinosaur events under my belt, and had had such a good time at both. Or my new alter ego, Pinky T-Rexadero, had. Yesterday's event was at the school and today's at the senior center in town.

Both times, I put on the inflatable dino costume and danced my huge pink inflatable heart out along with the others, including Nadia, Ruth, and Charlie. The students yesterday and the seniors today provided a lot of energy and they seemed to love our antics dancing around and faux bumbling into each other. Although some of the bumbling for me at least wasn't fake. It was tough to see in that suit.

No one seemed to mind, though, which made me happy and enjoy the shenanigans even more.

When I bounded into the rec center to see the kids yesterday, their shouts of happiness were infectious. I would have thought they were used to seeing the dino costumes by now since our group had visited them often, but a pink T-Rex was apparently new to them.

That was clear when they shrieked with delight when they saw me and yelled for "Barbie Dino" specifically to roar for them. What a heady feeling that they were happy because of me. It was the sweetest.

The other day, I saw a pink velvet T-Rex purse in the window of Velvet Rose, an accessories store in town where everything was made from, of course, velvet. Part of me wondered if I should buy it and have Barbie Dino carry it for an extra bit of fashionable dinosaur flair. But I'm only going to be here on Earth for a few more weeks. It wouldn't make much sense to do so, unless I was going to bring the pink T-Rex suit back up with me. There wasn't really much use for it there, even though I'd become accustomed to it now.

I felt like I'd tapped into another side of me in this costume. It was funny what being down here on Earth was showing me. I'd found my artistic side and my goofy side as well and I loved it. Hopefully, I'd be able to figure out a way to do both back up there. I couldn't believe we'd be back in just a few weeks.

Nadia had picked me up for both of the dinosaur events, which was sweet of her. After the one today, I stopped by work since it was just a short walk down the street, and put Pinky into the storage closet there. I could pick her up again tomorrow after work for the school event that evening.

From there, I headed towards Coffee Colony to meet up with Tom for coffee before visiting his store.

Pulling open the door to the coffee place, I saw him sitting at a table glancing at his phone. When the door bell jangled, he looked up, smiled, and waved when he saw me. I walked over to the table and he stood up and gave me a hug.

Huh.

Where were the instant sparks and that feeling that this was right?

Okay, give it time. You've only just met the guy.

But when Grace first met Jordan, there were instant sparks of electricity. Why wasn't I feeling that here?

"I'm so glad you could make it," he said. "How about we get that coffee?"

"Absolutely. Sounds great."

Just blowing him away with the wit there, self.

At the counter, Tom ordered a large hot espresso for himself. After smelling the hazelnut coffees Laurel and Amber had the past week, I was curious, so I ordered a medium hot hazelnut with extra cream and no sugar.

"How's your weekend been?" he asked as we waited for the coffees.

I thought about mentioning the driving, but realized it might be weird to him that I didn't drive, so I left that out.

"It's been good. We had two dinosaur shows for the Rec Department, so that's been fun. And I caught the tree lighting the other night."

"I hope the tree lighting was good. I was in the shop the whole time, so I didn't see it, but I heard people talk about it. As for the dinosaur shows… I've never seen one, but it sounds pretty funny. You weren't one of the dinos, were you?"

Would it be a problem for him if I was? It felt like he was judging the group, or me if I was part of the group. But maybe I was just overthinking. Wouldn't be the first time.

"Actually, I am one of the dinos and it's enjoyable. It was silly and goofy and just fun."

Tom looked a bit shocked, but quickly put on an easy smile.

"Huh. Looking at you, I wouldn't have expected that, I guess. But I'm glad you enjoyed yourself."

Okay, leave that statement alone, because I'm not sure I wanted to know what he would have expected by looking at me. I decided to turn the conversation over to him instead to a much safer topic.

"How about you? How's your weekend been?"

"Busy, busy as can be expected since it's Christmas shopping season and I run a toy store."

I felt a bit like an idiot. Right. If it wasn't a busy weekend for him, that would be a truly bad sign for the state of his business.

Tom's name was called and he went over to grab the coffees.

"Shall we go see my store? It's probably packed, like usual, but you'll get an idea about it."

"Sure, sounds good! I can't wait to see it."

As we left the coffee shop with our coffees in hand, Tom gallantly held the door open for me, and put his hand on the top of my back to guide me through the crowd that was coming in.

That feeling of his hand on my back should have made me happy. Instead, I felt off — like I wanted to be away from him instead of closer to him. This wasn't the idea.

I shifted away from his touch by moving my body to take a sip of the coffee. The scent of the hazelnut drew me in and I took a tentative sip, hoping I wasn't about to burn my tongue in the process.

Okay, so the smell and the taste matched up. That was a relief at least. I liked the hazelnut flavor and now I had a new coffee to drink in the morning sometimes while I was here. Sweet!

We crossed the street to go to his toy store and a flash of red hair caught my eye off to the side. Grace was walking towards the coffee shop. Oh, it would have been nice to see her. I wonder if she's grabbing a coffee or meeting someone like I was. Maybe Jordan? Okay, that was probably wishful thinking, but an angel could hope.

Thomas' Toys was indeed packed full with customers. Everywhere I looked, there was a swarm of parents and even some kids, who probably wanted to check out the toys for last-minute changes to their wishlists.

Tom stopped and muttered something under his breath.

"Sorry. I didn't catch that."

"It's busier than I thought it would be. Looks like it's picked up since I stepped out to meet you. Would you mind just walking around for a few minutes and taking a look at the layout while I help out at the counters?"

I was surprisingly fine with being left alone.

Yes, please, leave me alone so I can figure out why I'm not all that into you as I thought I would be. I wasn't about to put it that way, though.

"Yes, of course. Go take care of what you need to. I'll see you in a few."

I wandered the shop, taking care to not bump into any of the throngs of shoppers in the aisles.

As I walked through, I noticed that the aisles were placed a bit tightly together at the front of the store near the counter, but there was more space and a large open section in the back of the store near the big stuffed teddy bears, lions, and other creatures. I made a mental note to suggest flipping that, so there'd be more room for people up near the counter and people wouldn't feel as packed like sardines while checking out. Plus, using up some of that space in the back might give the aisles more space.

Other than that, I didn't have many suggestions to make. I walked over to their display window to see what was in it. Even further away in the store, the Christmas tree in the center of the display was an eye catcher with large stuffed animals, dolls, skateboards, and marble games around it. Running around the bottom of the tree was a train set. I stood there and watched it go by again and again.

"Chloe, hey." I turned when I heard my name to see Tom walking up to me.

"Sorry about that. Duty calls. Hope you didn't get too bored."

"All good. I had fun walking around the store and was just looking at your display. I love it, but it feels like it's missing something. Have you thought about adding a big board or sign that has 'Check Off Your List' at the top, with a bunch of gift ideas listed underneath it and checkmarks next to each one? It might be a good way to get even more people into the store when they are vividly reminded of their own list of presents they have to buy and provide ideas to the ones who haven't yet put together a list."

Tom pondered the idea for a moment, trying to see it in the display.

"I like it. Maybe you could sketch up the idea and we can talk about it over dinner some night this week since I don't think we're going to get much of a chance to chat today?"

His invitation should have made my heart melt, but I wasn't feeling it. I didn't understand that because he was such a perfect human. Maybe it was because I was going back up in just a couple of weeks, or maybe it was something else.

I felt goosebumps run up and down my arms, but they weren't about me and Tom. Instead, I had a flash of insight that I hadn't had before about him, and I'm glad it finally hit instead of waiting until after I'd accepted dinner.

He wasn't the one for me.

Instead, that spark I had felt in the office was between him and Laurel. I was just there standing in the way of what could be.

"Of course I'll sketch up the idea. As for dinner, thank you, but I'm busy pretty much every night this week with dino shows and other events for the department."

I was glad to see that sadness didn't cross over his face. If anything, he looked relieved and I was fully relieved to see that.

Based on what had come to me about his true interest, I had assumed he would be okay with me rejecting him, and I was happy to be right. Now it was time to test that theory out further and bring the two together.

"Even though I'm busy, I know Laurel isn't doing any of the dino shows this week, so she might just be free for dinner if you ask her."

Tom grinned. I'd gotten it right.

"That's good to know. Maybe I will."

I had to know, so I pressed further.

"Can I ask you something? From your reaction, I get the feeling you've wanted to ask Laurel out for a while now. Why did you ask me for coffee instead?"

"I've always thought she was pretty and seemed interesting — and very business-driven like I am. But I never got the sense she was interested in me, so I didn't want to risk her turning me down and then it being weird since we work together on things like the sponsorship. As for asking you for coffee, you're cute and I enjoyed working with you on the ad, so I thought I'd see if there was anything there with the guise of talking about the store. And I think I can safely and hopefully say neither of us thinks there is."

Okay, humans were weird. Laurel definitely liked him and he liked her, but neither thought the other was interested so they never pursued it. Talk about needing an angelic nudge.

"You are right. You and I work great together professionally, and I think we'd make good friends, but that's pretty much it. I'm glad you feel the same way. As for Laurel, trust me. Ask her to dinner. In fact, hold on..."

Tom looked at me quizzically as I pulled out my phone, found Laurel's number in my contacts, and texted her.

Leaving the toy store now. Tom's great but there's no sparks there. We're friends. That's it. He's going to text you and ask you to dinner. Say yes.

After I hit "send", I waited a moment and saw that it had been read. She replied quickly.

What? Are you sure? Well, that's exciting. Thank you!

I turned and showed my text to Tom, making sure to cover her reply as I didn't want to invade her privacy. His face lit up.

I was over the moon happy for him. Didn't expect that. I should be bummed that he's interested in Laurel instead of me, but I'm not.

"Consider this a nudge. Text her. Now. She's going to say yes. And I'll head back home and get started on that sketch. Oh, and also, a store suggestion for after the holidays — broaden the aisles up front a bit because you'll give the customers more room and they won't feel as packed in. Enjoy dinner with Laurel. Seriously. Now go text or call her."

"Thank you, Chloe, for all of that. I'm not sure how I got so lucky to get a chance with Laurel, but thank you."

"You're welcome. Have fun."

I walked out and headed down the street to the large Christmas tree in the center of town square where I could grab a bus back to the apartment. Looking up at it, I remembered the tree lighting with Mitch.

That was a special night. Heck, any time with Mitch was fun and special in its own right because he was such a great guy. I decided to give him a call and he instantly picked up, but was clearly surprised.

"I'm taking a wild guess you're butt dialing me here…"

"Hahaha. No, no. I meant to call you, silly. I was just thinking about you."

"You were? On your date with Tom. That doesn't sound like it went too well."

I chuckled. Well, it did for Tom and Laurel…

"It wound up being more of a friendly hang than a date. I gave him some ideas for his window display and layout at his store, and then a thought came to me, and I told him he should reach out to Laurel and ask her to dinner. Turns out he's been interested in her for a while and he just needed that nudge to do so. I can pretty much guarantee they're going to have dinner some night this week and that it's going to go well."

"You don't sound disappointed about that."

Understatement of the century.

"I'm not. I'm relieved. Sure he's hot, but that's not everything. He and I weren't meant to be and that's okay. I'd much prefer that he and Laurel get together, honestly. They seem better suited for each other."

"So what are you doing now?"

I looked up again at the Christmas tree, memories of the other night swirling in my head.

"I'm just a girl standing in front of a Christmas tree, remembering that I saw it light up the other night with you. And waiting for the bus to show up so I can head back to the apartment."

"No way. I'll come get you. You don't need to wait for the bus and I'll probably get there before the bus will."

"You're sweet. Thank you, Mitch. I'll see you soon."

I hung up and walked around the Christmas tree and the square since I didn't have to wait by the bus stop. As I walked and enjoyed seeing the lights start to glisten, my phone buzzed. Laurel.

We're getting dinner tomorrow night. You sure you're okay with this?

Yes! My heart felt light reading that, so I was absolutely okay with the news.

Absolutely. I'm more than okay with it. I'm happy for you. See you tomorrow at work.

I put my phone back in my purse and saw Mitch pull up into one of the spots in front of the tree. Happily, I ran over to him to head back home.

Twenty-Two

Chloe

As Mitch and I drove home from a late lunch after he picked me up in town, we crossed over the Crystal River bridge. With the afternoon fading, clouds of pink, dark blue, light blue, white, and gray blazed across the sky. It was the perfect view against the rushing river.

"I'm so happy," I said, curled up in the passenger seat as I looked out the window.

"Why's that? I wouldn't have thought you'd be so cheery after a date that didn't end well."

I thought about that. Tom had been hot, but he wasn't the one meant for me. From what I understood, he was meant to be with Laurel, and I'd given them the nudge they needed to make that happen.

"That was never really a date, so I don't think it counts. Sure, both Tom and I maybe thought it was at the start, but there wasn't that jolt. And when I got the sense that he belonged with Laurel, that made more sense, so I started thinking of him as just a friend. The two of them work together, so I'm happy that they're going out."

"You do know there doesn't always have to be that jolt, right?" Mitch said that kindly. I knew he wasn't trying to pick a fight. Instead, he was telling me how he felt. We just saw it differently, which was fine.

"There doesn't? That's what I've been searching for my whole life, mainly because I saw it when Grace met Jordan. I know it might sound silly but I believe in it whole-heartedly."

"I know you do." Mitch looked like he was about to say more, but a bright sign caught my eye as it flickered on and off.

"Mitch! Look! That sign! It's advertising karaoke Saturday night at that Chinese restaurant, and the sign is going off and on. I think we were meant to see that."

"I don't know, Chlo… Couldn't it just be that they're having electric issues with the sign?"

Maybe. But I preferred my view of it, mainly because it was how I saw it, and I strongly believed in nudges. Why didn't Mitch?

"I guess it could, but I really think this was for us. It will be a way to help the Rec Center. I'm going to call them and see if they'll offer karaoke for Friday night with a cover charge that will go towards the Rec Center — and maybe they'll allow a bit of the food/drink proceeds to go towards it, too. And I'm going to invite Grace and tell her to invite others. That way, Jordan will come if he's supposed to and they'll get their second chance."

Mitch kept his eyes firmly on the road, but I saw doubt on his face.

"What about Wyatt?"

"Wyatt, Schmyatt. Sure she can invite him as well if she wants, but I have no doubt that Jordan's going to be there."

I called the restaurant and asked to speak with the manager or someone in charge of events. They put me on hold for a moment, but shortly a voice spoke.

"Hi, this is Penny. I'm the manager here. How can I help you?"

"Hi Penny. I'm Chloe and I work at the Silverton Rec Department. I know this is super late notice, and might not be possible with holiday functions, but I was wondering if you were able to host a karaoke night the Friday before Christmas? We would bring in a crowd, and have a cover charge of ten bucks. Half of it would go to your restaurant and the other half would go to the Rec Department. We're trying to help the Department stay fully funded so my coworker Laurel doesn't lose her job, and so we can buy back the Rec Center before it's destroyed."

"Oh, heck yes. I heard about the Rec Center and I was horrified. It's where I spent most days after school as a kid to get help with homework, so I definitely don't want it to go away. Plus, all the events. I learned how to play double-dutch there so I'm glad to help. As it turns out, we literally just had a cancellation for a corporate holiday party that night, so that room is open. If you want to hold your karaoke event here, you've got it. And because I feel so strongly about the Rec Department, I'll even put 25% of the food and drink purchases towards the Department. Nope, scratch that. I'm feeling generous. 50%."

"Oh my goodness. You're an angel, Penny, and trust me, I know one when I encounter one. Thank you! Thank you! Thank you!"

"You're welcome, Chloe. I have your number here, so I'll text you to confirm and will include my email address. Send me your email when you get it, and

I'll send you a contract detailing everything we talked about. Oh, and the karaoke guy is my husband, Joe, so he's already signed up. I'll just tell him he is."

"You are the best! Thank you! So, 7 pm works for that night?"

"That's perfect, yes. We'll talk more, but consider it done."

I hung up the phone and grinned at Mitch.

"I'm going to assume that you set up karaoke for that Friday night?", he asked.

"I sure did. It's perfect, and I'm so excited!"

I got out my phone and texted Grace, telling her about karaoke at the East Palace and that we were doing a group event there that Friday night to help the Rec Department. Laurel would probably go with Tom, and maybe Amber would as well with her husband, but I wanted it to be a big event, so hopefully she could invite a bunch of people.

It took a few minutes for her reply to come back, but Grace was in.

Sure, sounds fun! Will be good to see everyone! I'll post about it and see who can go. I'm still at the coffee shop, so I'll text later.

So, that was her I saw going into the coffee shop. Hmm, glad she was having fun, but I was still hopeful it was Jordan she was seeing. Guess I'd find out soon enough at karaoke or before.

"She's in! Oh, I have to figure out a song or song to sing. You'll do a duet with me, right?"

Mitch's face crinkled up. "Hard pass there. You know I adore you, but no, I'm not singing."

I fake pouted.

"Pretty please. I don't want to be up there all by myself singing."

He grinned.

"That's not going to work on me, missy. You have a great voice, so you'll be more than fine."

I beamed at the compliment.

"Well, thank you, kind sir. I'm going to keep trying, though. Maybe you'll change your mind. I'll use my wiles on you."

"Good luck with that. I'm not singing. Sorry, Chloe, but it's not going to happen."

"You know me."

"That I do, so I fully expect you're going to keep mentioning it. Not changing my mind, though."

I grinned. He did know me.

"Guess we'll see…"

I sat back as we headed home and let songs run through my head as ideas.

Twenty-Three

Grace

The song "Into the Mystic" flitted into my head as I walked down the street after parking.

As I arrived at Coffee Colony, I saw Wyatt sitting at a table by the window. Was I late? I glanced at my phone and saw that nope, it was still five minutes before we were going to meet up. Well, he's as early as I am. I always thought that people who arrived earlier showed they were interested in being somewhere instead of being half-hearted about it by showing up late.

He was paying attention to his phone (Sally?), so he didn't see me walk past, but to his credit, he did look up at the door when I opened it and the overhead bell chimed.

Wow. That smile of his went straight to my heart. He was clearly happy to see me and I could only hope my smile in return was showing the same.

I weaved through the tables to join him and he stood up and gave me a hug.

Strong arms that feel really good around me. I could stay here forever, but okay, that would be weird. The hug did go on for a moment longer than regular hugs, though.

After the hug, we sat down at the little Formica coffee table. I unfurled my black fuzzy scarf from my neck and took off my coat, setting both on the back of my chair.

Glancing at Wyatt, I saw that he was wearing a black merino turtleneck sweater with black pants and a tweed jacket. Great look.

"It's really good to see you, Grace," Wyatt said. "I hope your friend's dad's wake and funeral went okay."

"Good memory. Yes, they did. And thank you for asking. I appreciate it. The wake was very sweet and had one heck of a wonky moment, and the funeral was as most funerals are — something to endure to be there for a friend. I'm sure you know how it is. How about you? I hope you had a good lunch with your dad and step-mom."

"Sure did. Always good to see them, and brunch included the fluffiest pancakes I've ever had and crisp bacon, so you can't go wrong with either of those."

"Ohhh, bacon. Now I want some and I'm pretty sure this place doesn't sell bacon coffee nor donuts with bacon on them. The horror. I agree with you, by the way, that bacon should be crisp. Soggy bacon just isn't the same."

Wyatt chuckled. "Is bacon coffee even a thing?"

He reached to pick up his phone, feigning to look. "Nah. You know what? I don't want to know if it is."

"I'm pretty sure it isn't. At least I hope it's not. Let's vow to never ever google it and just go with that assumption."

"That works for me. However, speaking of coffee… I waited to order until you arrived. What would you like? I'll go get it from the counter and be back in a flash."

What a gentleman. I wasn't used to this. Part of me wanted to tell him I'd go and get it, but I stopped myself. He was being courteous so I should let him be so.

"How about a coffee with extra cream and no sugar… and no bacon?"

I said the last bit with a mischievous wink.

"You've got it. Coffee. Extra cream. No sugar. Extra extra bacon. Perfect."

He was a goof. I liked that a lot.

While he was at the counter, I saw a notification come up on my phone from Chloe. I glanced at it only because Wyatt wasn't sitting there.

Huh? Karaoke. Well, that sounded like fun and anything for the Rec Center. Of course I'm in.

As I finished writing back to Chloe, Wyatt came back with two coffees, setting one in front of me.

"Coffee with extra bacon, just as requested."

I chuckled. "Why, thank you, kind sir. Now I won't have to put salt in my coffee today, as it will already have flavor."

A look of horror passed Wyatt's face before he realized I was joking.

"I know we don't know each other all that well yet, but you don't really do that, do you?"

I reached over for the salt shaker, looked at it and held it up to the coffee for a moment as if I was going to pour it in, and then put it back down.

"A girl's gotta have some secrets, doesn't she? Stick around long enough and I guess you'll find out…"

"This is true, and I look forward to sticking around long enough to find that out, although I'm hoping you're on the no salt in coffee side. I'm all for a good salt lick, but that seems a bit too far even for me."

Mmm, salt. Now all I could think of was some extra salty potato chips. I'd have to get some on the way home, since I don't think I have any in my apartment.

"So, tell me, Wyatt. When you get a craving for a snack, are you a salt person or a sweet person?"

"Oh, we're breaking out the tough questions, are we? Salty food is always going to win me over. How about you?"

"It depends on the moment for me. I've had moments of wanting nothing more than some spice drops when I'm having a sugar craving, and then there are other times when I want to dive head first into a hot salted pretzel."

"My mouth is watering and now I want to find a pretzel vendor. You're right. They are delicious. I think I saw one the other night when I was driving through town. Maybe some night after work, we could take a walk and grab a pretzel while looking at the Christmas lights."

Christmas lights made me think of the Christmas tree display. Strolling with Wyatt and looking at all the different themes of the trees sounded like a dream.

I needed to ask him if he was still in for the Festival of Trees.

"Speaking of Christmas lights… let me back up, because I didn't say yes to what you mentioned. Yes. I would love to look at Christmas lights with you in town and grab a pretzel."

"I'm glad. It's a date, then, if I'm not being too forward to call it such?"

For a moment, I saw his usual confident veneer slip and he looked somewhat anxious. It was endearing, and I rushed to assure him.

"It is absolutely a date. Yes. And to add to that, maybe before we walk through town, or as we're walking through town, we can stop at the Rec Center for the Silverton Festival of Trees and look at all the different trees there. Remember I told you about that? Every one of the 200 plus trees is decorated in a different theme and they're sure to be impressive and whimsical. I hope that sounds like fun to you, because it's something I've always wanted to take a date to, but we've never done one here til now."

Oh, gosh. Now I was the one who was anxious. Would he think it was silly or childish to want to see the trees? Sure, we'd talked about it before, but I don't think he knew what it involved.

"I'd love to. And I do remember us talking about it after our dinner. Yes, that sounds like fun. I'm looking forward to seeing the trees with you, Grace. I never take the time to decorate a Christmas tree, so it will be fun to see them decorated, and also spend more time with you."

"Perfect. I'm glad."

What he said about not decorating Christmas trees struck a chord with me. I still had to decorate my own Christmas tree in my apartment and the one I was donating to the Festival. Inspiration struck.

"Wyatt, do you have any plans after coffee?"

"I don't. Why do you ask?"

"Mentioning the Festival of Trees made me realize that I haven't yet decorated the tree that I'm donating to them to try and help out the Rec Center, nor my own tree. Would you like to come back with me and decorate two trees?"

As the words came out of my mouth, I realized how forward that sounded that I was inviting him back to my apartment after the second date. Ugh.

I quickly added, "As I said that, I heard my own words. That sounded like an invitation that I'm not ready for yet. I really did mean just to decorate the trees. I'm going to invite my neighbors, Chloe and Mitch — the ones you met at the restaurant — to come decorate as well."

Wyatt looked a bit relieved, which was good to see that he wasn't expecting something.

"Sure. That sounds fun. It's been years since I decorated a tree, so why not?"

"Great. Let me text Chloe real quick to make sure they'll be home by then. They were out and ooh, that reminds me of something else to tell you about. One sec."

I texted Chloe about tree decorating and the "!!! YES !!!" that she quickly wrote back indicated to me that she was looking forward to it. Very cute! Writing back, I told her we'd be there in about an hour and that I was happy.

Turning back to Wyatt, I said, "Okay, Chloe and Mitch are in. We'll meet them at the apartment in about an hour, if that works."

"Absolutely. Do you need to stop anywhere on the way back for decorations, or are you set?"

"Nope, all good. I have everything I need to decorate both, so that part is thankfully set. As for that other thing I mentioned, how do you feel about karaoke?"

"Can't say I've ever been, actually. Why do you ask? Do you have a karaoke machine at your apartment that you're going to dig out?"

I chuckled at that thought. "No, no. But that would be fun! Chloe texted me while you were grabbing our coffee to say she thought of another potential way to help the Rec Center. She's having a karaoke event at the East Palace on the Friday before Christmas. Have you been there?"

"I'm not sure. I may have been some night after work with the guys, but it's not ringing a bell. Where is it?"

I pictured the location right near the river with the gazebo overlooking the waterfall and couldn't help smiling.

"It's right by the Silverton River. In the parking lot by the East Palace, there's a section of the river with a waterfall and a gazebo that sits and looks out over the waterfall. It's one of my favorite spots, actually. Whenever I'm feeling thoughtful or like I need a moment of peace, that's where I go, and I sit in the gazebo and watch the water rushing along. Makes me feel like I'm not alone in the world and like everything's going to be okay, even if just for a moment. And, my gosh, I just told you way too much, didn't I? I need to stop talking."

I put my hand to my forehead in horror that I'd just told Wyatt on our second date that I wasn't happy-go-lucky all the time. Ugh. He's going to think I'm a trainwreck.

Feeling his hand resting on top of the hand I still had on the table, I tentatively glanced up at him. His eyes were kind, which is what I needed to see at that moment. Maybe he actually understood and wasn't going to judge me for having feelings or discussing them.

"Never apologize for talking. I enjoy hearing you talk, and I'm glad you felt comfortable enough to share that with me. Your gazebo at the waterfall sounds wonderful. I've never noticed that spot, so I look forward to seeing it at some point. Hopefully with you. And I hope you know you're not alone in the world, but I understand that feeling all too well. We all have those moments."

My heart twinged a bit hearing that, and I turned my palm over to lace my fingers through his.

"Thank you for saying that. I appreciate it. Sharing my feelings and thoughts is a bit new to me, thanks to times when people talked at me instead of talking to me, and they certainly didn't want to hear what I had to say."

Like, oh, Jordan, and any guy I'd dated before him. It's a miracle I knew how to have conversations with people at all.

"I'm not whoever that was, Grace. I know you have no reason to believe me about that yet, but over time, I hope you'll see that. I want to hear what you have to say, and I want to listen and learn while doing so."

I exhaled. He was so nice and just thoughtful. And not Jordan. I needed to remember that.

"I appreciate that. I appreciate you. Thank you, and I want to listen to you, too, by the way. I don't think that should ever be one-sided. Oh, and for the record, since you did listen, I guess I'll reveal something else."

I took a dramatic pause just for effect.

"Okay, here it is. Are you ready? I've never put salt in coffee in my life."

Wyatt rubbed his forehead in mock relief and I snort laughed, and then covered my mouth. That was way too loud and not at all ladylike or "perfect." I expected Wyatt to cringe or at least politely ignore it.

"That I made you snort laugh just made my day," he said, stunning me. "It's really attractive because I know you genuinely found what I did funny with that reaction."

Wow. Can I actually be myself around him? This would take some getting used to.

"How do you know exactly what to say?"

"I'm glad I do. Shall we get going so we can get to tree decorating?"

"Absolutely! I'm excited, and I'm glad you're going to decorate the trees with me."

Twenty-Four

Chloe

"Rockin' around the Christmas tree…"

I sang along to the radio in the car as Mitch drove. This song had come on right after Grace texted about Christmas tree decorating, and it felt appropriate.

"This is going to be so much fun! We should bring something, right? Can we stop off at Arrow on the way back to the apartment?"

Laurel and Amber had mentioned their obsession with the department store, Arrow, since it had everything, but I hadn't yet been. Luckily, there was one on the route to our apartment, so hopefully Mitch would be okay with running in with me. We'd been to the local supermarket a few times for groceries, since it's not like our fridge could get magically replenished after the first time. But we hadn't yet visited an actual store. I was curious to see how it would go.

"Of course we can. But we can't stay too long."

"Hmm, it sounds like you think I'm going to just stroll up and down every aisle and look at every single thing. Which, okay, I totally want to, but I won't because we need to get back to decorate the tree with Grace and Wyatt."

I thought about that for a second. Could I give a little nudge for Wyatt to not be able to make it and Jordan show up instead?

"Chloe, no…" It was like Mitch read my mind. I guess he did know me really well.

"I wasn't really going to nudge Jordan to show up. Okay, so I thought about it, but I didn't do it. I'm not going to interfere."

Suddenly I saw a bright blue arrow in the sky.

"Ooh! There it is! Mitch, there's Arrow!"

Mitch chuckled. "Yes, I see it too, Chloe."

He pulled into the vast parking lot. It was pretty busy as it should be during December with Christmas shopping. We did manage to find a spot that opened up right on the side along the wall.

"Look at that little divine intervention of finding a spot!" Mitch beamed after he parked and we got out of the car. "I'm glad the spot was there because we'll be able to find the car easily when we come out by just heading towards the wall."

"Good plan! You're really smart, Mitch."

I looked at the electric lights beaming from the store. It was like a beacon drawing me in. I turned and grinned at Mitch.

"Are you ready for this, mister?"

He laughed. "Not in the slightest, I'm sure! But let's go."

The store was everything I thought it would be and more. Arrow was brimming with chaos and what felt a bit like magic with people all in good spirits, despite the crowded aisles and lines.

And I didn't have a clue on where to start to look for something to bring to Grace's apartment. The clothes were directly in front of me, and I almost turned into the section to look at everything, but stopped myself. That wasn't the plan for today and it's not like I'd need Earth clothes for much longer.

Mitch kept pace with me easily as we wound our way through the store.

"Hey, Chloe, there's a huge Christmas tree over this way. Maybe there'll be something there."

I glanced where he was looking and saw the tip of a lush green faux tree peeking out from above the shelves.

"Oooh, perfect. Yes! Let's go!"

I grabbed Mitch's hand without even thinking to make our way to the Christmas section of the store. There were so many people in the aisles that we could easily have lost each other... well, besides that we were probably the tallest people in the store. I did know that he'd keep me on track instead of wanting to stop and look at everything.

The Christmas section was filled with people, so we made our way gingerly through the crowd to look at the ornaments and decorations. Grace clearly didn't need another Christmas tree, so we needed to find something else.

Although...

I stopped in front of the trees, gazing at them. "What do you think, Mitch? Should we get a tree for our apartment? I hadn't even thought of that."

"What would happen to it when we leave?" he asked me, and okay, he had a point. It's not like we were going to be staying here and would have a place to store it, and it would have no place up there.

"I do have an idea, though…" added Mitch. "What if we bought one of the trees and some decorations and decorated our own tree for the Festival of Trees?"

I squealed and threw my arms around his neck.

"Yes! You're the bestest! I love that idea. We need a theme. Oh, and we need a carriage first because there's no way we're carrying all of this through the store."

I grabbed Mitch's hand, sped back to the front of the store for a carriage, and then hustled back to the Christmas section. We quickly found a pre-lit tree and then turned into the ornaments section. So many options. Seashore. Classy. Sports. Animals.

Oooh.

A shiny pink ornament caught my eye, so I picked it up and showed it to Mitch. He groaned.

"Chloe.. I know you've been enjoying being a pink T-Rex, but I'm not all that sure about a dinosaur tree. That might be a bit quirky even for us. Well, me. It has you all over it."

I wasn't sure if I should take that as an insult or not. Yes, I was quirky, but that wasn't what I meant with the T-Rex ornament.

"No, silly. This is something I'm thinking of getting for Grace since the first time I met her, I was wearing that inflatable suit. We'll get her something else, too, but I really like this."

Mitch smiled. Good, he liked the idea.

"That's very thoughtful of you. I'm sure she'll appreciate it. And while you were looking at that, I think I've found our theme."

"Oh. What is it?"

Mitch swept his hand out to the side, revealing what was there on the hooks. My eyes lit up.

"Angel everything! Oh my gosh, Mitch! This is perfect! Yes! An angel tree. Let's do it!"

Mitch and I gathered up an angelic tree topper and a whole bunch of angel decorations for our tree. We also found an ample supply of white garland to wrap around the tree and a fluffy white tree skirt that would sit underneath as a cloud of sorts.

"This is going to look — dare I say — divine."

I grinned at Mitch's pun. "Very punny, sir. But it will. I can't wait to put it together. Okay, now we need to find something else for Grace."

My eyes swept through the Christmas decor. Nothing else seemed right. Walking up and down the aisles, we found ourselves in the Christmas food section.

"Hmm, wait. What about this?"

I held up a Ghirardelli chocolate set for approval.

"Based on how you gravitated to it, I'm thinking that's a good call and will also work really well for Grace. Do you want to also buy one for us?"

I thought about it for a moment and picked up another one, placing it in the cart.

"I mean… I wasn't going to, and wasn't even thinking about doing so. But since you mentioned it and all, you clearly wanted some chocolate and I just want you to be happy."

Mitch chuckled. He picked up a gift bag and tissue paper in the same section so we'd have something to put the little ornament and chocolate set in.

"So thoughtful you are. Okay, are we good here?"

I looked longingly around the store, thinking of all the things I couldn't buy.

"I guess so. We do have to get back to the apartment after all as we told Grace we'd be there soon."

Mitch patted me on the shoulder.

"I know you want to look around some more, but yeah, we should get going before you buy the whole store. How about we come back some night this week when we have more time?"

"Yes! It's a date!" Realizing what I'd just said, I quickly backtracked. "You know, it's on the calendar and there are dates on the calendar, so it's a date on the calendar when we'll come back. Not like we're going on a date since we're friends. Friends don't do that."

Mitch shook his head, trying and failing to hide his laughter at my awkwardness. Thankfully, he was used to my antics by now.

"Okay, goofball… C'mon. Let's go pay and get out of here. We have a date at the register."

He said the last bit with a wink. I groaned.

"You're not going to let me live that one down, are ya?"

"Not a chance."

Twenty-Five

Grace

Is there a chance that Chloe and Mitch are here already?

I felt nervous as we got out of our cars at my apartment building, even though I'd made it clear Chloe and Mitch would be there, too.

Wyatt walked over to me as I stood at the doorway stairs.

"So, I realized on the drive over here that you didn't tell me what your theme is for the tree. It's bacon, isn't it? Tell me it's bacon, and it's a bacon-scented tree."

"Well, shoot!" I replied. "There goes the surprise. I was actually going to fry up pieces of bacon, too, for the tree, although maybe I shouldn't go that far considering it'll be sitting on the tree for a week and would be a bit rotted by the end of it."

"Yeah, no. No one will want the fly-laden tree. That would be sad. Yours would be the sole tree without any raffle tickets in it."

"Wait. You wouldn't put in a pity ticket just because it was my tree? How dare you. That's it. We're done."

I jokingly huffed and turned to walk away, and then turned back and grinned and grabbed Wyatt's hand for a moment.

His hand felt right in mine and he gave my hand a squeeze before speaking.

"Oh, I would, but I wouldn't be able to take it home, as my apartment has a no pets policy and I'm pretty sure flies count. I'd just have to donate it to a local trash bin."

"Funny man."

We walked up the steps to the entryway and I unlocked the outside door. I didn't see Chloe or Mitch as we got to the top of the first floor stairs, and hoped they weren't still out. The last thing I wanted was to give Wyatt the wrong impression about why he was in my apartment. Sure, I was attracted to him, but we were still getting to know each other.

I took my keys out of my purse to unlock the door and heard the door across the hall fly open.

"Yay!" said Chloe! "You're here! Not that I've been waiting at the door watching the hallway through the peephole. Nope. Not me. Hi!"

"Hi, Chloe," I said, and then saw Mitch come out of the apartment behind her. "And, hi, Mitch. You guys remember Wyatt. Looking forward to tree decorating?"

I opened the door, thanking past me for putting away the clothes I'd tried on, so I didn't have to dash around putting anything away now.

"Okay, quick apartment tour then. This is the kitchen and that's the living room, which is where we'll be decorating the trees." I continued walking through the apartment as I spoke.

"This is where I paint, and also where the trees currently are and all the decorations; over here is the closet. Wyatt, you can either hang your jacket in here or drape it over one of the kitchen chairs. Up to you. My bedroom is here and that's the bathroom."

"Your apartment is great," Wyatt said. "It suits you."

I beamed. "Thank you."

"Yes, we agree," said Chloe. "This is basically a mirror image of our apartment, and I love what you've done with it. It feels like a home."

"Thank you, Chloe. That's the intent, so I'm glad it came across. I think it's important that you enjoy where you live and make it a place of respite to enjoy."

Wyatt turned to Mitch. "How about we work together to move the trees out into the living room?" He then turned to me and continued.

"Umm, I don't mean that you couldn't move them on your own or that you and Chloe couldn't move them. I just saw the trees there and offered to move them."

"Total caveman lawyer move there, sir." I laughed. "Yes, you're correct considering that I got them into my apartment myself, but I'm more than fine with having you guys move them from the spare room into the living room. You okay with that, Chloe?"

"Absolutely I am! We'll help by moving some of the decoration boxes."

"Perfect. Then, yes, we're all good here."

As the men went into the spare room, I turned to Chloe, who was standing at my kitchen table.

"Thanks for coming over, Chloe. I figured it would be easier to have this as a group."

"Hey, you're welcome. I'm glad to. We're glad to. It'll be fun to decorate trees. Mitch and I even picked up our own tree to decorate and donate to the Festival of Trees. You inspired us. Oh, we got you two things, by the way."

She handed me a gift bag she was holding, and I opened it to find a box of chocolates and a little box inside. Those chocolates would be fun to dig into!

I opened the box and laughed, pulling out the pink dinosaur ornament.

"Aww, who's a cute little dinosaur? Thank you, Chloe! That's so sweet. It's going to look adorable on my tree here and I'll always think of our first meeting when I see it."

Chloe beamed.

"You're welcome. I'm glad you like it. Our meeting certainly was memorable, huh?"

"Definitely! One for the record books."

I turned to set down the chocolates and dinosaur on the table as Wyatt and Mitch brought one of the tree boxes into the living room.

"So, where should we put this one?" Wyatt asked. "Since this one has 'Grace tree' on it in faded print, I'm assuming it's the one you've had for a while."

"You would be correct. The box also has the tree stand in it, so how about you put the box down right in front of the window next to the TV, and we'll work on decorating that one after the one for the Festival of Trees, which can go here in the kitchen. Chloe, can you help me move the table and chairs over against the wall, so we'll have some room here to work?"

I lifted up one end of the table after we pulled the chairs back, and Chloe lifted the other end. We brought the table over to the wall and then placed the chairs there, too, leaving space for the second tree.

"Thanks, Chloe! Okay, let's go get the many, many boxes of decorations."

"Sounds good! I can't wait to see everything."

There was a lot to see. I was grateful to past me for organizing it all into different boxes clearly labeled with either "mine" or "festival". That would make it easier to decorate, and it would be a lot easier to decorate the tree with Wyatt, Chloe, and Mitch, instead of doing so on my own. This was going to be fun.

Twenty-Six

Chloe

This is so fun!

There was a lot that went into decorating a Christmas tree? Who knew! We didn't have Christmas trees up there, but now I was wishing we did.

We started with decorating the tree she was going to donate since they had to be dropped off tomorrow.

"I love your idea for this tree, Grace," I said as I held up one of the postcard prints in a little wooden frame that would attach to the tree with an ornament hook.

The print was of a woman with long dark hair sitting with a serene look on her face and her hands crossed over each other. It looked familiar, so I didn't think it was one of Grace's paintings, but I didn't want to ask.

"Oh, the Mona Lisa by Leonardo da Vinci," said Grace. "One of my favorites. It's not at all my own style of painting since I tend to do landscapes and the like, but I wanted to put more than just my own paintings on the tree in order to draw attention to it."

"Your paintings are so good that they would catch everyone's eyes," said Mitch, who was holding one of the ornaments. "Like this one of a house on a beach. I love it."

Wyatt came over and looked at the ornament he was holding. "Oh, that's the painting you were standing in front of when we first met in person, Grace. It's definitely my favorite."

Grace blushed. "Thank you. I appreciate that. It holds an even more special memory for me because of that."

Shoot. They looked so smitten.

Maybe one of these paintings was one that reminded her of Jordan. I looked through the ones that were still in the box, but there weren't any that were clearly about Jordan and included an art painting class or anything else that I knew about them.

And I sure wasn't about to ask Grace about Jordan because Mitch wouldn't be pleased and we were back on solid footing. I didn't want to mess that up, even though I had sent just a little nudge to Jordan that he should see Grace's post about karaoke and decide to go.

Despite what Mitch had said, and as nice as Wyatt seemed, he wasn't the one for Grace. Jordan was.

We made quick work of decorating the tree to be donated and then Grace took a few pictures of it for posterity.

"Do you want me to take a picture of you in front of the tree?" I asked. Taking pictures with my phone was becoming easy after Mitch had shown me how to do so, and I loved capturing images to see later.

"Thanks, Chloe," she said. "But I'd love instead to get a picture of all four of us in front of the tree. Hold on. I'll go get my tripod that I use to take pictures of my class at the end of the year."

She went over to her kitchen closet and pulled a black cylindrical bag out of it, taking out the tripod and setting it up for her phone to rest on.

"I have the remote here," she said, holding up a tiny device. "Okay, everyone come stand with me in front of the tree. Wyatt, here on my right, and Chloe on my left with Mitch next to her."

Once we were standing in line, she said, "Say trees!" and we all grinned and said the word for the picture. I thought that she'd only taken one but she showed us a number of images.

I had to admit that we all looked cute and happy in the picture.

"I'll text these to you, Chloe and Wyatt, and Chloe, you can text it to Mitch since I don't have your number."

"Sounds good," said Mitch. "Thanks!"

"Okay, now we have to very, very carefully disassemble the tree to keep the ornaments so we can bubble wrap each section. That way, it will be safe for me to transport it to the Rec Center tomorrow after work and then easily reassemble it there with the ornaments already on."

Grace continued talking as we set to work on separating each of the three pieces of the tree and setting them down to wrap them up.

"This reminds me. Do you guys need bubble wrap as well for your tree? I have way more than I need for this one tree."

"Yes, please," I said. "I hadn't even thought of how we'd get the decorated tree there. Mitch and I can bring our tree in with us when we go to work since we're working over at the Rec Center anyway to set up for the Festival. Do you want us to bring yours over, too? We certainly can."

"No, that's okay, but thanks for asking. I don't have a problem bringing it over tomorrow night, and that way I can catch up with Amber and Laurel in person anyway and help out with the set up if necessary."

"Do you want any help with that?" asked Wyatt. "I don't think I have to work late tomorrow night, and an extra pair of hands would probably help… not that you need it, of course. But we could grab dinner or at least coffee after dropping off the tree and helping with any setup."

I watched Grace's face light up and had to admit that she was pleased.

"That sounds great," she said. "Thanks. Do you mind meeting me here at like 6 tomorrow night then?"

Wyatt pulled out his phone and checked his calendar, typing in something.

"Works for me. My last meeting is at 3, so I just blocked off from 4 on so I don't get any last minute meetings added in that would prevent me from doing so. Yes, I'll be here."

"Awesome. Let's wrap up these trees and get to decorating my own tree and then I can help you guys decorate your tree if you want?"

"Yay!" I said, thankful that our apartment was tidy. "Yes, let's do that."

Mitch made an almost imperceptible noise next to me and I glanced over at him. Grace and Wyatt hadn't noticed, but I had. He looked at me and then at Wyatt and then back at me again.

Fine.

"Wyatt, you're welcome to join us in decorating our tree as well if you're not busy?"

"Thanks, Chloe. That sounds like fun."

"Great!"

I looked back at Mitch as if to say "happy" and the smile on his face showed that he was. Even though I didn't want Grace and Wyatt to spend more time together than they needed to, it was obvious that Mitch wanted to include him and I couldn't discount that.

We moved onto decorating Grace's own tree, which surprisingly didn't have any artwork on it. Instead, the theme seemed to be no theme as the ornaments were all over the place, from red and green ball ornaments to little animal characters; wooden sleds with her name on it and a year to tiny white porcelain ballerinas. I held up one of the ballerinas as I was about to put it on the tree.

"Were you a ballerina, Grace?" I almost added that I didn't know that about her, but thankfully stopped myself because I shouldn't know everything about her.

"Oh, no," she said with a bit of a flush on her face. "I wanted to be as a kid, which is when my parents bought me those ornaments. But later, I tried ballet classes and they just weren't for me. I'm too much of a klutz to ever be a ballerina."

"You're not a klutz," said Wyatt. "At least I've never seen it if you are and I've now hung out with you a few times. You didn't drop anything at dinner nor at coffee, and haven't dropped a single ornament."

Grace looked thoughtful. "You're right, I haven't. Huh. That's one of the reasons why I was so careful with bubble wrapping the tree — because I have been called a klutz in my life so often that I just associate it with myself."

I bristled. "That's awful. Who called you a klutz? I haven't met them, but just from how you are, I can't imagine your parents calling you that."

"No, no. My parents have never said I was a klutz although I'm sure they've seen me be clumsy at times. No, it wasn't them… It was just something that kids called me back when I was younger and then someone I dated for a while as well. It was always ironic to them and him that my name is Grace."

Jordan did that? No way. That can't be possible. But now that I thought about it, I did remember something from one of their conversations I'd seen where he'd mentioned something about being graceful and her light had diminished for a moment. I'd assumed it was just from clouds in the sky, but maybe it was instead from what he had said.

Was it possible that I was wrong about Jordan and Grace belonging together?

Wyatt put his hand on Grace's arm and I saw her lean into it a bit. Now I was second-guessing everything. I glanced over at Mitch, but he was looking at the two of them with happiness in his eyes. What the heck?

"From the brief time I've known you, you've been nothing but the epitome of your name," said Wyatt. "If you have clumsy moments, that's okay. You're human. We all have them and it's nothing to be ashamed of and it's certainly nothing that anyone should be using against you. That's on them and shows their character. It has nothing to do with you."

There was a gentle ferocity in his tone that showed how strongly he felt about what he was saying.

From the look on Grace's face, it was clear that she was taking what he said to heart.

"Thank you, Wyatt. I know I can be clumsy, but I appreciate what you said. Thank you. Really."

Wyatt was about to say more when the sound of an old-fashioned phone ringing filled the air. He pulled his phone out of his pocket, said "That would be me. Sorry. I thought I turned the ringer off." and glanced at the screen.

"Pardon me for one second," he said as he stood up. "I'll just go into the hallway."

"That's okay," said Grace. "You can go into the spare room where the trees were."

Wyatt walked over that way and we heard "Hey, Sally…" as the door closed behind him.

Who the heck was Sally? I glanced at Grace and she shrugged her shoulders. Maybe Sally was someone Wyatt worked with at the law firm.

The door opened back up and we heard Wyatt say "I'll be right there."

He put his phone back in his pocket and came back over to us.

"Grace, I'm sorry, but something's come up and I have to head out. This has been so much fun today, and thank you for including me. I should be able to still help you bring the tree over tomorrow night and we'll attend the Festival as planned."

Turning to me and Mitch, he added, "I'm also sorry I won't be able to help decorate your tree, guys, but I'll look forward to seeing it at the Festival."

"I hope everything's okay," Mitch said.

"Thank you. Me, too…" Wyatt looked lost in thought.

"We totally understand," Grace said. She went over to the closet and got his jacket and handed it to Wyatt. "And I do hope everything's okay as well."

"Thank you."

They stood in front of each other for a moment, and then both leaned in for an almost perfunctory hug, before Wyatt stepped back to put on his jacket and headed out the door.

"Safe travels," Grace said.

"Thanks. I'll text you tomorrow to confirm that I can make it to drop off the tree."

"Sounds good."

Grace closed the door behind him and stepped back inside with a frown on her face. She shook her head as a way to shift her mood, and came back over to us.

"Let's get this tree decorated. I should put on some Christmas music. Why didn't I think of doing that before?"

Grace opened the music app on her phone and started up a Christmas playlist. Soon, festive music took away the silence.

"Are you okay, Grace?" I asked, tentatively.

"Of course. Just a little confused, honestly. I'm left wondering if this Sally is someone else that Wyatt is dating and I'm someone he dates when she's busy."

This would be the perfect time to try and nudge her away from Wyatt and towards Jordan, but I was still stuck on those second thoughts about Jordan.

"I'm sure that's not it," I said. "At least that's not the impression I get from him."

"Me neither, but based on my past, I guess I'm having a bit of a hard time trusting that. I want to trust him and he hasn't given me any reason not to trust him, but…"

"Sally could easily be someone he works with," said Mitch. "Maybe there was an issue with a contract at work or something."

Bless him.

"Yes, that could be the case," said Grace. "Thanks, guys. I'm worrying over nothing, hopefully. Let's finish up this tree and then we'll go decorate your tree and I'll see if I hear from Wyatt tomorrow."

Twenty-Seven

Grace

Sure enough, I did get a text from Wyatt the next day while I was taking lunch in between classes.

I'll be there at 6 tonight if that's still okay? Look forward to seeing you.

I quickly wrote back after I read his text:

Of course. See you then.

I wanted to add more and ask if everything was okay, but didn't want to seem like I needed to know. Even though every little bit of me wanted to know.

Chloe and Mitch had done a great job distracting me the night prior, especially when we were decorating their tree for the festival. Their angelic theme was a great one and the tree was so beautiful that I knew it would do well in the raffle.

The work day flew by, as it tended to right before Christmas break. Even though my students were excited about the holidays, they also knew they still had schoolwork to do. Thankfully the majority of them were always invested in my class and interested in the subject, which helped.

When I got back to my apartment, I had time to eat a couple of the chocolates Chloe and Mitch had given me before grabbing a shower and changing out of my dress into an emerald green v-neck sweater and black jeans. That seemed better for carrying in pieces of a tree and bending down to put the tree together at the Rec Center.

At 6 on the dot, my apartment buzzer sounded, and I let Wyatt in as my nerves flared up.

Be cool, I told myself. He's just here to bring the trees over and he didn't cancel. This is all good.

I took a deep breath and released it just as Wyatt knocked on my door.

When I opened it, I saw him standing there with a festive bouquet of red and white roses in a beautiful red vase decorated with red ornaments, candy canes, berries, and pinecones among the flowers. He smiled and held out the bouquet to me.

"For you, as an apology for my having to leave early last night."

"Oh, my goodness," I said as I took the bouquet and placed it on the center of my table. This is beautiful. Please come in. Thank you so much, but no need to apologize at all. I hope everything is okay?"

"Yes, it is, thanks. It's a long story, but yes, all is okay now. And I'm glad that I was able to make it tonight."

"Me, too."

I felt a bit awkward having him in my apartment without Chloe and Mitch there, so I walked over to where the wrapped up pieces of the tree were.

"So, how do you want to do this? Put a few in my car and a few in yours?"

"I can fit all of them in the backseat and the open trunk-like space of my SUV and we can just take my car if that's easier," he said. "Then, after coffee or dinner, I can drop you back here and of course only just walk you to the front apartment door to make sure you get in okay. That is if you're okay with that. If you're not, we can totally just take two cars."

"That works for me and is easier. Thanks for offering."

I grabbed my keys and picked up the biggest section of the tree and headed towards the door, leaving Wyatt to choose from the two smaller sections or the stand. He picked up the bigger of the two sections and the stand and joined me in the hallway.

"Do you want to lock this behind you before we go to put these in my car and come back for the other one?"

"No, we don't have to. I trust my neighbors and plus, we'll only be out there for just a moment or two. I do need the keys to get back into the building so I'm glad I remembered to grab those."

"Okay. Sounds good."

Wyatt went ahead of me to hold the doors open for me with his elbow. How gallant.

His SUV had plenty of room in the back for the big and second biggest sections to fit comfortably, and he put the stand on the floor in front of the back seats, leaving space on those seats for the smallest section to rest.

I ran back inside for the smallest section and locked my apartment door behind me. After I had placed that in his car, Wyatt held the passenger door open for me and I hopped inside.

Oh, he had heated seats. That was especially lovely on a chilly evening like tonight.

As Wyatt walked back over to the driver's side, I reached over and opened the door for him from the inside. It was a bit tricky to do so from the passenger side so I had to lean over the console and two coffee cups that were sitting there, but I wanted to do something nice for him.

"Thank you," he said, as he got in. "You didn't have to do that, but it was sweet of you."

"You're welcome. It was a bit more awkward than I thought it was going to be, but I'm glad I didn't — and also glad I didn't knock over your coffee. Must have been a busy day to need two cups of it."

As I said that, the thought struck that perhaps the second cup had belonged to someone else, like Sally, and I stopped speaking. Okay, now I definitely felt awkward.

"Oh, only one of those is mine," said Wyatt. Well, I guess that answered that…

"I wasn't sure if you drank coffee at night, but since it's chilly, I figured a hot cup of coffee couldn't hurt. The one by you has extra cream and no sugar, but sadly no salt nor bacon."

He'd remembered my order and our joke about that. Wow.

"Oh, well, now I can't possibly drink it," I joked. "I'm going to have to run back inside and get some bacon bits to sprinkle on it. No, seriously, that was very thoughtful and appreciated. Thank you."

"You're welcome."

He opened up the GPS app on his car's screen and scrolled down to where the Rec Center was listed a few spots down. I wondered why he'd been there, but didn't ask, as it wasn't my business. It was entirely possible that he had put it into his GPS a few days ago so he'd know how to get there. That was something I'd do.

Our conversation flowed easily on the trip over to the Rec Center and we chatted about everything from our favorite ice cream (chocolate for him and bubble gum for me) to college days and Christmas plans. Wyatt was going to his dad and step-mom's house and my plans were with my parents. There wasn't a moment of silence and instead lots of questions on both sides, which was a nice change.

Before I knew it, we had arrived at the Rec Center and found a spot right by the ajar door to the gymnasium where the trees would be set up. We brought the start of the sections into the warm building, and saw Laurel standing by the front of the decorated trees. Mitch and Chloe had clearly already been here, as I recognized their angelic tree that had even more sparkle than I remembered from the night prior.

"Grace! Hi! You can bring your tree over here."

Laurel pointed to an empty spot by her that had my name listed on a placard.

"Hi Laurel! This is Wyatt. He was kind enough to help me decorate the tree along with Mitch and Chloe and offered to help bring this tree over."

Wyatt set down the section he was holding and shook Laurel's hand.

"It's a pleasure, Laurel. Nice to meet you. Everything looks great here."

"Thanks so much. A pleasure to meet you, too."

"Grace, no need for both of us to walk back outside. I'll run back out and get the last section and the stand and bring them in."

"Thanks, Wyatt. That sounds great."

I set to removing the bubble wrap with Laurel, who was beaming.

"Okay, spill. You're always cheerful, but that seems to be amped up tonight, Laurel. What's going on?"

"You know Tom Tinker, the toy store owner, right?"

"Of course. He's a sweetheart and hot. What's not to like?"

"Well, he asked me out and we're going out to dinner tonight when I'm done here."

"What? How fun! I'm happy for you. Wait. You're not going to be late because of us being here, right?"

"No, no. We're good. I'm meeting him at 8. There's plenty of time."

"Phew. Good. I was going to kick you out the door if that was the case. I hope you have such a fantastic time. And if things work out — which I'm sure they will since you're awesome and he's awesome — you guys can visit the Festival and see all the trees, because that's super romantic."

Laurel sighed. "I can just see it, which is a good feeling because that means I'm optimistic about the date and him."

"I totally get that."

"Ohhh, is this about Wyatt? He's definitely cute…"

I glanced over at the door to make sure Wyatt wasn't about to walk in, and saw we were clear.

"That he is, and he's great. We'll see, you know. He did tell me he'll see the trees with me."

"I do know and I get it, but I think optimism is a good thing here, too. Oh, about the Festival. I almost forgot."

"What's up? Can I help?"

"It would be great if you could, but if you already have plans, that's okay. We had two people who were going to man the Hot Chocolate booth here for part of the event on Saturday, but they had to drop out. Any chance you could do so? I can see if Chloe or Mitch can help out, too, so it's not just you."

"What's this about hot chocolate?" Wyatt asked as he came back in. "I'm free on Saturday if you're able to do so, Grace, and then we could see the trees either before or after. Sounds like fun."

"That would be great, Wyatt. Thank you. Grace? Are you in?"

"Of course. Sounds like fun! Let's do it. Text me with the information on when we need to be here, the hours you need us, and we'll figure out the rest."

Laurel clapped her hands. "Yay. Thank you! That's perfect. You guys are the last drop-off of the evening, so I can help you set up the tree."

I grinned. She was definitely looking forward to dinner with Tom, and I was happy to see that. And now I knew I'd see Wyatt again on Saturday for the hot chocolate booth and Festival of Trees after the children's event. Something to look forward to as even more Christmas magic.

Twenty-Eight

Chloe

The Christmas magic was strong with this children's event. I could just feel it.

I was standing in one of the classrooms of the Rec Center along with the other members of the dinosaur group, having a drink before putting our suits back on.

The eyes of every child there had lit up when we first pranced into the room to the tune of 'Jingle Bells' with necklaces of bells for added effect around our dinosaur necks.

We danced for all of the kids, and then Amber told them we'd be back in a half hour, giving us a break out of the suits so we didn't get too warm. The suits were fun, but they were certainly toasty after dancing around.

While we were having a break, the kids decorated Christmas cards for their parents and would write their Christmas lists to put in Santa's mailbox during the next break.

"Don't you just love it?" Ruth said as she came over to me with a few bottles of water, and she handed one to me.

"I sure do. The energy is off the charts high, and I love making the kids happy."

"You're a natural dino. The kids can tell who loves what they do and who's doing it just to be involved. Anyone who doesn't love being a dino gets weeded out pretty quickly, and for the past couple of years, we've just had all the good ones, including you."

"Aww. Thanks, Ruth. You and Charlie are absolutely the good ones, too."

"Thank you, my dear. Speaking of, I should get this water to him to make sure he hydrates. Drink up and sit down for a while to rest your dancing feet."

I walked over to the desk next to me and sat down. It was the type of desk that had a section in it to hold a purse or notebook when not in use. I went to place my phone there and accidentally turned on the flashlight, which highlighted a piece of paper.

Unusual. The cleaning people were pretty good about making sure nothing was left behind, but they must have missed this as it was pretty far back.

I took the paper out to throw away or give it to Amber in case it was anything important. As I pulled it out, the words "Rec Center Sale" stopped me.

Well, this was definitely important. I shouldn't be looking at this. I knew that. There was nothing I could do to stop the sale, but maybe there was a nudge I could give one of the involved parties to at least delay it to give Amber and Laurel more time to raise the funds they needed.

Armstrong and Son.

Okay, so that was probably the law firm involved. I'd have to figure out who they were or how to contact/find them. My eyes swept down the page to the two names at the bottom of the letterhead.

Marcus Armstrong, Esquire. Founder of Armstrong and Son.

Wyatt Armstrong, Esquire.

Wyatt?

No.

It couldn't be.

He had helped Grace with decorating the tree for the Festival, which was set up to help raise the funds they needed to keep Laurel's job.

Why would he do that if he was one of the ones involved in selling the Rec Center?

That didn't make sense, but I was right.

He wasn't the one for Grace.

And now I had proof that he'd been keeping his involvement secret. Did I really want to show this to Grace and be the one to tell her?

No, I sure didn't, but I felt like I had to.

I don't think Amber and Laurel knew because Laurel had mentioned that she met Wyatt and she thought she was great.

Ugh.

I folded up the piece of paper and put it into my pants pocket, sending an angelic nudge to Wyatt and his dad to spill the beans.

That's all I could do for the moment.

The kids came first and Pinky had to dance.

Figuring out what to do about Wyatt and the Rec Center would have to wait. There'd be time for talking to Grace about this later.

Twenty-Nine

Grace

"Maybe we won't have as much time to talk as I thought," I said to Wyatt as we walked into the Rec Center and saw the Hot Chocolate booth.

The Center was full with people and merriment and it seemed like every person had a cup of hot chocolate in their hand, or was standing in front of the booth. Okay, so we were going to be busy. Glad it wasn't just me that would be handling that crowd.

"I love talking to you, and we'll have plenty of time to do so when we're looking at the trees after our shift," Wyatt said.

I looked around to see if Chloe and the other dinosaurs were dancing anywhere so I could see them, but no luck. I did see a tree that was decorated in the shape of a dinosaur with little dinosaurs all over it. How cute! If somehow Chloe hadn't seen it, I'd grab a picture to show her later.

It was the last day of the Festival, and I could tell already that it was a huge success by the crowds and the number of people putting raffle tickets into the containers in front of the trees.

Hopefully this would at least save Laurel's job. If not, that combined with the proceeds from my art show and the upcoming ones from the karaoke night should all help.

We made our way over the hot chocolate booth, where Laurel and Tom were busy passing out hot chocolate to the customers. Well, that was a great sign that they were together at the event.

There was a timely lull in the crowd in front of the stand, and Laurel pointed over to the side of the booth, where there was a door for us to enter. Looking at the inside of the booth, I was glad that I hadn't asked Chloe and Mitchell to help out as well. The booth was spacious but for two people at most with all of the hot chocolate machines and carafes, cups, and accompaniments of whipped cream, sprinkles, and candy canes.

We waited right outside the booth as Laurel and Tom exited.

"Thank you guys so much," said Laurel. "It's been pretty steady, but then there was just a wave of people after people that only just slowed down. Hopefully it will just be steady for you guys instead of that insane."

"Fingers are crossed," I said. "Anything we need to know about?"

"I think you're good. The prices are on the poster in front of the stand and also on the counter as well for the customers to see, and the cash register has the prices as well. We also have a payment app on the phone that's there in case people want to pay that way. It's charged, but it's also connected to the charger so you won't have to worry about it running out of power. Amber and I will be back in two hours to take over, and you should have everything you need there, but if you run out of anything, just text either of us and we'll bring it over. But now, I'm going to go wander around and look at the trees with Tom."

She comfortably took his hand.

"Have so much fun, guys! We'll be fine here. Stop back here if you want some hot chocolate."

I added the last with a laugh because I was pretty sure they were probably sick of hot chocolate for a while, and everyone chuckled.

Wyatt held the door open for me, and waved his arm into the booth.

"After you."

"Well, thank you, kind sir."

"You're welcome."

Wyatt stopped and stood still for a moment.

"Everything okay?" I asked.

He blinked and looked at me, as if he was uncertain where he was.

"Yes. Sorry. That was so weird. I had the strangest feeling that I was supposed to tell you something, but I don't know what. It's gone now. Ever had a feeling like that?"

"Oh, yeah. Usually for me, it's that sense of deja vu. It happens. I always say it's because something happened in an alternate universe. The only explanation I can come up with."

"Huh. Well, hopefully, in that other universe, I told you whatever it was I was supposed to."

"I'm sure you did. Now let's go serve some hot chocolate."

We grabbed two clean red and white striped aprons off the hooks and put them on. Looking at some of the other hot chocolate-dabbed aprons that were sitting on a chair, that seemed like a smart idea.

The timing worked out well as no one had been standing there when we were talking with Laurel and Tom, but a few people were walking over towards the booth as we shut the door and got to the counter.

Laurel's prediction was correct and it was a steady group of people, with just a few moments of lulls here and there.

During one of them near the end of our shift, Wyatt held up one of the candy canes and turned to me.

"Have you ever had hot chocolate with pieces of smashed up candy cane in it?"

"No, I can't say I have. I've had it with a candy cane resting in it, like we do with these, but that sounds interesting. Where'd you hear of it?"

"My mom always made hot chocolate for me at Christmas when I was a kid, and that was the only way she'd serve it. Her parents did so for her when she was growing up, and she wanted to do so for her kids, which was me. I haven't thought of that in forever and haven't had hot chocolate in ages since she passed away years ago, actually, but this candy cane made me remember that."

"Oh, Wyatt, that's a lovely memory to have. Do you want to recreate that hot chocolate with candy cane pieces here? If so, I'd love to try it."

"I'd like that."

He got two paper towels, and put one down on the side counter behind us with a candy cane on top of it, and then placed the other paper towel on top of that. Looking around, he saw one of the empty metal carafes and brought it over.

"This might be a bit loud. Do you think that's okay?"

The Rec Center was already loud with happy people talking away as they walked through and the sounds of the Christmas music piped in.

"I'm sure it will be fine, and it probably won't take all that long to break, right?"

"It's been a long while since I've done this," admitted Wyatt, "so I'm not entirely sure. But let's find out."

With the childlike grin on his face, I sure as heck didn't want to stop him from recreating a past treat. I only hoped it would be as delicious as he remembered.

Thankfully, with just a few whacks of the large carafe, the candy cane was shattered into multiple pieces and it hadn't impacted the counter at all. As anticipated, the sounds of the music and the people muffled the noise, so no one was annoyed by it.

Wyatt gently lifted the top paper towel away from the pieces and then took two cups. He turned the second paper towel into a funnel of sorts and placed pieces of the candy cane into each cup, topping those pieces with hot chocolate.

I grabbed one of the cups and brought it up to my nose, taking a big whiff.

"If it tastes even just a bit as good as it smells, it's fantastic."

"Wait," said Wyatt, taking the cup back from me. "There's two more things that it needs."

"What's that?"

"No cup of hot chocolate is complete without whipped cream on top and then a few more of these broken up pieces sprinkled on top of that."

He quickly added the whipped cream and some candy cane pieces to the top of the two cups and returned mine to me.

"Cheers," he said as we clinked cups and each took a sip.

That was the most delicious drink I'd ever tasted.

"Okay, every single cup of hot chocolate I drink from now on needs to be just like that," I said.

Wyatt was chuckling and staring at my face.

"What's so funny?"

"You have some whipped cream on the tip of your nose and above your lip," Wyatt said. "Hold on."

He stood closer to me and reached over and wiped the whipped cream off my nose with his finger, and then did the same to the top of my lip.

I suddenly lost the ability to speak, realizing how near he was.

"There's still one more bit on your lip," he said.

I wanted him to kiss me and it seemed that was his intention as his face came closer to mine.

I closed my eyes and pursed my lips a bit.

"Wyatt? What are you doing here, son?"

I heard a male's voice and my eyes flew open as we jumped away from each other.

Standing in front of us at the counter was an older man with salt and pepper hair that was thick, and shorter on the sides than the top.

He looked so familiar, and it took me a moment, and then I remembered.

The man I spilled coffee on in the halls of this very Rec Center.

Wait.

Son?

That was Wyatt's dad. Now I wanted to close my eyes for an entirely different reason.

What a way to meet his dad. My face lit up like a fire.

"Dad. Hi! What are you doing here? I didn't expect you'd be at a Christmas festival. Oh, Dad, this is Grace. Grace, this is my father, Marcus Armstrong."

"Hello, Grace."

He had only looked briefly at me, but clearly didn't remember me, which was a relief. He turned back to Wyatt.

"I'm as surprised as you are to find myself here. I was about to sit down with a scotch and read the paper when I felt the need to attend. And what do I find but you working at a hot chocolate stand that's raising money in the building that our law firm is handling the sale of? I worked a long time to find the right buyers for this place and it's going to make quite a profit for us."

They're what? Wyatt's law firm was the one that was taking the Rec Center away. And he hadn't mentioned that?

How could he!

I placed my hands over my face and backed away a little bit as Wyatt reached out to me.

"Grace. Wait. I can explain…"

"There's nothing to explain," I said to him, realizing how cold I sounded and I didn't care. "I hope you and your dad enjoy the money you're making by selling this place and turning it into whatever it becomes, instead of the place it's been that's full of memories for everyone who has ever been here."

I stopped as memories of working in the hot chocolate booth with Wyatt and that almost kiss ran through my head.

"That includes the memories of today, which have now been forever tarnished. I can't forgive you for that."

"Grace. Please…"

"Let her go, son. You can come have a scotch with me away from this place. I don't know why I'm here. I avoid it since it reminds me of your mother as we met here."

I opened the door to find Amber and Laurel standing there. They were about to come in and had heard everything, clearly, since they were glaring at Wyatt and his dad.

"Are you okay, Grace?" Amber asked.

I shook my head yes, fearful that I'd burst into tears if I even tried to speak.

"Wyatt, it's time for you to leave. You're no longer welcome here," said Laurel with ice dripping from every word.

Marcus was already walking away towards the door as Wyatt went to follow him.

But he stopped, and turned back towards us.

"Grace. Everyone. I'll fix this. I will. Or at least I'll try."

"There's nothing to fix," I said. "What we had was a lie because while I was working so hard to help the Rec Department and save the Center, you were actively working this whole time to sell it. Nothing will fix that. Nothing."

I turned and Amber grabbed me in a hug. This was not at all the time to break down, because everyone was having a wonderful time and I didn't want to ruin that for everyone.

"How about you and I go into one of the back rooms here and you can have some water before you head out?" she said into my ear.

"Thanks, Amber. Yes, please."

I let her lead me through the trees into the back while Laurel manned the booth. I knew that Wyatt wouldn't try to come talk to me as he knew he was no longer welcomed there, and I needed a moment of peace before heading home.

Thirty

Grace

When I got home, I walked slowly to my apartment.

My heart was heavy, and I hadn't even looked at any of the trees after Marcus' reveal about their law firm. I was supposed to have been walking through all the trees and marveling over them with Wyatt.

Instead, I got out of there as quickly as possible and headed home.

As I put the key into my lock and started to turn it, I heard the door behind me open.

"Are you okay, Grace?" Chloe said.

I turned towards her and she saw the look on my face, causing her own face to fall.

She crossed the hallway and pulled me into a big hug.

"Oh, Grace. It's going to be okay. What happened?"

"Do you mind if we go in my apartment to talk? It's easier than out here in the hallway."

"Of course." I let go of the hug and let Grace open the door, following her lead.

She closed the door behind me and sat down at my kitchen table, looking at the Christmas bouquet that Wyatt had given me.

"That's so pretty!" she said.

Seeing the bouquet brought everything rushing back and I sat down, trying my best to hold back the tears.

"The flowers were from Wyatt, back when things were good between us. Or at least when I thought they were."

"What happened?"

"It's a mess. Things were going so well at the hot chocolate booth, and we even almost kissed. But then his dad showed up and announced that their law firm was the one handling the sale of the Rec Center and that he'd even found the company that was buying it."

"Wait, so Wyatt didn't tell you? His dad did?"

Chloe looked confused, which was confusing to me. Why did she care who told me?

"Yeah, his dad burst in and just announced it to us. Wyatt said he wanted to explain, but I wouldn't let him. Really, what could he say? Nothing. He's the one who kept the secret that his firm was the one that made the sale happen. There's nothing he could say that would justify that."

Chloe reached into her pocket and pulled up a folded up piece of paper and started unfolding it.

"In the realm of being honest, there's something I need to tell you. I found out earlier today that Wyatt's firm was the one involved."

"What?" I stood up. "And you didn't tell me or even text me?"

Chloe stood up as well and handed me the paper.

"I wanted to, but I didn't know how to tell you, because I knew it would ruin things with you and Wyatt and you seemed so happy. I found this paper in our room at the Rec Center during one of the breaks and wanted to tell you, but the thought of causing you this much hurt gave me pause. I know it was wrong and I should have told you the second I found out. I'm sorry. I'm a bad friend for not telling you."

I took the paper from her, and remembered that I had had something I should have told a friend the second I found out about it. But I didn't because I didn't want to hurt Abigail and mention that it looked like Ethan was still on a dating site under a different name.

All the anger I was feeling towards Chloe for not telling me fell away.

I sat back down at the table while she remained standing cautiously at the door, like she thought I was about to yell at her to leave.

"You're not a bad friend," I said. "Well, no more than I am. I understand why you didn't tell me and I am sure it was getting to you that you hadn't. It's okay. You only just found out today and I'm guessing you were waiting at your door for me to come home to talk to me then."

"I was," Chloe said as she, too, sat back down. "It's been killing me that I knew something that was going to hurt you. But I wanted to protect you from that. I didn't want to hurt you. That doesn't justify it, though. I'm sorry."

Reaching over, I placed my hand on top of Chloe's and squeezed it.

"It's okay. I forgive you. I can't forgive Wyatt, though. He lied and I can't get past that."

Thirty-One

Chloe

"How can she ever get past that?" I said to Mitchell as he drove us to work.

All week, that had been our main topic of conversation. Well, that and that I was the one who nudged Wyatt's dad to tell the truth when I'd found out. He was still mad at me for that because it broke up Wyatt and Grace.

But they were going to break up anyway once the truth came out. I just made the truth come to light sooner than it would have otherwise.

Thankfully, at least, it wasn't an offense bad enough that Emmy would make us both stay down here instead of coming back up. It shouldn't be anyway.

We got to the Town Hall and headed upstairs to the Recreation Department. As we neared the open door, the sound of cheering came from inside.

What was that?

We poked our heads inside and saw Amber and Laurel dancing around.

Okay, this was new.

"What's going on, guys?" said Mitch.

Amber ran over to us. "Mitchell! Chloe! You're just in time to hear the great news."

"Great news? What is it?" I asked.

"Wyatt's our hero," said Laurel.

I'm sorry. What?

"How exactly is he a hero?" asked Mitch.

"Go ahead, Amber," said Laurel. "It's your department so it's your story to tell."

"Well, you just missed Wyatt," started Amber. "He came by to tell us personally that the Recreation Department was fully funded and the Rec Center wasn't being sold."

"But how?" I was eager to know just what had gone on this morning.

"I'm getting to that… He's been busy this week since his dad revealed it was his law firm. Wyatt was never involved in the sale itself. He deals more with reviewing leases and rental properties instead of the sales, so he didn't know until his dad mentioned it."

Oh, no. He really didn't know. My heart sank.

"He has been down in the basement of this building looking through old documents," continued Amber. "And that paid off for him when he found a document that stated this building was part of a previously unknown underground railway that ran through here and up into Canada. He worked with the historical society, and they were quite happy to learn the news. That gave this building even greater historical significance than it had before, and they deemed that it couldn't be demolished, which made the sale impossible. Laurel, want to tell them the rest?"

"Yes! Wyatt found open land nearby that can instead be used as the place for the company's new building instead of this one. And, even bigger news for me personally… My job is safe! Wyatt donated his bonus to the Recreation Department and got his buddies to do the same with part of their bonuses, so between that, Grace's gallery show proceeds, and the Festival, we're fully funded and I'm still employed."

"That is huge news," I said. "I'm so happy for everyone and especially that your job is safe, Laurel, and that the Rec Center will stay the wonderful Rec Center that it is. Has anyone told Grace yet?"

"No," said Laurel. "Wyatt said that he'd texted her a few times and tried to call, but she's blocked his calls and texts. We thought that you might want to tell her."

"Thank you," I said. "I'll do that right now. She's going to be so shocked. Mitch, you were right. Wyatt is one of the good ones."

Thirty-Two

Grace

I was right. He really is one of the good ones.

Now I just had to reach him.

When Chloe called to tell me the news, I couldn't believe it. But then she handed the phone to Amber and she confirmed it.

No wonder Wyatt had said he could explain. He could have, but I probably wouldn't have believed him then and just assumed he was trying to say anything to get me not to leave.

I instantly tried calling him, but he didn't answer. I guess I wouldn't have either if it was me.

He had to know, though, that I would have heard by now and was reaching out to apologize. Right?

I left a voicemail saying how sorry I was, and that I'd heard the wonderful news about his findings and what he'd done to save the Rec Center and Chloe's job.

I again mentioned karaoke night tonight and that I really hoped he'd come out, because I missed him and wanted to apologize to him in person for just believing the worst.

I then sent a text with essentially the same thing in it, but not really expecting a reply.

I could only hope he'd call me or come to karaoke night.

Thirty-Three

Grace

⁂

Karaoke night was here.

The East Palace restaurant in Silverton was located in a strip mall-like shopping plaza next to the Crystal River and waterfall. Considering that it was the weekend before Christmas, I was shocked to find some parking spaces. I figured that stores would be busy with people buying last-minute gifts.

I pulled into a spot a few rows back from the entrance and glanced at the time. 6:35. Okay, good. I'd spent enough time primping at my apartment. Karaoke didn't start until 7, but we were getting there early to get a good table and grab some drinks.

I wondered who I was going to see inside.

I knew Chloe and Mitch would be there because it was her idea, and Abigail had texted me earlier that she'd see me there. I'd posted the event on my SocNote, and 30 friends had clicked "interested". But we all knew that meant nothing and that I most likely wouldn't see a single one of them. Joshykins and Zack RSVPed yes, which made me happy. Always loved seeing them.

Amber and Laurel were both out at a celebratory dinner with Amber's family and Tom. I was so relieved for them that the Rec Center and Laurel's job were both safe. Any funds that came about from the karaoke night tonight would go towards further funding for the Rec Department.

Would I see Wyatt here? Yes, I'd called and texted him with my apology and mentioned karaoke night, but he never got back to me. I couldn't blame him because I'd been so mad, but based on what I knew at the time, I'd had every right to be.

I stopped overthinking and got out of the car. It was unseasonably warm, so my black and gray floral top, black jeans, and black boots worked well. I'd been at this restaurant before for meals, and seemed to remember the crowd all tended to dress down anyway.

The karaoke room was on the side of the restaurant behind the bar. I immediately saw Chloe; Mitch; Joshykins; his partner, Zack; Dani; Jessie; and Abigail sitting at one of the long tables, with paper slips to request songs in front of them. I didn't see Wyatt yet, but hoped he was going to make an appearance.

Waving, I headed over.

"Hey, Grace!"

No. Why was he here?

I stopped and turned, seeing Jordan sitting at one of the side tables with a lovely woman with long black hair and a sweet smile.

What was he doing here? And who is she? Is this the woman he's been dating?

She's cute. Of course she is…

Plastering a grin on my face, I walked over to them.

"Jordan, hi. What are you doing here?"

"I saw your post about it, and thought it sounded fun. I didn't RSVP because I wasn't sure I'd be able to make it, but I was telling Nina about it and she was interested. Oh, Nina, this is Grace, who organized this karaoke night. Grace, this is my friend, Nina McKensie."

"Friend, huh?", said Nina, chuckling. "Thanks, dude. I'd say we're more than that since we've been dating for months, but hey, sure, friends."

I hoped my face didn't show my pain hearing those words. I knew Jordan had been dating someone else, even while he was still dating me, but to meet her in person was something else entirely. Seemed like he hadn't changed much in the commitment department though.

"Nina, it's a pleasure to meet you," I said, sticking my hand out to shake hers, probably a little too vigorously. "I'm so glad you guys were able to come out and I hope you have a great time."

I turned to walk away, but then realized I should be nice and invite them to join the group, so I turned back to the twosome.

"A bunch of my friends are over at that table. I'm heading over to join them and you're welcome to join us if you'd like."

"Sure!," said Nina. "I'm always up for making new friends." She looked at Jordan with that last word.

"Babe, c'mon…"

Jordan at least had the decency to look guilty.

They got up and followed me over to the table. I sat down in between Abigail and Josh, and Nina and Jordan sat across from Chloe and Mitch.

"Okay, quick introductions here," I announced to my friends, pointing to each one as I said their names. "This is Jordan and Nina. These folks are Chloe, Mitch, Dani, Jessie, Joshykins, Zack, and Abigail."

"Yeah, some of us have met Jordan before," said Josh. "Surprised to see you, dude, but nice to meet you, Nina."

I kicked Joshykins under the table to stop him before he went further with that. Maybe inviting Nina and Jordan to our table wasn't such a great idea.

"Good to see you again, Josh and Zack," said Jordan. "Think the last time I saw you — and you, Abigail — was at your barbecue over the summer. Good times."

"Nice to meet you all," said Nina. "I guess I didn't realize you all knew each other."

"If it helps," chimed in Chloe, "Mitch and I are meeting everyone for the first time, too. Well, minus Grace, obviously, since we met her through being neighbors. I talked her into this karaoke night because I've always wanted to do so. I'm glad everyone was able to come out because it's going to be so much fun!"

"Glad I'm not alone in being new then," replied Nina. "Thanks, Chloe and Mitch. So have any of you done karaoke before? When Jordan mentioned going tonight, I was surprised but figured it would be good for a few laughs if nothing else."

"Oh, I thought Jordan said it was your idea," I said.

"It sure wasn't my idea. We had plans to go out to dinner tonight and just as we were going to walk out the door, Jordan said that we should go get Chinese instead at this karaoke thing a friend of his was putting together."

"Okay, that's true," said Jordan. "I wasn't planning on going, but just then it struck me that it would be funny to see people singing off-key and I'd get some laughs out of it. You know there are going to be some awful singers… not that I'm talking about anyone at this table. Well, maybe Grace."

"Jerk," I said with a smile on my face. "You just can't help yourself, can you? And I'll have you know I have a great singing voice. Well, at least I think I do when I sing in the shower and in the car. Hmm, I hope I do anyway."

"No matter how it happened that you guys are here," Chloe said, "I'm happy everyone came! The more the merrier. Right, Grace?"

"Of course! So are we all going to sing?"

"I'm out," said Abigail. "I'm here just for the moral support, and figured it would give me something to do since Ethan is out doing last-minute Christmas shopping with his brother."

"Awww," I said. "Are you sure I can't get you to do a group song with me? Pretty please. We could be the Spice Girls with Jessie and Dani."

"I love you, my friend, but it's not happening," said Dani. Jessie shook her head as well.

"Zack and I are singing," said Josh. "We already put in our duet song with the DJ."

I turned to Chloe. "This was your idea, missy. Tell me you're singing."

"Of course! I'm just looking through their songbook online to see what I want to sing, and I'm going to try to get Mitch to sing, too."

Mitch groaned and looked at Chloe. "Please, no. We've talked about this. You know I don't sing…"

While they bickered like an old married couple, followed by Chloe walking over to the DJ with a slip of paper, I turned to Jordan and Nina.

"So, how about you guys? Jordan, I'm pretty sure you told me once that you've done karaoke before."

"Shut the front door," said Nina. "You have? Well, no wonder you wanted to come here tonight. I had no idea. You won't even sing in the car."

"Thanks, Grace," said Jordan, fake glaring at me. "That was one time during a friend's bachelor party weekend in Mexico. We were drunk and sang something. I think it was Vanilla Ice's "Ice Ice Baby" as a group, but I honestly don't remember."

"You've got half a beer in front of you," I replied. "Have another one and then you'll be at the least buzzed with liquid courage before you sing. So no excuse. You're singing."

I pushed the sign over to them that listed the website for the DJ's online songbook, and started looking at it on my phone to see if they had a song I'd always wanted to do. Bingo! There it was! I jotted it down on the piece of paper and brought it up to the DJ, and then came back to the table.

"So, whatcha singing?" asked Jessie.

"I'm not saying a word, but it's one that you all know really well."

"Hmm, that could be anything since we have so many songs that we've known since our college days," said Abigail.

"True, true, but it's a good one," I replied. "Hopefully it still will be after I sing it…"

"I have faith in you, my dear. Are you doing a solo or a duet? Which reminds me, is Wyatt going to be able to make it?"

"Signed up to do the song myself. As for Wyatt, I'm not sure."

Way to be blunt, Abigail. What were the chances Jordan hadn't heard that?

"Is Wyatt your boyfriend?" asked Nina.

Ooof.

Well, if Jordan hadn't heard what Abigail and I said, he was sure listening now with his eyebrows slightly raised. Can't say I hated the thought of him being a little jealous.

"We haven't had that discussion yet," I replied, keeping my eyes firmly away from Jordan. "But I've been seeing him for the last couple of weeks."

No need at all to mention that I'd broken up with him based on the wrong information, because I was hoping to rectify that.

"Awesome. I hope he can make it and I'll look forward to meeting him."

"Me, too," said Jordan.

He gave me a look that I didn't want to try to fathom. Was he surprised I'd actually moved on from him? Was he jealous? I couldn't tell from his inscrutable expression.

The waitress came over to grab our drink orders. After she left, I glanced back across the table when I heard Nina speak.

"I might be talked into doing a duet," said Nina. "But I'm not singing on my own."

"Fair enough," replied Jordan. "I'm going to look through the songs and see if I want to sing a solo and blow you all away with my singing skills, or maybe I'll just write down everyone at this table and make you all sing."

He continued scrolling through the website and stopped to write down a song on the slip of paper, and brought it up to the DJ. As he came back, he had a slightly wicked grin on his face.

"Oh, no, no, no," said Nina. "We're all going to wind up singing the Backstreet Boys, aren't we? That seems like your go-to."

"Shoot," said Josh. "That's what I was thinking of doing. I even had the frosted tips like them back in college."

"You sure did," I said, and laughed. "I can never unsee that picture, but, now that I'm thinking about it, maybe you should sing Britney Spears..."

"Hey, now! A guy dresses up as Britney Spears for one Halloween and it haunts him forever."

"You're the one who showed me the pic, Joshykins. I can't unsee it. And you know I love you for your silliness."

"I love you, too, Grace. You're a friend who's become family over the years."

I reached over and hugged Josh.

"Don't you dare make me cry. I need to get into party singing mode, unless I'm singing 'Tears of a Clown', and I'm not doing that."

"I'll make you laugh instead. I spent this morning pondering the name of my future restaurant when I open my own. It should be a tapas restaurant called Snacking on Nonsense."

"Oh, no. Should I even ask what you were eating when you came up with that idea, since I know your meals are strange ones?"

"You know I'm going to tell you anyway. I was eating grapes, watermelon, marinated mushrooms, and beef jerky as breakfast at the time."

"What am I going to do with you? I'm just grateful you haven't made any of these strange food combinations the chef's choice at Subtle Savors."

"I would be fired in a hot minute if I did that. But when I own my own restaurant where I make the rules… game on. And you are going to be there first in line opening night."

"I have no doubt at all that you'll make that happen, Joshykins, and of course I will be. I wouldn't miss it."

A hush fell over the crowd as the light on the stage went on and the screen lit up. The DJ, who called himself DJ Joe, started speaking. He introduced himself to all of us and said he was looking forward to the singing and laughs we'd all have tonight.

"First up, we have Josh and Zack. Come on up, guys."

"Yaaay!", I yelled, clapping my hands. "Go get 'em, Joshykins and Zack."

They walked up to the stage and took the mics from the DJ. The title of "I Got You, Babe" took over the screen and we all cheered.

The two of them were complete hams and got into the song with Zack being Sonny Bono and Joshykins performing as Cher. The crowd loved it, and I was happy that they started off the night and got such a great response.

At the end of the song, both bowed and everyone clapped with delight.

"Okay," said DJ Joe. "Let's hear it for Josh and Zack. Nicely done! Next up, we have the vocal stylings of Chloe."

"Thank you, Chloe," said Mitch. "I'm glad I don't have to sing."

Chloe headed up, gave DJ Joe a big smile, and turned to all of us with the mic in her hand.

"Hallelujah" came up on the screen.

Oh, Chloe… I hope you know what you're doing. That takes vocal range that I know I could never pull off.

Under the table, I crossed all of my fingers and even crossed my thumbs to send her some good luck.

Chloe started singing and my jaw dropped. In fact, the entire audience of 50 or so people seemed like they were also struck silent.

Her voice was beautiful, stirring, and blew me away. I felt like I was sitting listening to the person who was meant to sing that song and every note was heartfelt.

As Chloe sang: "Well your faith was strong but you needed proof.," I felt a tear come to my eye.

That song always evoked strong emotion in me and tonight was no exception. Was it possible that I could find the proof and faith I needed that love would come my way? Or had it come my way already through Wyatt and I just wasn't ready to trust that after being hurt before? I wasn't sure, but my soul felt a sudden glimmer of hope hearing Chloe sing.

To ease my tears, I took a sip of water. While I did so, I glanced down the table and saw that Mitch's eyes were glued on Chloe and love shone in his eyes. He looked mesmerized.

Chloe told me he was gay, but there's no way he is. Does she not know he's straight and clearly in love with her? Maybe my friend needed a knock on the head to see what was in front of her.

When Chloe stopped singing, it was like the whole crowd came out from under a spell. In unison, we jumped to our feet and clapped, yelling "Woo hoo!.

Chloe was blushing happily at the reaction her voice brought about, and waved to everyone as she walked back to our table.

"Chloe!" I said. "You were amazing. You should be a professional singer."

"I'm in the choir back where I'm from, but everyone sounds like me, there. I never thought of it as being anything special. But thank you, my friend."

"Who has to follow the divine Chloe?," said DJ Joe. "Ah, here it is. Come on up, Grace!"

Oh, no.

No, no, no.

Of course I have to be the one after Chloe's performance. I'm going to embarrass myself.

I walked up to the stage, grinned awkwardly at DJ Joe, and took the mic. Turning, I faced the crowd and wondered if it was too late for a sinkhole to open up beneath me.

"Mamma Mia" came up on the screen.

Too late.

It's starting.

The piano chords that started off the song gave me a few more moments to find my courage. I took a deep breath, and started singing as the words came up.

During the first lyrics about being cheated on and knowing something had to end, I kept my eyes glued to the screen and firmly away from Jordan.

Shoot. Is he going to think I'm singing about him? Why didn't I go with my second choice of "Sk8terBoi" or "Miss Me More"?

Okay, "Miss Me More" probably would have been worse as a "Look at me. I'm totally over you" mentality.

Grr. Focus, Grace. Think of Wyatt and how you want to look up here if he walks in right at this moment. He's the one you want to think about. Not Jordan.

"Go, Grace!" I looked over and saw Abigail standing up and cheering, prompting Joshykins and Zack to get up, too.

That gave me the confidence boost I needed as the line *"Just one look and I can hear a bell ring"* started, which seemed appropriate as that line was always the one that had a bit more gusto… I felt stronger, and even more so as I sang louder and with more theatrics like I was an actual singer at a concert.

That feeling heightened when a bunch of women who were there for a bachelorette party came out onto the non-existent dance floor and started dancing and singing away in front of me. Wow. Okay, now I understand why this is so addictive.

I forgot completely for a few moments that Jordan was there and performed for the crowd, who were loving it.

When I stopped singing, the crowd clapped heartily. I did a little bow and walked back to the table, looking at the door first to see if Wyatt had snuck in. I was bummed that he hadn't been there to see me sing, especially with that kind of response from the crowd.

"Ladies on the dance floor," said DJ Joe. "Don't leave. I'm going to take a little break and get a drink, so the dance tunes will keep playing."

He put on "Wannabe" as he left his podium, which kept the girls dancing and singing along.

"Amazeballs," said Josh. "You killed it. And your hair should be bigger because you're clearly filled with secrets, or just secret talents."

"Totally agree," added Zack. "Minus the hair thing. Also, I'm glad you didn't sing like Pierce Brosnan."

"Stop it," I said. "First, I'm going to make 'fetch' happen, Joshykins and clearly you can sit with us. And Zack, he's easy on the eyes, so he can get away with it, and he sang pretty well in that second film. The first one did cause my ears to bleed."

"Gotta hand it to ya, Grace," said Jordan. "You weren't bad, and you surprised me because I thought for sure you were going to trip either walking up there or back, or fall off the stage."

"I have to try and live up to my name, somehow. We all know I'm a klutz, but singing up there was fun and easy. Looking forward to doing so again at some point. And thank you, all. I appreciate it. I was nervous til you guys stood up and cheered me on, so thank you. Really."

"That's what we're here for, babe," said Abigail, patting me on the shoulder. "I'm still not singing, though."

"No worries, my friend. I have another one in mind — probably not for tonight, but another visit here, because we're coming back."

"Still not singing then, either," grinned Abigail.

"I won't make ya do so," I replied. "That's what friends are for. We have each other's back."

Thirty-Four

Chloe

"Be right back, Chloe," said Mitch. "I'm going to go use the facilities. If the waitress stops by when I'm gone, can you get me another water?"

"Of course. See ya when you get back."

As Mitch walked off, I followed his movements with my eyes to see if any of the guys in the room caught his eye, but nope. Instead, I saw a few female heads turn as he walked past.

What the heck? I could feel myself bristle, which didn't make sense. I couldn't be jealous.

This was Mitch. Sure, he's handsome and great, but… no. Just no.

Mitch was my buddy. My confidant. The person I went to whenever I needed to talk about anything, good or bad, and who I felt like myself most around. That wasn't love. That was companionship. Right? There was no way I was mistaken about Mitch's type and how I felt about him.

My thoughts turned away from that awkward train of thought when I saw a couple walk over to me. The woman had a big smile, long light brown hair, and was holding the hand of the tall dark haired man next to her.

"You don't know us at all," said the woman, "but your performance of 'Hallelujah' was beautiful."

"Oh, thank you. That was my first time doing karaoke, so I wasn't sure how it would go."

"Are you kidding me? Wow. I thought you were a professional singer. That's amazing. That song is one of my favorites, so much so that my husband, Ryan, and I considered it as our wedding song. But we went with the Hawaiian 'Somewhere Over the Rainbow' instead."

"I don't know that song, but I'll need to look it up now. What's your name, by the way? I'm Chloe."

"I'm Maura. It's a pleasure to meet you, Chloe. I hope we'll see you sing again sometime, and next time, sing with your boyfriend. He couldn't take his eyes off you and was enamored. It was really sweet."

"I'm sorry. Who?"

"The man with the dark blonde hair that you were just talking to you. Are you guys not dating? Ugh, nice job Maura. I'm sorry — actually scratch that, I'm not sorry — I have a tendency to say sorry too often when I'm not, but Ryan has helped me with that. Anyway, if you're just friends and you're not interested at all in him, I can confirm he's interested in you as more than a friend."

"No, he's gay, but are you sure you have the right guy? Mitch has icy blonde hair. He has no interest in me."

"If I'm wrong, I'm wrong, but I don't think I am. I'm talking about the guy that's been sitting across from you. He has dark blonde hair. That boy loves you from the look in his eyes, and a tip — if you see him as having icy blonde hair, that might be because you see him in a different light than anyone else, and there's a reason for that."

"That boy's not gay," said Josh, who had been listening in. "Trust me, my gaydar is on point and he's straight, and hooked on you. Did you not know that?"

"Okay, Maura, it's probably time for us to head out," said Ryan, as Mitch walked back to the table.

"Think about what I said, Chloe," said Maura as she turned to leave. "I know I'm right."

"What's she right about?" inquired Mitch as he sat back down, having heard the last words.

Could I be wrong and he's not interested in guys at all, and is instead interested in me? But he's my bestie. The one I turn to when I need a laugh and who gives me the best hugs and understands me and gets me.

I sputtered. "Ummm, she said she loved my singing and that I should be a professional singer."

"Well, she is right. You have a fantastic voice. One would even call it angelic, but you surpass all the other angels, at least to me."

Oh, I was so confused. My head felt like it was spinning. That sounded like I meant something special to him. Was there any chance he thought of me as more than just a friend?

"Thank you, Mitch. There's something I need to…"

I stopped talking as DJ Joe came back from his break.

"Hmm," he said, looking at the piece of paper. "There's probably a rule against this since she's already sung once, but since it's a duet, that's fine. Let's welcome Jordan and Grace to the stage!"

Grace got up with a dazed look on her face.

"Me? Are you sure about that?" she asked Jordan.

Jordan grinned. "Yeah, you."

Jordan and Grace walked up to the stage, with Jordan ignoring Nina, who looked like she'd been smacked.

"Chloe, did you have anything to do with this?" Mitch whispered to me across the table as Grace and Jordan walked up to the stage. He looked really mad. "You know you're not supposed to interfere."

Well, if he was interested in me, he sure isn't now. Ugh.

"I didn't. I promise. I'll admit that I did give him a little nudge to want to show up tonight, but I had nothing to do with him writing down Grace's name on that duet instead of Nina's."

"I want to believe you, but I'm not sure I can."

"Mitch, please believe me."

My words fell on deaf ears as "Summer Loving" from "Grease" came up on the screen, and Jordan and Grace started singing.

Their chemistry was still off the charts, but now I was starting to doubt everything. Was I so determined to be right and the perfect angel matchmaker that I had only looked at the chemistry, not focusing on everything else that is important in a partnership?

Once Grace started singing, it was like she'd never left the stage. I was proud to see her happy and singing away up on the stage with Jordan hamming it up, but I could also see a little bit of confusion in her eyes. We were all pretty confused at the table, wondering why Jordan had so blatantly disrespected Nina by writing down Grace's name instead of hers.

Halfway through the song, Nina got up and left the table with her shoulders slumped.

I looked up at the stage, but Grace and Jordan hadn't even noticed she'd left. Their eyes were on each other.

"Excuse me, I'm sorry…" I heard Nina apologize as she bumped into someone coming in as our table was right near the entryway.

Glancing over, I groaned. I thought I was silent, but Mitch heard me and looked over in that direction. Wyatt was standing there in the entrance staring at the stage. He looked crestfallen seeing Grace and Jordan together singing.

"Shoot," whispered Mitch. He turned to me, leaned in, and whispered. "I really hope you didn't cause them to sing together, Chloe, because now my charge is the one hurting."

"Wait. What? Wyatt is your charge? I didn't know."

"You never exactly asked."

"You're right. I didn't. That was selfish of me. I'm sorry. I've been so hung up on myself and Grace that I forgot you also came down here because of a charge. What are you helping him with?"

If Mitch was going to reply, he didn't get a chance, as the song ended, and Grace and Jordan came back to the table, flushed with happiness from the song. But I saw Grace's grin turn into a frown when she noticed Nina wasn't there.

This wasn't what I wanted at all. Shouldn't I be glad Jordan had chosen Grace?

Thirty-Five

Grace

"I'm glad you guys sang that because now Josh can't make me do another duet," said Zack as we came back to the table.

"Hey, we would have killed that," said Joshykins, "but I'll give you your moment, Grace. I'm going to start calling you Sandy after that."

"Thanks, Joshykins," I said. "Does that make Jordan Danny? I think he needs a lot more hair gel and a leather jacket for that."

"Be glad I didn't do what I was going to do," said Jordan. "I thought for a moment of telling you that you would be singing Danny's part and I'd do Sandy's. But I'm not sure my voice would go that high. Would have been funny, though…"

"I think I might have liked that better," I replied. "I'm a natural alto, so part of that was tough. But I think I killed it anyway."

Looking around the others at the table, I saw that Chloe and Mitch were looking anywhere but at each other; Abigail was giving me a quizzical look, which told me I was going to get an earful later about Jordan; and Nina wasn't there.

Singing with Jordan had felt great and was fun, but now it was like I'd hit a crash after a sugar high. When we were singing, I hadn't thought about Nina and now I felt guilty about that, because she was the one who had come to the event with Jordan, and he was dating her.

"Umm, where's Nina?" I asked to no one in particular at the table.

"She walked away from the table about halfway through your song," said Dani. "I have to say that she didn't seem too happy. In fact, she looked sad."

Dammit. As happy as I was that Jordan had chosen me in a sense, I didn't want to hurt someone else in the process.

"Aww, she'll be okay," said Jordan, chuckling. "I didn't think she'd want to sing, and I knew Grace would have fun with it, so I decided to write her name down instead. Plus, heck, nothing wrong with making her a little jealous."

"Wait," I said. "No. There is indeed something wrong with making women jealous. It doesn't make you better than them. It doesn't give you the upper hand at all. Instead, what you're doing is showing that you're not interested in a relationship and playing a game to see if the woman is worth keeping around and toying with further or not. No woman — and no person — wants to play games with the person they're interested in. It makes them feel cheap."

Jordan looked like he was about to interject, but I was on a roll and kept going because this needed to be said.

"No, I've let you talk long enough and do whatever you want to do, without taking anyone else's feelings, including my own, into account. Singing with you was fun, yes, but now that I'm seeing that you sang with me to toy with

Nina serves as a stark reminder to me of who you are and what I most certainly don't want. Nina seems like a great woman from the few moments I've spent with her and you're going to lose her if you don't grow up. Maybe you already have. She's not a plaything. No one is. You like her? Tell her. You want to text her? Text her without doing your stupid game of waiting a few days because you don't want her to think you like her too much. If you're dating her, date just her and stop with this nonsense. And leave me out of it. Stop texting me and sure as heck, don't invite me up on stage to sing with you just to make someone else jealous. For a minute there, I thought that maybe you'd changed your mind and were interested in me. But now I'm seeing otherwise."

Jordan looked stunned, but he got back to his game face quickly.

"Okay, that was a lot you just threw at me. Maybe I'm playing games, as you call it, but you are, too. It's not like you haven't been replying to my texts and still being flirty. Also, didn't you say there was some guy you were seeing? Where is he tonight? And why did you invite me here if you didn't want me to show up as some way to make me jealous if the other guy did show up? So it's not just me playing games."

Ugh. Where was Wyatt? Why hadn't he shown up? He was the one I really wanted there. Was he instead off texting, talking, or hanging out with Sally?

"You're right. Well, not about inviting you. I posted about the event on SocPost as a public event, so you were invited with a slew of other people. As for replying to you, you're right about that. Maybe I shouldn't be doing so or texting you, but I don't like just ending communication with people. It was an effort to see if we could be just friends, but clearly that isn't the case and could never be the case. Now that I'm saying all of this, it's sounding defensive to me and it probably is. I guess I did wonder if we still had a shot down the road. But we don't. That's clear to me now."

My head was spinning, but I heard Mitch say, "Chloe, I need to know. This is the only way."

"Jordan, why did you really ask Grace to duet with you instead of Nina?" continued Mitch.

"Basically, I wanted attention and thought I might be losing Nina's interest, so I figured I should keep Grace around thinking she had a chance. Plus, I heard her mention that she was seeing someone else, and that made me realize I was losing my hold on her. So I wrote her name down to make her forget about the other guy and keep paying attention to me so I could string her along until I find someone I actually want to be with and then I can fully ignore her," replied Jordan.

"So, there was no other reason? You didn't feel compelled to do so in any way?"

"No. The only time I felt like I wasn't the one really making a decision was when I decided to come here tonight, and maybe when I sent her a text the other week. But writing Grace's name down was all me, and I'm sure it worked and she'll be wrapped around my finger again."

I put my hands up to cover my eyes, feeling exhausted. At least I finally knew Jordan's intentions or complete lack of intentions. Hearing it sure hurt, but it was good to know the truth. Although I wondered why he was actually spouting off this truth.

"Wow," said Nina, who had come back into the room during that conversation. "Dude, we are done. I was done already when you blatantly disregarded my feelings and chose Grace to do a duet. But now, I'm so far past done that done is a dot way out there in the distance. Especially after hearing you say you're stringing Grace along until you find someone you want to be with, since that's clearly not me. You're a jerk."

"Nina, I'm sorry," I started to say, but she cut me off.

"Don't sweat it," she replied. "I had my own version of Jordan stringing me along in my life at some point and thought I got away from that. Not so much. Guess I have a type. And this isn't on you at all. This is all about Jordan's antics. I think you're great, Grace, and we're good."

"Thank you," I said. "I'm guessing you probably don't want Jordan to drive you home. Abigail, any chance you could give Nina a ride home?"

"Of course," Abigail said. "Glad to. Are you ready to go now, Nina?"

"I sure am." She grabbed her purse off the back of the chair. Abigail, Dani, and Jessie went to follow her out the door after giving me a hug and saying bye to everyone, with the exception of Jordan, who had slunk down in his chair.

As they headed off, I heard Abigail say to Nina, "You can do way better. Hey, I should introduce you to a guy I know, Nick…"

Pretty sure I wouldn't be seeing Nick come up on the dating apps any more the second he met Nina. They'd look good together.

"What the heck just happened?" said Jordan. "Why did I say all of that?"

"Was it not true?" I asked him.

"No, it's true. All of it. I just never planned on telling you or Nina that. I liked the attention from both of you, but neither of you were the one I really wanted long term. I'm not sure I actually want anyone long term or that I'm capable of a real relationship since I like just messing with people and seeing what happens. What the heck. Why do I keep talking?"

"Let's call it a little nudge from above," said Mitch. "Nina and Grace both needed to hear the truth, and I needed it for a different reason."

"Whatever, dude," said Jordan. "I'm outta here."

He walked out without talking further to any of us, which was good riddance. Joshykins and Zack followed shortly thereafter making me promise to text them that I got home okay. That left me with Chloe and Mitch at the table.

"A nudge from above?" I said. "What do you mean? Angels? Also, what was I thinking?"

"We'll talk about that first part later," said Chloe. "I'm sorry, Grace. I thought Jordan was the right guy for you due to your chemistry, but I was clearly so wrong. Chemistry is just one part of it. I understand that now."

I caught her look at Mitchell with those last words.

"It's okay, Chloe," I said. "It's not your fault. I was so convinced as well that fate wanted us together that I didn't give much credence to all the red flags I was seeing with Jordan. I'm glad we didn't wind up together honestly, and I've finally realized that what I want or I should say who I want is Wyatt. I wish he'd shown up tonight so I could have told him that and apologized about the Rec Center and figured out if he feels the same or if his heart is with Sally."

"Shoot. Grace, Wyatt was here. He came in for a moment during your duet with Jordan, but then turned around and left when he saw you singing together."

"Oh, no! I wonder if there's any chance he's still out in the parking lot. I need to go see. Excuse me, please, and I'll see you guys tomorrow."

"Go get him," said Mitch. "I'm sure you'll find him."

Please, please let me find Wyatt so I can tell him how I feel.

Thirty-Six

Chloe

Time to tell Mitch how I felt.

When Grace left, I realized that left me at the table with Mitch. Guess it was time for us to talk, as much as I didn't want to because I was nervous he might not at all feel the same way I did.

"I should have told you," started Mitch.

"Something's on my mind," I said at the same time.

We chuckled as we both stopped our sentences.

"Ladies first," said Mitch with a wave of his arm.

"No, no, I want to hear what you have to say first. But now that I've said that, there's something else I need to say before you speak first. Yeah, that makes no sense. Go with it. I didn't cause Jordan to pick Grace for his duet. I did, however, nudge him to consider showing up here tonight, and a nudge to text her before when I thought she was losing interest. But only because I really did think they belong together, and I didn't know then what a complete toad he is. But, Mitch, I need you to know I had nothing to do with that duet. Nothing."

"I believe you, Chloe. Okay, so I had to give him a little nudge to make 100% sure, but after I got over that moment of anger, I believed you and just wanted confirmation. I was angry because Wyatt is my charge and I thought you were so bent on putting Jordan and Grace together that he didn't stand a chance, since you're a bit of a bulldog when you want something to happen."

"I'm sorry I made you angry. That wasn't my intent. I didn't know about Wyatt but I understand why you didn't tell me. You're right. I was being stubborn because I felt that they belonged together, but I don't believe that now. Maybe she does belong with Wyatt. Maybe she doesn't, but we shouldn't interfere with how our charges behave, even with little nudges — unless they're going to do something that destroys their lives, of course."

"Always looking for a way around the rules," chuckled Mitch. "But yes, let's try not to interfere at all. We can send insights and direction since that's what we're supposed to do."

He stopped for a moment and glanced towards the parking lot and continued.

"I really hope they found each other. I have a good feeling about those two."

"Did you nudge him at all to stay around, hopefully?"

"No, I didn't. I'm not you." Mitch grinned that grin that always made me feel better. "I'm going to let this play out the way it will. If they don't find each other right now, I'm hopeful they will figure it out eventually."

Oh, gosh, speaking of figuring things out…

I bit my lower lip, unsure if I should bring this up or if it would make things awkward. But I had to know.

"I understand that. Sometimes it takes people longer than it should to figure things out."

"What do you mean by that? If you don't mind my asking…"

"This is hard, because I'm scared."

"Whatever it is, you can talk to me about it, Grace. You know I'm always here for you and will listen to whatever is going on judgment-free."

"I know that and I appreciate it, Mitch. I appreciate you. That's part of it. I appreciate you and I appreciate our friendship. You make me happy and I don't want to lose that."

"You're not going to lose my friendship. Why would you? What's going on?"

"I guess it has to do with the whole Jordan thing. I was convinced that Grace belonged with him because I saw this spark of chemistry between them when they first met, so I thought that was a sign of true love. And over the years, I've dated guys here and there but they never progressed because they didn't have that spark — and honestly, they weren't the right guy for me anyway looking back. Maybe that's why the spark wasn't there. But I thought I'd know when I met my love. I'd just look at him and I'd know. But Jordan being the anti-true love opened my eyes that they just had chemistry. That's all it was. It wasn't true love. And then I thought about what love might actually be if it wasn't that spark, and maybe it's the person you feel most yourself with, who's there for you in your good news and bad, who makes you laugh, who makes you grow, and who you think is so handsome that you see his hair as icy blonde because he shines so bright to you, and you didn't realize no one else saw him that way but you, but you never gave him a chance because you just always thought of him as a friend and you also thought he was into guys, but then there was one moment when you saw him turn female heads and you felt jealous and realized you might actually have already found the love of your life, and you didn't know it. And now you're rambling like a fool and are so scared you've ruined things forever and he doesn't feel the same way and you'll look like an idiot…"

Mitch was speechless. Shoot. I clearly ruined things, and now he'd want to stay down on Earth instead of going back up and having to see me every day. Or maybe I should stay down here, so I could avoid him. This was awful.

"Oh, gosh, you don't feel the same way at all, do you? I'm a fool. I'm sorry. Can we please forget I just said anything at all? Can I give you a nudge to forget this? Is that possible?"

I felt tears beginning to fall and I closed my eyes. I opened them only when I felt Mitch place his hand gently atop mine. When I looked up, he had tears of his own in his eyes, but he was smiling so broadly.

"Chloe, I wasn't talking not because I don't feel the same way, but because I was dumbstruck that my dream was coming true right in front of me. I've been in love with you for as long as I can remember. I just knew you didn't see me that way, so I didn't say anything and figured I'd deal with us just being friends, and if you ever felt differently, I'd be there."

I turned my hand over to lace my fingers with his.

"I feel like my eyes have just been opened to what's been standing in front of me the entire time. I love you, Mitch. When I think about it, I've always loved you, but I thought you were gay because you never showed interest in any female, so I just assumed…"

Mitch laughed.

"I'm not gay. I never had eyes for anyone else because all I could see was you, Chloe. It's always been only you. That important thing I was going to tell you when we were walking… the thing I want more than anything else in the universe… It's you. I want you. I love you."

I got up from the table and walked over to Mitch's side to sit down next to him.

"You've got me. I just didn't know it. And I'm so glad my eyes have been opened. This is the best Christmas present ever… to love you and have your love."

We both leaned over and gently kissed, breaking apart only when we heard the sound of angelic cheers coming from above.

I shook my head, laughing as I rested my forehead against Mitch's. "Okay, I guess they approve. Now shoo and let me kiss him some more."

And with that, we did kiss some more while thoughts ran out of my head.

Thirty-Seven

Grace

Thoughts ran through my head as I raced out into the parking lot, looking frantically around for Wyatt. He wasn't there.

Why would he be because he left while I was singing with Jordan, and that seemed like a lifetime ago now. I cursed myself for being blinded by Jordan for even just a moment when I shouldn't have let him turn my head.

Just when I realized I wanted to fight for Wyatt and was firmly done with Jordan, this had to happen. I had to find him and explain myself in person so he could see that I was telling the truth.

I hoped that he was sitting in his car somewhere in this parking lot and hadn't left yet, but there was no way to tell because there were so many dark cars there and I didn't want to be a creeper checking each car. Plus, that seemed like a quick way to get abducted or worse by someone who was sitting in one of the cars.

I wasn't ready to go home, though, and walk into my apartment. The first thing I'd see would be that Christmas tree that Wyatt, Grace, and Mitchell put up, which would remind me even more of Wyatt. I knew I had to go home eventually, but not right now.

This was my fault for singing with Jordan. I knew it was wrong and that I shouldn't have done it, but I did. And now I had to tell Wyatt that it was him that I wanted, if he'd only give me a chance.

Feeling dejected, I walked over to my waterfall to sit in the gazebo and think about what I wanted to say before I called or texted him. As I walked, I looked at the beauty around me, which still caught my eye despite how I was feeling. That waterfall was glistening in the moonlight and the lights on top of the gazebo had that same ethereal glow that I'd seen in the restaurant on my first date with Wyatt.

That had to be a sign that this wasn't over yet. Didn't it?

Or was I just reaching, which heaven knew I'd done far too often over the years. All I could do was hope it did mean that I still had a chance with Wyatt and that he wasn't on his way to go choose Sally and live happily ever after with her.

"Grace?"

A voice from the gazebo pulled me out of my reverie. How did I miss that someone was there?

To my shock, Wyatt was sitting there in the back of the gazebo, closest to the railing that separated the gazebo from the rushing water. He looked as surprised as I felt, and stood up, coming to the front of the gazebo as I stopped outside of it.

"You're here," I said. "I was just looking for you and here you are. Chloe told me that you came into the restaurant and then turned and left, so I wanted to find you. But I didn't see you outside, so I came here to think."

"Yeah, I came in and saw you happily singing with a guy that I can only assume is Jordan, so I left. I didn't think anyone saw me. I was going to head straight home, but I remembered you mentioned this waterfall and gazebo, so I thought I'd check it out to cool off before I drove."

"It was Jordan, yes, but our duet didn't mean anything. He put my name down to sing with him without my knowledge until it was announced. And then it became this whole thing, which is a long story, but in the process I saw his true colors and they weren't appealing at all. I don't plan to ever contact him again. Yes, there were lingering feelings there as we had dated for a while, but that's completely over."

"Are you sure? I don't want to get in the way of your happiness, and I kind of figured I deserved it after the Rec Center thing even though I swear to you I didn't know until my dad mentioned it."

"Gosh, no, being with Jordan could never make me happy, and he kept far too much from me already. He doesn't get me and never wanted to. He wanted almost like a Stepford Wife who didn't have a personality of her own, and who he could just talk at instead of learning anything about. That's not me. Jordan is my past and I'm never going back. When I'm around you, though, I know that you do see me and enjoy spending time with me. And I've learned to actually communicate and talk, and I know you want to listen to me and you seem to hear me, which is new to me, so I'm still trying to figure that out. But I'm willing to learn how to communicate even better. With that said, I don't want to keep you from being happy either, so if you're better off with Sally, I'll step aside and we'll part as friends. I just want you to be happy, Wyatt."

"Sally? Why the heck would I be happier with Sally?"

"I know she's someone who you talk to often through calls and texts that have come through when we've been out. And I figured she was who you were also seeing."

"Oh, Grace, I wish you'd mentioned this before. I'm not dating Sally. That would be a bit gross considering she's my sister."

"Your sister? I'm an idiot. With the number of calls and texts, I just assumed…"

"I get it, and that's partially on me. I should have mentioned who she was. She's been calling and texting a lot because she was pregnant with her first child, and she was nervous about it. Our mom passed away in childbirth with Sally — right before Christmas, no less, so her pregnancy at this time has been a difficult one for her knowing that."

"You mentioned that your mom died when you were younger. I had no idea she'd passed away when your sister was born. How awful. Umm, you mentioned she was pregnant? Did she lose the baby? I'm so sorry if that's the case."

"No, no, no. I'm sorry. She was pregnant in the past tense because she had her baby today. And everything is fine. Sally and her husband, Sam, now have a beautiful daughter, Emerson, who is named after our mother. I'm sure we'll all wind up calling her Emmy. That's why I was late getting here. I was at the hospital waiting to hear how it went, and of course was nervous for my sister considering what happened to my mom. When I got the news and met Emerson, all I could think of was how much I wanted to tell you. You're the first person I want to tell anything to, so I came here. And then…"

"I'm so happy for your sister, brother-in-law, and new niece. And I'm so sorry that I didn't ask who Sally was, but I was trying so hard to not get hurt again that I couldn't ask and risk knowing you were dating someone else. I love that I was the first person you wanted to tell your good news to. That's what

I want."

"I don't want to date anyone else, Grace," Wyatt said. "I just want to date you. Just you. Is that okay?"

"That's more than okay. And as luck would have it, I only want to date you."

"One more thing. The Rec Center. I'm so sorry that I didn't know my law firm was the one handling the sale. When I found out at the same time you did, I felt so guilty because I knew how hard you were working to keep it, and that's when I knew I needed to save it. So, I went and dug through the old records — we're talking so old that they were on dusty paper —- at Town Hall and found out about the underground railway, which makes it a historical monument. Once I knew that, I went to the company and told them that they couldn't buy it and raze it to the ground like they were planning. They suddenly became much less interested, to no surprise, and we found a different building for them in the form of the old mall land that wasn't in use anymore. I tried to call you and tell you, but..."

"I know. Amber told me. It's okay. I understand. I was mad at first, obviously, but I get why you didn't tell me. It's why I didn't ask you about Sally until just now because I didn't want to know, but communication is so important. I realize that now because we could have easily cleared up that miscommunication at least if I'd just asked you one little question about who Sally was or simply if you were dating anyone else. I spent so much time not speaking up when anything bothered me that I didn't know that I should or actually that I could. But with you, now I know that I can, and I'm grateful. And even more grateful that you saved the Rec Center. You are a superhero, Wyatt. At least you're my superhero."

Wyatt leaned in and kissed me gently. It was the best kiss I'd ever had to date and I swore the lights in the gazebo flickered.

I broke the kiss for a moment only to say, "What took you so long?"

"I was stuck in traffic," Wyatt said with a grin before pulling me back to him for another kiss.

As we kissed, snow flurries fell lightly around us.

Acknowledgements

This tale has been in my head in one form or another since my senior year in high school. I was taking a Creative Writing class at Cape Cod Community College and was asked to write a scene of a novel. For that scene, I wrote the first version of what is now Grace first meeting Wyatt in person at the art gallery, standing in front of her painting. The teacher loved it, but I wasn't sure if I'd ever do anything with it.

That changed about 15 years ago, when I found the print out of that scene as I was going through old papers. I took it and posted it to my personal Facebook account as a "note", and my friends loved it and wanted to read more. Slight problem. There wasn't more at the time.

I went on to publish my first book, "Some Horrific Evening," and there was no place for that tale in it. The thought, however, continued, and I jotted down ideas around the painting and that art gallery in countless notebooks over the years.

One of those ideas made its way into a novel idea I put together for a writing class. In that class, this tale involved the Three Fates, and I learned so much about writing and to not include so much info-dumping. The first version of that tale included a deep dive into Grace's family, which wasn't needed at all in the first chapter.

I went back and forth and back and forth in notebooks and in the notes section of my phone with ideas for this story and others.

Finally, this tale took form when I was thinking of how much I love Hallmark Christmas movies. I wanted to write my own and to make it a sweet Christmas tale that anyone could read.

Because of that, the story of Grace, Wyatt, Chloe, and Mitch now stands before you.

I hope it gives you as much joy reading it as it gave me to write it, and that it provides some hope.

About the Author

Mary E. Hart is the author of the haunted house novel, "Some Horrific Evening" and the 1980s themed horror tale, "Not Your Barbie Dino," in the collection "Totally Tubular Terrors." She has also had her flash fiction tales, "Left at the Bus Stop" and "Destination Anywhere" accepted and read on the Sudden Fictions Podcast. When she's not writing about technology in her full-time job, or creating stuffed animal political debates with her son, she is writing down tales like this one.

You can connect with me on:

🌐 https://www.maryehhart.com